M000317593

THE GHOST

AND LITTLE MARIE

HAUNTING DANIELLE

THE GHOST OF MARLOW HOUSE

THE GHOST WHO LOVED DIAMONDS

THE GHOST WHO WASN'T

THE GHOST WHO WANTED REVENGE

THE GHOST OF HALLOWEEN PAST

THE GHOST WHO CAME FOR CHRISTMAS

THE GHOST OF VALENTINE PAST

THE GHOST FROM THE SEA

THE GHOST AND THE MYSTERY WRITER

THE GHOST AND THE MUSE

THE GHOST WHO STAYED HOME

THE GHOST AND THE LEPRECHAUN

THE GHOST WHO LIED

THE GHOST AND THE BRIDE

THE GHOST AND LITTLE MARIE

THE GHOST AND THE DOPPELGANGER

THE GHOST OF SECOND CHANCES

THE GHOST WHO DREAM HOPPED

THE GHOST OF CHRISTMAS SECRETS

THE GHOST WHO WAS SAYS I DO

HAUNTING DANIELLE - BOOK 15

THE GHOST
AND LITTLE MARIE

BOBBI HOLMES

The Ghost and Little Marie
(Haunting Danielle, Book 15)
A Novel
By Bobbi Holmes
Cover Design: Elizabeth Mackey

Copyright © 2017 Bobbi Holmes
Robeth Publishing, LLC
All Rights Reserved.
robeth.net

This novel is a work of fiction.
Any resemblance to places or actual persons,
living or dead, is entirely coincidental.

ISBN 978-1-949977-14-1

To Grandpa Pete, because I borrowed your buggy whip story.
I figured you were born about the same time as Walt,
and it would have been something he would have done as a kid.

And to Steve Biehn, for answering all those pesky trust questions in
spite of the snarky comment I left in your high school yearbook!

ONE

S hadowy light from the rear corridor made its way into the darkened room through the partially open doorway. There was no illumination coming from the adjacent bathroom in spite of the fact its door was open. The bathroom night-light had burned out several days earlier, and no one thought to replace it. After all, it wasn't as if she could get up in the middle of the night without assistance and use the bathroom.

While she preferred to sleep in total darkness, Marie Nichols found comfort in the hallway light. These days she preferred to sleep with one eye open, and it helped if she could actually see something. It would have been different had she been able to lock her door. A locked door meant a secure space. Yet patient rooms were never locked in this place. As far as she was concerned, any of the patients —or residents, as the staff called them—could enter her room at any time—even when she was sound asleep. Since coming to Seaside Village two weeks earlier, Marie hadn't had a decent night's rest.

Aside from her lack of sleep, Marie hadn't gotten used to the smell of her temporary home, a mixture of urine and disinfectants. She found her keen sense of smell a curse. If they would only open the windows once in a while and let in the fresh air. But for some reason the staff insisted on keeping the place tightly locked up— preventing fresh ocean air from entering and residents from escaping. She doubted it was possible to open the windows even if it was allowed.

Worse than the smell was her bed—smaller and firmer than her mattress at home. Yet it wasn't the size or hardness that troubled her, it was the fact she had to sleep on her back. After a person had been used to sleeping on her side for over ninety years, curled up in a fetal position, sleeping flat on one's back made it difficult to fall asleep. Unfortunately, she had no choice.

Now she wore a metal pin in her hip, making it uncomfortable to lay on her injured side. Unfortunately, it made it equally uncomfortable to lay on the opposite side. Marie cursed herself for her moment of carelessness. In a hurry to answer the phone, she had failed to pay attention to what she was doing and ended up falling, resulting in a broken hip.

Marie found Adam's first phone call—which had been the catalyst for the broken hip—a bit ironic. Her grandson Adam had been calling to check on her. Since she had failed to answer his initial phone call—and then the second and third call—he had come right over and had found her—which meant she wasn't left to suffer endless hours on her kitchen floor and had received emergency medical care within a few hours.

However, had Adam not called her that morning, she wouldn't have been rushing to answer the phone—therefore she would never have fallen or broken her hip. While she didn't discuss the irony with Adam, she did with her dear friend Danielle Boatman. Danielle would find dark humor in the situation, while poor Adam would just feel guilty.

Making Adam feel guilty was the last thing Marie wanted to do, especially after the past week. It had given her a new appreciation of her eldest grandson and his attentiveness towards her. Her son and his horrid wife—Adam's parents—along with Adam's brother, Jason, and Jason's fiancée, had descended on Frederickport earlier that week, under the guise of looking after Marie and spending Thanksgiving with her. However, unlike Adam, who continued to assure Marie she would be going home as soon as her physical therapist deemed her capable, she had caught her son and daughter-in-law taking a tour of the rooms for the permanent residents. At the time, Marie had a good idea they weren't looking at the rooms for themselves. It turned out she was right.

Glancing to the nightstand, she looked at the illuminated

numbers on the alarm clock. It was a few minutes past three in the morning. She momentarily considered taking the pain pill she had tucked in the pocket of her dressing gown. But then she decided against it. While the ache in her hip was bothering her more than usual and keeping her awake, Marie was reluctant to rely on pain pills.

If they had their way, they would keep us all drugged up, Marie thought. She smiled, proud of herself for being so crafty, the way in which she hid the pill under her tongue and pretended to swallow it. It was something she had started to do the third night at the rehab center, when she realized her pain was not severe enough to warrant taking drugs. However, the medical staff had disagreed with her and had insisted she continue taking the pills at regular intervals.

Each time the nurse would leave the room, Marie would remove the pill from her mouth and slip it in the pocket of her dressing gown. The next time Marie visited the toilet, she would flush the unwanted pain pill.

Pondering her unfortunate stay at Seaside Village was not helping her sleep. Restless, Marie tried to get comfortable. Sitting up briefly, she removed one of the pillows from under her head and tossed it to the foot of her bed. Settling back on the remaining pillow, she pulled the sheets and blankets up to her chin. Her hands, now under the bedding, she folded together and rested on her belly.

Just as she glanced to the partially open doorway, she heard it—steps coming down the hallway, in her direction. The sound of footsteps stopped. Marie stared at the doorway. She watched as a dark figure pushed open the door to enter her room. Without her glasses on, she was unable to see who it was, but she assumed it was the night nurse making her rounds. Not wanting the nurse to know she was awake—thus risking the chance of another pill being forced on her—this time a sleeping pill—Marie closed her eyes and feigned sleep.

She lay there a few moments, her eyes firmly closed, listening. There were no more sounds of footsteps. She wondered briefly if the nurse had quietly moved down the hallway. Just before she was about to open her eyes, she heard it again—more footsteps. They weren't walking down the hallway; they were coming toward the bed.

Still playing possum, Marie could feel the nurse hovering over her. With her eyes firmly closed, she remained motionless. After a few moments of complete silence, Marie wondered if the nurse had left her room. Fluttering open her eyes ever so slightly, Marie found herself looking up at a pillow hovering over her face. Before she could utter a sound, the pillow abruptly covered her eyes, nose and mouth—cutting off the oxygen—followed by a person's body weighing down her covers, holding her in place.

With Marie's hands both trapped under the blanket—crushed by the person applying the pillow—Marie could not reach out and push at the attacker. In a panic, she struggled under the pillow's suffocating confinement.

Just when Marie was certain she was going to die, the pillow was removed from her face. She then heard the person run from the room. Taking a deep breath, the suffocating oppression gone, Marie opened her eyes and looked to the partially open doorway. Once again, she was alone in the room.

Without thought, Marie jumped up from the bed and quickly made her way to the door leading to the hallway. She didn't consider using the walker, which stood near her bedside. For the last week her physical therapist had insisted she use it, telling her she needed to get used to the fact she would never again walk without one. Yet, at the moment, the walker was the last thing on Marie's mind.

She looked down the dimly lit hallway. In view was a nurses' station. As usual, it was vacant. The nursing home—or rehab center, as Adam insisted on calling it—had two nurses' stations. The one that was always staffed was located in the front of the large building. It was in that section of the nursing home where the permanent occupants resided. A good majority of those were patients suffering from Alzheimer's or were elderly patients who were no longer able to live alone and needed full-time care. It irked her to think her own son expected her to move into that part of the nursing home instead of moving back to her own lovely house.

The back section of the center, where Marie was staying, housed those who were temporary residents, there for rehab until they could once again go home. Most of the patient rooms in her section were currently vacant. It was one reason she found sleeping at the center so creepy.

"Adam says I'll be going home quickly if I do what the doctors tell me. But if I stay here another night, I won't be going home at all!" Marie muttered as she hurried down the hallway, toward the rear lobby. It was in this section of the lobby where she usually sat when her family members or friends came for a visit.

Just as she reached the end of the hallway, she heard a woman call out, "Where do you think you're going?"

Marie turned toward the voice. She found a nightgown-clad elderly woman standing at the open doorway leading to one of the patient rooms. The room had been vacant earlier that day, so Marie assumed it had to be a new patient.

"Did you see someone running down the hall?" Marie asked.

"Yes. They went out the back door." The woman pointed in that direction.

Marie peeked around the corner and spied the doorway. She didn't see anyone. Whoever it was must have already left the building. The back door was always locked, and the only way to get in—or out—was to use the keypad. Of course, the staff normally would not share the code with the patients, for fear they would escape. However, Adam knew the code, and he had shared it with her.

"They must have a good reason for not wanting the patients to have the code," Adam had said.

"Naturally they don't want their Alzheimer's patients to escape," Marie had snapped. "But I doubt those people would remember the number anyway. But what if there's a fire, Adam? You want me to get trapped in this god-awful place?" The mention of a fire had been enough for Adam to give Marie the code.

Marie was still thinking of Adam and the key code when she remembered the woman watching her. She turned back to the new patient, but she was no longer there. Marie assumed she had gone back to bed.

Instead of returning to her room, Marie decided to get out of this place before the homicidal maniac returned. Calling Adam and asking him to pick her up was not an option. He would just think she had been having a bad dream and tell her to go back to sleep. And she definitely could not call her son or daughter-in-law. They would probably accuse her of being delusional and use that as an excuse to force her to stay longer.

Glancing one more time back to the room of the woman who had talked to her a moment ago, and then down the main hallway leading to the occupied nurses' station, Marie was confident the woman really had gone back to bed and not down to find a nurse to wrangle Marie back to her own room.

Making an effort to move quietly and stay out of sight, Marie made her way to the back door. A few minutes later she was standing outside under the moonlight, in the center of the rear parking lot. Only three cars were parked behind the building, and there were no other people in sight. Whoever had tried to smother her had obviously driven off already. That was assuming, Marie reminded herself, that the woman was correct when she told her someone had exited out the back door.

Marie glanced back to the building and frowned. For some reason, she couldn't remember punching in the password to open the back door—or even opening the back door, for that matter. *But I must have*, Marie told herself, *or I wouldn't be outside now*. With a shrug, she continued on her way.

It wasn't until Marie started down the sidewalk, away from the rehab center and toward the police station, did she question her own judgment in leaving through the same door her attacker had gone through just minutes earlier. What if he had been still lurking in the parking lot?

Marie considered the possibility for a brief moment and then shrugged. For some reason, she wasn't afraid anymore. Of course, that didn't mean she wasn't going to report the incident to the police, nor did it mean she intended to go back to that place.

She was halfway down the street when she realized how remarkably well she felt. Pausing for a moment, Marie stretched. "Stupid therapist," she grumbled. "I don't need to use that damn walker, and I certainly don't need any more physical therapy. I'm walking wonderfully! In fact, much better than before, I don't even need a cane! Those people are just trying to bilk Medicare for more money!"

With a lighter step, ninety-one-year-old Marie Nichols cheerfully skipped down the sidewalk—under the moonlight—making her way to the Frederickport Police Department.

TWO

Tapping on the kitchen window caught Danielle's attention. About to turn on the coffee pot, she paused and glanced toward the sound. The curtain was drawn, but she knew it was still dark outside. Danielle looked up to the wall clock. It was not quite six a.m. She heard another tap, followed by a voice.

"Dani, are you in there?" It was Lily's voice.

Danielle turned on the coffee pot and then walked to the kitchen door and opened it. Standing on the doorstep was Lily, wearing a long green robe, fuzzy slippers, and holding an empty coffee cup.

"I saw the kitchen light was on, and I'm out of coffee," Lily said as she walked into the house, holding up her mug for Danielle to see.

"You're up kind of early, aren't you?" Danielle asked as she returned to the kitchen counter.

Lily shut the door behind her and walked over to the coffee pot, waiting for it to finish brewing. "Sadie woke me about a half an hour ago, she needed to go out. Ian sleeps like the dead. I have no idea what poor Sadie did when she had to go out before I moved over there." Lily shook her head and chuckled.

"Ian still sleeping?" Danielle reached up to the overhead cabinet and grabbed herself a mug.

"Yes. After I took Sadie out, I tried to go back to sleep. But by that time, Ian was snoring like my grandpa. I figured I better get up, or I'd end up shoving a pillow on his face."

Danielle chuckled. "So, the honeymoon's over?"

"Nah, I didn't smother him, did I? I got up because I love him. Unfortunately, when I went to the kitchen, I discovered we were out of coffee. Dang, I really miss having someone like Joanne to keep the pantry stocked."

"Yes, I lead the life of luxury and privilege," Danielle said with dramatic flair as she filled Lily's cup with coffee.

Lily giggled and took her full cup to the table and sat down. A moment later, Danielle joined her.

"So why are you up so early, anyhow?" Lily glanced around the room. "Is Walt here?"

Danielle shook her head. "I haven't seen him this morning."

"So why are you up so early?" Lily repeated.

Danielle drank some coffee and then said, "I promised Marie I would pick up some cinnamon rolls at Old Salts this morning and bring them to her."

"How is she doing? Ian and I were talking about going over there this afternoon." Lily sipped her coffee.

"She's anxious to get out of there. I can't say I blame her. I was hoping the cinnamon rolls would cheer her up."

"Is she for sure not coming over for Thanksgiving dinner?" Lily asked.

Danielle frowned. "No. Can't say I'm particularly fond of her son. I thought Adam was a jerk when I first met him, but now I know where he gets it from."

"Ah, come on, you and Adam are friends now."

"I know. In fact, I really like him. He sort of grows on you…like fungus." Danielle grinned.

Lily laughed. "I think I'm going to tell him you said that."

Danielle smiled softly and shook her head. "No, please don't. Adam seems stressed enough with his entire family showing up. Anyway, his father's jerkiness isn't really how I used to see Adam. Even when I thought Adam was a sleazy crook, he was good to Marie."

"And his father?"

"We've lived in Frederickport for almost a year and a half, and this is the first time Marie's son has come to see her."

"At least he came now. A broken hip can be pretty dangerous for a woman Marie's age. He's probably worried about his mother."

"I'm not sure about that." Danielle was about to take a sip of coffee but instead slammed the cup back on the table. "Do you know what Marie told me last night when I talked to her on the phone?"

"What?"

"Her son and his lovely wife—no wonder poor Adam has issues —took a tour of the permanent facilities of Seaside Village."

Lily frowned. "So?"

"Looking at rooms for Marie."

"Why? Marie already has a room there."

"The section where the full-time residents live. Marie thinks he wants her to move there permanently."

"I can't imagine that. Marie would hate living there. She loves her house. When I was there the other day, the physical therapist said she was doing great, thought she should be home before Christmas. Did he tell Marie she shouldn't be living alone anymore?"

"No. But I think she was right about what her son's up to. I didn't tell her, but when I stopped by Adam's office yesterday morning, her son was there, grilling Adam about Marie's house. You know, how much it was worth now, how good the market is. He certainly was talking like someone getting ready to list property."

"It's not his house to list," Lily snapped.

Danielle shrugged. "I know. But families are funny. And from what I've seen so far, Adam's dad seems like the kind of guy who pretty much rolls over anyone in his path."

"That's probably why he and Adam aren't that close."

"I guess Adam and his parents had some sort of falling-out. And from what Marie once told me, she took Adam's side, which didn't help the relationship with her son. I've no idea what it was about; I didn't ask."

"I still don't understand why she isn't coming for Thanksgiving," Lily said. "I thought you asked her therapist about it, and he said she could come for the day, she just had to be back by midnight."

"I know." Danielle smiled ruefully. "At the time Marie made a joke about being Cinderella and having to be back before her carriage turned into a pumpkin. But I guess her son made a huge fuss, said the entire family had come back to Frederickport to be with her, and he couldn't imagine she would spend Thanksgiving with strangers instead of family."

Lily let out a snort. "Strangers. What a jerk. You did tell him they were welcome too, didn't you?"

"Of course. But I guess he told his mother he wanted to spend Thanksgiving with her, not with strangers. I think he guilted her out. Apparently, he made a big deal about it."

Lily shrugged. "Well, at least Marie will get out of that place for Thanksgiving. If she can't come here, that's okay. It might be nice for her to spend this time with just her immediate family."

"That's just it, she isn't getting out for Thanksgiving. They're eating Thanksgiving dinner there."

"At Seaside Village?"

Danielle nodded. "Apparently, Marie is not the only one in that family who doesn't like to cook. And I guess he said he was not going to take Marie out for the day just to go to a restaurant, when they can eat a perfectly good Thanksgiving dinner at Seaside Village."

Lily groaned. "Poor Marie. She was so looking forward to getting out of there for a day."

"I know Adam isn't happy either. We all made these Thanksgiving plans before Marie had her fall."

"I guess this means Adam and Melony won't be here for Thanksgiving dinner either?"

"Not sure about Melony. But Adam won't be coming now. I could tell he wasn't thrilled about the change of plans."

"You're telling Lily about Thanksgiving dinner?" Walt said when he appeared in the kitchen the next moment.

Danielle glanced up to Walt and smiled. "Morning, Walt."

Lily looked to the spot Danielle had just greeted. "Hey, Walt."

The chair between Lily and Danielle moved out—and then in—as Walt sat down at the table.

"Where's Ian?" Walt asked.

"Still sleeping," Danielle explained.

"Oh, there was another reason—other than coffee—for me coming over here." Lily set her cup on the table and grinned.

"What was that?" Danielle asked.

"I was planning to come over later to tell you, but when I couldn't go back to sleep this morning and I was out of coffee, I figured I might as well come over and tell you the exciting news now."

Walt arched his brows, his mouth curling into a smile. "A baby?" he whispered.

Danielle's eyes darted to Walt and then back to Lily. Before she could respond to Walt's comment, Lily blurted, "I'm going back to work!"

Visibly disappointed, Walt slumped in the chair.

Unable to suppress a grin, Danielle reached over and patted Walt's hand. Unfortunately, her hand went through his, touching the table. Ignoring the unsuccessful pat, Danielle said, "Gee, Walt, that's kind of sweet."

Lily frowned. "What?"

"Umm, Walt thought maybe the something you wanted to tell us was that you were having a baby."

"A baby would be nice," Walt grumbled. "I've always heard babies are more apt to see spirits. We could become great friends."

"A baby?" Lily squeaked. "I've only been married a couple of months!"

Walt shrugged. "Plenty of time to get pregnant." He then added, "Of course, if you make a habit of leaving your husband home alone in his bed while you're over here, less chance there'll be a baby."

Turning from Walt to Lily, Danielle said, "Oh, don't mind Walt. He just gets sentimental sometimes. So tell me about this job?"

"Sentimental?" Walt frowned. "What is that supposed to mean?"

"Remember Ray Elliot? I introduced you to him at that museum function?" Lily asked Danielle.

"The principal from the elementary school?"

Lily nodded. "Yes. I met him when I was helping the museum do that project with the local schools. Ray contacted me yesterday and asked me if I might consider taking a second-grade teaching position at his school. I guess one of the second-grade teachers is pregnant and won't be coming back after the Christmas break. They were going to use one of their regular subs, but for some reason the sub can't take the job now."

"Can you even do it? Don't you need an Oregon teacher's license?"

"Oregon has a reciprocity agreement with California. It'll involve some paperwork, but no big deal." Lily grinned.

"So you're going to do it?" Danielle asked.

"Ian and I talked about it last night. I've been missing teaching. I wasn't sure I wanted to go back—I'm still not one hundred percent sure. But I can easily take over this teacher's class, finish out the year, and come summer, I'll have a better idea of if I want to go back permanently or move on to something else."

"Wouldn't it be easier to just take on one baby instead of a class full of second graders?" Walt grumbled.

Danielle suppressed a smile. Walt seemed sincerely disappointed to hear Lily's announcement wasn't a baby.

"Oh, and guess who'll be one of my students?" Lily said excitedly.

"Who?" Danielle asked.

"Evan MacDonald." Lily grinned.

Walt let out a sigh and leaned back in his chair. "Evan and Lily in a classroom together. That might prove interesting. I wonder what trouble those two will get into."

Danielle rolled her eyes. "She's going to be his teacher, not his new partner in crime."

"What are you two talking about?" Lily frowned.

"Walt is just being silly, ignore him."

"Not hard to do, considering I can't see or hear him," Lily grumbled.

THREE

Twilight teased the eastern horizon. The parking lot lights at the Frederickport Police Department continued to burn, waiting for the morning sunlight to take over their job. Chief MacDonald pulled into the lot, parking under one of the bright lights. After turning off the ignition, he and his two young sons climbed out of the vehicle.

"I don't know why I can't just wait in the car," Evan whined, resenting being pulled from his bed a half an hour early.

"I told you, I don't want you waiting outside in the car alone," the chief reminded him.

Reluctantly, Evan trailed behind his father and older brother, Eddie, as they made their way to the front door of the police station.

"Good morning, Chief," Holly Parker greeted him when the chief entered the inner offices. She was the newest employee at the station, starting her third week as dispatcher.

"Good morning, Holly," the chief said brightly as he held the door open, waiting for both of his sons to enter.

"Hi, boys. I'm surprised to see you all here—especially so early!" Holly said.

"Eddie left his backpack here," Evan grumbled.

The chief chuckled and ruffled his youngest son's hair. "Don't be such a grump; I promised I'd take you out to breakfast before I drop you off at school."

Evan shrugged.

Suddenly remembering something, Holly snatched several slips of paper from her desk and offered them to the chief. "I have these messages for you. Don't know if you want them now, or…"

"No, now is fine," the chief said as he reached to take the papers. He paused a moment at the desk and read the notes. After a moment, he looked over to his sons and said, "I need to make a phone call when we get to my office."

"What about breakfast?" Eddie groaned.

"Don't worry, we'll have plenty of time for breakfast." Folding the notes, the chief slipped them into his shirt pocket and smiled at Holly. "Thanks."

The three made their way down the hallway to the chief's office. Halfway there, Evan said, "Dad, I need to go to the bathroom."

"Okay. Meet us back in my office."

Evan gave his dad a nod and then raced down the hallway, passing the closed door leading to his father's office. A few minutes later, after using the bathroom, Evan was back in the hallway again. It was quiet in the police station; only a few people were on duty. Most of the employees hadn't yet come in for work.

Remembering that his father's co-workers occasionally brought in donuts or cookies and left them in the lunchroom, he wondered if any were there now. Taking a slight detour, Evan headed off in that direction in search of something to eat.

The moment Evan entered the lunchroom, he froze. An elderly woman sat alone in the room, sitting at the table. She turned to look at him. He immediately recognized her. She was a friend of his father's—Marie Nichols.

"Good, I suppose this means your father is finally here. I've been waiting forever for him!" Marie greeted him impatiently.

Evan nodded and then frowned. He suddenly realized she was wearing some sort of robe-like nightgown, and he could see her feet under the table. They were bare.

"My dad is in his office," he stammered.

"Good. It's about time." Marie frowned a moment and tilted her head slightly, studying him. "Why are you here? Shouldn't you be at home getting ready for school?"

"My brother left his backpack in my dad's office," Evan explained. "We had to stop by here and pick it up. Then Dad is taking us out to breakfast before taking us to school."

Marie smiled. "That's nice. I always enjoy it when my grandson takes me out to breakfast. I hate cooking. Does your dad like to cook?"

Evan shrugged. "He likes to barbeque."

Marie shook her head. "I never tried that, myself. Barbequing is a man's job."

"You want me to go get my dad?" Evan asked.

"No, that's alright. I can find him myself. Your name is Evan, right?"

Evan smiled and nodded.

"The younger son?"

"Yes."

"So what grade are you in now, Evan?" Marie asked.

"Second." Evan smiled.

"It looks like your dad is doing a fine job raising you and your brother. Not an easy thing for a father alone. But Danielle speaks very highly of you and your brother. Although, I suspect she is especially fond of you."

Evan's smiled broadened. "I like Danielle and going over to Marlow House." Evan almost said he liked visiting with Walt, but instead said, "And I like going over there to play with Sadie."

"Sadie?" Marie asked, and then she remembered and smiled. "Right. Ian's dog. But Sadie lives across the street, doesn't she?"

Evan nodded. "Yes, but she spends a lot of time at Marlow House."

"Do you know I used to live across the street from Marlow House, where Sadie lives?"

Evan's eyes widened. "You did?"

Marie nodded. "Yes, my parents lived there when I was born. But we moved when I was just a baby."

"My dad said Ian and Lily just bought that house."

"Yes, yes, they did. They bought it from me. And I must say, my father would be quite shocked at what I got for it." She chuckled.

"I better go to my dad's office. He's probably waiting. Do you want to go with me?"

Marie considered his question a moment, her forehead furrowing into a frown. "Is your brother with your father?"

"Yes."

"Evan, perhaps you should tell your father I'm here, and have him come to me, so we can talk in private. I have some unpleasant

15

business to discuss with him, and I would prefer to talk to him alone."

"Oh, okay." Evan nodded. "I'll go tell him."

"Thank you, Evan. I'll wait here."

Evan turned and dashed from the lunchroom, heading to his father's office. When he arrived, the door was open, and his father was standing by his desk while his brother was sitting on a chair, looking through his backpack.

"I was just coming to look for you," MacDonald told Evan. "Where were you?"

"I was talking to someone in the lunchroom."

"Who?"

"Umm..." Evan frowned. "I know her name...but I can't remember. She's a friend of yours."

"Why is she in the lunchroom?"

Evan shrugged. "She said she needs to talk to you. I think it's important. Sounded like a secret."

"Secret?"

Evan nodded. "I told her she could come with me to your office, but she said she needed to talk to you alone. She wants you to go to the lunchroom. She's waiting for you there."

"Can we go to breakfast now? I'm hungry," Eddie asked as he zipped up his backpack.

"Just a minute, Eddie." The chief picked up the office phone and called the front desk. When Holly answered, he asked, "Who's waiting for me in the lunchroom?...Evan was just in there, and he said a woman was waiting to talk to me...no...are you sure?" With a frown, the chief hung up the phone. He looked at Evan.

"Dad, can we go now?" Eddie whined.

Ignoring his eldest, the chief looked at Evan. "According to Holly, no one has come in this morning to see me. You don't know this woman's name?"

Evan shrugged. "I don't remember what it is. But she's really old."

The chief let out a sigh. "When you say old, do you mean my age or your grandparents'?"

Evan wrinkled his nose. "Older. Oh...she said she owned the house Ian and Lily just bought!'

"Ahh...Marie Nichols," the chief said.

"Yes! I remember now. That's her name."

The chief chuckled. "Well, if anyone could sneak past Holly, it would be Marie." MacDonald then frowned, as if he just remembered something. "Was her grandson with her?"

"I didn't see anyone else," Evan said.

Eddie let out a sigh and slumped back on the chair, clutching his backpack.

The chief frowned. "That's odd. I thought she was still at the nursing home. And she doesn't drive…"

"Dad, she's wearing her pajamas," Evan told him.

"Her pajamas?"

"I think they're her pajamas. Like the kind Aunt Sissy wears. And she doesn't have any shoes on."

"You boys stay here. I'll be right back."

———

CHIEF MACDONALD LEFT his sons in his office as he made his way to the lunchroom. Once there, he stood in the doorway and glanced around. It was empty. Leaving the lunchroom, MacDonald moved down the hallway, poking his head in the various rooms, looking for Marie. At the women's restroom, he knocked loudly. When there was no answer, he inched open the door and called Marie's name. Still no answer.

Instead of returning to his office, he headed to the front desk to talk with Holly. While he believed Evan, he still didn't understand how Marie managed to get from the care home to the police station, and why she was wearing pajamas. But if she were in fact barefoot and wearing pajamas, the only thing that made sense, she had somehow escaped. If *escaped* was the correct word. It wasn't as if she was an actual prisoner, MacDonald told himself. However, he knew that was how she felt staying there.

By the time he reached Holly's desk, MacDonald had come to the conclusion that Marie had indeed slipped out of the care center, still wearing her nightclothes. He didn't believe it would have been possible for her to have walked all the way to the station; he didn't see how, considering she was recovering from hip surgery. But she very well could have called a taxi. It sounded like something Marie would do. From what he knew, Marie didn't seem to get along with her son and his wife. But why had she come to him? If Marie had found it necessary to steal away in her pajamas to come to the police station instead of just calling Adam, why? *Something is going on,* MacDonald told himself.

"Sorry, Chief," Holly said when MacDonald once again asked her about a woman visitor. "I didn't see anyone leave. Of course, I did step away for a moment to get something from the supply room. I suppose if someone was here, it's possible she left without me seeing."

"And you didn't see her arrive? She's an elderly woman wearing a nightgown."

Holly smiled. "I'm sure I would have noticed that. But you can ask Officer Tanner. He was here when I got in this morning. I suppose it's possible he let her in and forgot to tell me when he went home."

MacDonald glanced at his watch. "I think I better give Adam a call."

FOUR

Adam Nichols pulled up in front of his grandmother's house and parked behind his parents' car. He stayed in his vehicle a few moments, looking up to the house. He didn't see his brother's rental car and wondered if Jason had parked it in their grandmother's garage.

With a heavy sigh, Adam exited his vehicle and slammed the door shut behind him. Seeing his parents the first thing in the morning was not how he wanted to start the day, but he didn't have a choice. When he reached the front door, he found it unlocked. Entering the house without knocking, he glanced around, listening for voices. The only sound came from the ticking of the nearby grandfather clock. None of the downstairs lights were on. He wondered if everyone was still asleep, yet quickly dismissed that idea because of the unlocked door.

If I'm lucky, maybe I can get in and out of here without having to deal with them, he told himself.

Moving stealthily down the hallway, past the living room, Adam found himself holding his breath, not wanting to make any unnecessary noise. Just as he reached sight of the open doorway leading to the kitchen, he noticed light coming from that room. Letting out the breath he had been holding and resigning himself to the fact he probably would not be able to get in and out of his grandmother's house without dealing with family, he continued on.

When Adam looked into the kitchen, he was relieved to find his brother, Jason, standing at the kitchen sink, filling the coffee pot with water. He appeared to be alone.

Jason glanced briefly to the doorway. "You're here early." He continued to fill the pot.

Three years younger than Adam, Jason bore a striking resemblance to his older brother. Yet unlike Adam, who had dark brown, almost black eyes, Jason's were hazel. Adam tended to wear his hair short and neatly trimmed, whereas Jason's brown hair was in constant need of a haircut, curling just above his collar. In personality, they were nothing alike.

"Are Mom and Dad up?" Adam asked in a whisper as he entered the room.

Jason shook his head. "No, still in bed. I don't expect them up, not after the night they had."

Adam frowned. "What do you mean?"

Jason shrugged and poured the water into the back of the coffee maker. He set the pot on the coffee maker's burner and then turned to face his brother. "Same old thing. One hell of a fight. It would have been nice had they toned it down a little. After all, this is the first time they've met Sondra."

"I guess some things never change." Adam opened an overhead cupboard and pulled out a coffee cup.

"So why are you here so early?" Jason asked.

"I think I left my cellphone here." Adam glanced around the kitchen, looking for the phone. "You haven't seen it, have you?"

"No. Did you try calling it?" Jason asked.

"I'm pretty sure it's dead. The battery was low last night. And what am I going to call it with? I don't have a landline."

Jason shrugged. "Well, I haven't seen it, but I haven't been looking."

"If it's not here, then I must have left it in Grandma's room last night."

Jason poured himself a cup of coffee and then poured Adam one. The brothers took their steaming mugs to the kitchen table and sat down.

"Is Sondra still sleeping?"

"No, she was gone when I got up this morning." Jason sipped his coffee.

Adam arched his brows. "Gone?"

Jason chuckled. "She got up early to go running along the beach. I knew she was going. She told me last night."

"And you didn't go with her?"

Jason laughed. "Seriously? Running on the beach in this weather, while the sun is barely up? Not my idea of a good time."

"Did she take your car? I didn't see it in the drive," Adam asked.

"Yes. She said she was going to stop afterwards and get something to eat down at the pier."

"I'm surprised you didn't go with her."

"I don't like to eat this early. Anyway, she'll be fine on her own. This is Frederickport. Nothing happens here."

"You've obviously been away for a while," Adam muttered under his breath.

Jason looked up from his coffee. "What?"

Adam flashed his younger brother a smile. "Nothing." He took a sip of his coffee and then asked in a soft voice, "So what were Mom and Dad fighting about last night?"

Before answering, Jason glanced over to the open doorway. He looked back to Adam and whispered, "Grandma. She really pulled Mom's chain last night when she told them she was going to change her will."

Adam scoffed. "Grandma is not going to change her will. She's just pissed that Dad seems determined to keep her at Seaside Village. She wants to come home, and frankly, I don't blame her."

"Come on, Adam, Grandma is ninety-one. Don't you think she's a little old to be living alone?"

"She's been doing perfectly fine living on her own up until now. She should be able to live where she wants."

"Adam, Grandma broke her hip," Jason reminded him.

"So? I remember you broke your leg when you were in junior high, and no one talked about keeping you in the hospital for the rest of your life."

Jason frowned. "Hardly the same thing."

"Anyway, why does anyone care?" Adam snapped. "It's not like it inconveniences any of you. Hell, I'm the one keeping an eye on Grandma."

"She is Dad's mother. I think as her only child, he should have the ultimate say in what is best for Grandma. It's not your responsibility or mine."

"Is that why he's visited her so frequently since they moved to California?" Adam snarked.

"Well, to be fair, some of that is your fault."

Adam glared at his brother and took another sip of coffee. He then set the mug on the table and asked, "So they were fighting about Grandma?"

"Not at first."

"What else were they fighting about?" Adam asked.

"They were in the bedroom; they didn't actually have the fight in front of us. Of course, with the thin walls in this house, you can hear about everything. When they first started raising their voices, they were talking about the shop."

Adam frowned. "The shop?"

"I don't think it has been going well with the business. Has either one of them said anything to you about it?" Jason asked.

"Me?" Adam said with a snort. "Are you serious? I'm the last one Dad would discuss business problems with."

"Well, from what Sondra and I overheard, I think Dad's having some serious cash-flow problems. And then they started talking about Grandma. Mom thinks she's senile and not capable of making decisions. She told Dad he waited too long to step in and do something about her estate."

"Her estate is fine."

Jason shrugged. "I just think Mom's afraid Grandma might do something stupid, you know, like leave her money to that cult your old girlfriend was hooked up with."

"Grandma is not leaving her money to any cult," Adam scoffed. He took another sip of coffee and then said, "So that's why they really came? Figured they could leave Grandma in the home and then start selling off her assets to save Dad's business?"

"Come on, Adam. Grandma is ninety-one. It's not like she's going to live forever. They naturally assume that when she goes, they'll get half of her estate. You can't blame Mom for freaking out at the idea Grandma might change her will at the last minute and leave the money to someone else."

"Grandma wouldn't have made that threat if Dad hadn't tried pushing her to move permanently into that place."

Jason shrugged. "Like I said, she's ninety-one. And you know, we're both pretty lucky Grandma set up her will like she did. I sure as hell don't want her to change it."

"Lucky how?"

"Grandma could just as easily have left everything to Dad. That's pretty common. Everything goes to the children, and the grandchildren have to wait until their parents check out to get a share. And considering how Mom spends money, and how Dad's business is sinking, there wouldn't be anything left for us when they eventually kick off."

"Ahh...so you're looking forward to a quarter of Grandma's estate?"

Jason grinned. "Hey, Grandma has lived a long life. And yeah, I have to admit it is a nice feeling knowing there is a substantial nest egg waiting for me. I don't make a lot of money as an associate professor. Face it, if it was all going to Mom and Dad, we'd never see it. I suppose we should be happy Mom and Grandma never really got along."

"I can see you're going to miss Grandma when she goes," Adam grumbled.

Jason shrugged. "Hey, I'm not saying I want Grandma to die or anything. But come on, Adam, it's not like her and I are that close. You were always her favorite."

"I was always the one willing to help her when she needed something," Adam reminded him.

Jason stood up with his now empty coffee mug. "And I imagine you got paid well for it. You've been making money all these years on her properties. Look at that fat commission you made on her Beach Drive house. I can't believe that went for over a million!"

Adam frowned. "How do you know what it went for? Grandma said she wasn't saying anything."

Jason walked to the coffee maker and refilled his cup. "Then I guess Grandma should have locked her file drawers before she broke her hip."

"Damn, Jason, have you been going through Grandma's files?"

"Not me. Dad went through them the first night. But you can't blame him. Mom says it's common for someone to pass away not long after they break a hip. Dad was just trying to figure out where Grandma's estate stood, and what he'll need to do when she's gone." Jason returned to the table with his cup of coffee and sat down.

"I've been handling Grandma's estate for a long time now. He could ask me."

"Come on, he did ask you questions when they first got here. You gave him that bull about not being able to discuss your client's personal business. He's her son, for heaven's sake, and your father!"

Adam shrugged. "Like you said, he asked me questions when they first got here—about her money situation. He should have been asking how she was doing health wise."

"Adam, you know Dad."

"So how did the fight end?"

"One of them slammed out of the house. Took off. When I went to bed, the car was still gone. It was in front of the house this morning when I woke up, so whoever left obviously came back."

"Who left? Mom or Dad?"

"I don't know."

Adam stood up. "I'm going to look for my phone and then get out of here before I have to deal with Mom and Dad."

"Well, good morning to you too," Chloe Nichols said from the doorway.

Adam turned to his mother. He found her staring at him through eyes very much like his own—yet hers showed traces of the makeup she had applied the day before. Clad in a satin, floor-length robe, its design a rich assortment of golds, oranges and reds in swirling paisley, she looked like a woman preparing to meet her lover. Chloe rested her right hand on one slender hip, while her left hand casually gripped the edge of the door jamb. Adam thought she looked regal. She had always reminded him of one of those beautiful—albeit evil—queens in a Disney movie.

Adam couldn't quite recall what her natural hair color was. Growing up, he had seen his mother as a blonde, brunette, and redhead. Her current hair color was inky black, the same shade as Heather Donovan's. This morning Chloe wore her hair down. It fell several inches below her shoulders. Her choice of hair length and color was not flattering to many women her age. Yet her slender form along with a better-than-average plastic surgeon allowed Chloe to embrace styles often reserved for much younger women.

"Good morning, Mother. You haven't seen my cellphone, have you?" Adam asked with a smile.

FIVE

A dam pulled into the rear parking lot of Seaside Village at the
same time as Danielle. They parked their cars next to each
other, turned off their ignitions, and got out of their vehicles.

"Are you stalking me?" Adam teased Danielle as he slammed his
car door shut.

Standing next to her red Ford Flex, Danielle held up her paper
sack from Old Salts Bakery. "I come bearing gifts for your
grandmother."

"Cinnamon rolls?" Adam perked up. "I hope you brought
enough for me."

"When are there ever enough cinnamon rolls?" Danielle teased.
Together she walked with Adam toward the back entrance of the
care facility.

"I know Grandma will appreciate them."

"What are you doing here so early? Did Marie tell you I was
bringing cinnamon rolls this morning?" She paused with Adam by
the back door while he keyed in the password.

"You know she wouldn't do that; then she'd have to share."
Adam chuckled. "I think I left my cellphone here last night. It was
either here or Grandma's house. If it isn't here, I'm screwed. I
already checked Grandma's house."

Finished entering the password, Adam quickly opened the door
and held it open for Danielle to enter first.

"Did you try calling it?"

"Why does everyone ask that?" Adam grumbled as he followed Danielle into the rear lounge of the care home.

"Because that's what people normally do when they lose their cellphones."

"That's hard to do if there isn't another phone around. And it only works if the cellphone is charged and on. I'm pretty sure my battery is dead."

"I can relate. My phone's not holding a charge these days. I have it plugged in so much it's starting to feel like another landline."

Together they walked towards Marie's room. The lounge and hallway on Marie's end of the building seemed deserted. Down the main hall, in the far distance, was the front nurses' station. Danielle spied staff and patients milling in that area.

When they arrived at Marie's room, it was empty, and her sheets were stripped from the bed.

"Kind of early for Grandma to be at breakfast," Adam said as he walked into the room and glanced around. He spied his cellphone sitting on the dresser. "There it is!"

"I'm surprised she went to breakfast," Danielle said with a frown. "She knew I was bringing cinnamon rolls."

"That's one of Grandma's bitches about this place. She says they insist she go down to the dining room during the meals even if she isn't hungry." Adam picked up his phone and looked at it, turning it from side to side. As he suspected, the battery was dead. He tucked the phone in his back pocket.

"I know. But the exception is if she has guests—like when I brought sandwiches for lunch, and we ate them in the back lounge. I'm surprised she didn't tell them I was coming with breakfast."

"I don't imagine they consider cinnamon rolls a healthy breakfast." Adam glanced up at the wall clock and frowned. "But it is kind of early to be at breakfast."

"Maybe she's off visiting," Danielle suggested.

"Grandma, visiting, here?" Adam said with a snort. "She complains there's no one here she can have a decent conversation with. But let's go find her. I want one of those cinnamon rolls."

Together Danielle and Adam headed out the doorway to the hall. Just as they did, they came face-to-face with SeAnne Eason, one of the younger nurses working at Seaside Village.

"Mr. Nichols!" SeAnne gasped. "I thought that was you who came in. They finally got ahold of you. I'm so sorry."

Coming to an abrupt stop, Adam frowned. "What are you talking about?"

"Your grandmother...umm...they did call you, didn't they?" SeAnne stammered.

Adam pulled his cellphone out of his back pocket and showed it to the nurse. "I haven't had my phone since last night. I forgot it here. What about my grandmother? Has something happened?"

Color drained from the nurse's face. "Then you don't know?"

"Know what?"

"I'm so very sorry. Your grandmother passed away in her sleep last night. It was very peaceful. I know they've been trying to contact you all morning. The only number they have is yours."

At the news, Danielle let out a gasp before looking around, wondering if Marie's spirit was lingering nearby.

Visibly stunned, Adam stared at SeAnne. "What do you mean she passed away? I saw my grandmother last night. She was perfectly fine!"

"Mr. Nichols, I am so sorry for your loss. But your grandmother was ninety-one. It's a blessing, really, that she went so peacefully."

"Blessing, my ass!' Adam shouted. "Where is my grandmother?"

Tears now filling Danielle's eyes, she reached out and took hold of Adam's right hand, giving it a reassuring squeeze. Feeling him tremble, she held on tightly.

"The funeral home picked up her body a few minutes ago."

"Why in the hell did they do that?" Adam roared.

"Well...umm...when your grandmother checked in...umm... that was the instruction...umm...you know, if something happened...Maybe you should go talk to the front desk. My supervisor, Sunny Hartman, is the one who found her this morning, I believe she's at the front nurses' station."

Without another word, Adam started for the front desk, dragging Danielle along with him, her hand still clinging to his.

"How can she be dead?" Adam asked.

"I'm so sorry, Adam. I really loved your grandma," Danielle whispered.

Adam walked a few more steps, and then he stopped abruptly and turned to Danielle. He smiled sadly, tears now streaming down his face. "I know you did. And she loved you. You were the daughter she never had."

"I like to think...granddaughter." Danielle smiled up at Adam, her glistening tears threatening to escape. "I'm far too young to be your aunt."

"You are so vain, Danielle Boatman." Adam laughed in spite of the tears, and then he reached out and drew Danielle into his arms. They held each other for several moments. When the hug ended, Adam wiped his face with the back of his sleeve. Instead of holding Danielle's hand, Adam casually draped his arm around her shoulders. Together Adam and Danielle walked to the nurses' station, looking for answers.

ADAM AND DANIELLE each took a seat in Sunny Hartman's small office. Sunny shut the door for privacy and then took a seat at her desk. With a heavy sigh, she folded her hands on her desktop, sat up straight in her office chair, and looked across the desk at Adam and Danielle.

When Danielle had first met Sunny Hartman the prior week, she wondered if Sunny was her real name or a nickname earned because of her perpetually sunny disposition. The nurse's cheerfulness had annoyed Marie, who complained to Danielle that she would like to slap the smile off the woman's face.

"She acts like she's working at Disneyland, and this is the happiest place on earth!" Marie had scoffed.

"I think she's just trying to keep the residents' morale up," Danielle had suggested.

"If she wants to do that, she should start by making it smell better!" Marie had countered.

"I FOUND her this morning when I was making my rounds. At first, I thought she was sleeping. I'm very sorry," Sunny explained.

"What happened?" Adam asked.

"She died in her sleep. I'd like you to know she looked very peaceful when I found her. I don't believe she suffered."

"I was here last night," Adam argued. "She was perfectly fine. She told me she was ready to go home."

Sunny smiled sadly. "I know Marie was anxious to get home. But she was a very old woman and more fragile than she liked to admit. It was simply her time. I know that isn't much comfort now, especially when it's so unexpected, but I believe she went peacefully."

Danielle reached to Adam and took his hand, giving it a reassuring squeeze. "She's right, Adam. Your grandmother put up a good front, but she was feeling her age. We talked about it. She didn't want you to know, especially now."

Adam looked at Danielle and frowned. "What do you mean?"

"She didn't want to stay here any longer than she had to," Danielle explained. "She was afraid if your father knew she wasn't as strong as she tried to put on, he'd do something so she couldn't go home. Marie always told me that when it was her time, she prayed she would simply go in her sleep. I think that's what we all want." Danielle gave his hand another squeeze and then released it.

Adam slumped back in the chair and let out a heavy sigh. "Now what?"

"No one else in your family has been contacted. We called your number several times and left messages. We don't have your father's phone number, so we couldn't call him," Sunny explained.

"I left my phone here last night. That's why I stopped in this morning, to find it. My parents and brother have been staying at my grandmother's house. Did you try calling there?"

Sunny shook her head. "I'm sorry, when your grandmother was admitted, the only number she gave us was yours. She said you would contact any other family member if necessary."

"I don't think she wanted Dad to come to Frederickport. She was afraid he'd try to interfere. She knew she could manage me." Adam couldn't help but chuckle at the fact his grandmother had been adept at managing him.

"I really liked your grandmother," Sunny said. "She was a character. There was nothing senile about her despite her age. Maybe her body gave out, but her mind remained sharp to the end. If your father would have asked my opinion, I would have told him she needed to go home when the physical therapist felt she was ready."

"I was told the funeral home already picked up her body?" Adam asked.

Sunny nodded. "Yes. Your grandmother made her funeral arrangements some time ago with the local funeral home, through her church. Long before she came here. When she was admitted, she made it very clear who we were to call if she died here."

Adam chuckled. "That sounds like Grandma."

Danielle stood up. "I'm going to go call Lily and let her know. You should probably call your parents."

DANIELLE STOOD IN THE HALLWAY, just outside the closed door of Sunny's office. After pulling out the cellphone from her purse, she called Lily.

"She died?" Lily gasped after Danielle gave her the news.

"They found her this morning. It looks like she simply died in her sleep."

"I thought she was doing good? She said she was going to be home by Christmas," Lily said. "Do you think she got some infection from the surgery? I know that happens sometimes."

"It might not have anything to do with the broken hip or surgery. It could have simply been old age. Or maybe the trauma from the injury and surgery simply overtaxed her body."

"Are they doing an autopsy?"

"I doubt it. I don't see the point, under the circumstances. They've already taken her to the funeral home."

"Wow...have you seen her?" Lily asked.

Danielle glanced down the hall to her right and then to her left. "No. She wasn't in her room, and I haven't seen her in the hallway. But she might have gone with her body to the funeral home. That often happens."

"How is Adam doing?"

"He seems to be in shock. He was pretty close to his grandmother despite the fact she often drove him crazy."

"Yeah, I get that. My mom drives me nuts, yet I don't know what I'll do when she's no longer here," Lily said.

Danielle's phone began to buzz, indicating another incoming call. She quickly glanced at it and then put it back to her ear.

"Lily, the chief is calling. Let me answer it."

A moment later Danielle was disconnected from Lily's call and talking to Chief MacDonald.

"I've been trying to contact Adam, and he isn't answering his cell," the chief told her. "You mentioned you were going to see Marie this morning."

"Chief, I'm at the nursing home now, and so is Adam. Marie passed away last night."

"Excuse me?"

"She died in her sleep. One of the nurses found her this morning when she was making her rounds."

"Well, I suppose that sort of explains it," MacDonald murmured.

"Explains what?" Danielle asked.

"Why Marie was at the station this morning—in her nightgown —and Evan was the only one to see her," MacDonald explained.

They were both silent for a few moments. Finally, Danielle asked, "Umm, Chief, why would Marie's spirit go to the police station?"

SIX

Morning sunlight streamed through the east-facing window. Quivering leaves blocked a portion of the incoming light, their shadows dancing along the far wall. Max crouched nearby, preparing to pounce, his golden eyes fixed on the flickering shadows as his black tail twitched in anticipation.

Without warning he leapt from his place by the bed and raced across the room, his paws slipping along the wood floor, making it difficult for him to maneuver. Unable to stop when he reached the shadows, Max's right shoulder bounced rudely against the wall, sending him darting in another direction. He raced out the doorway and into the hall. Without pause he flew toward the stairway, sailing through Walt, who was just preparing to go downstairs from the second floor.

Walt paused and looked down, watching as the cat continued down the stairs after having just moved effortlessly through his legs. Had Walt been a living man, he might now be toppling headfirst down the staircase after the cat, which could, in effect, leave Walt in the same condition as he was now—*dead*.

"Crazy cat," Walt muttered as he continued down the stairs. When he reached the first-floor landing, he heard someone at the door. He was fairly certain it wasn't Max, because as far as Walt knew, Max hadn't figured out how to open the front door, and by the sound of the rusty hinges, someone had definitely just opened it.

Aside from Max, Walt was alone in the house. Danielle had gone to visit Marie, and they didn't have any houseguests. Danielle had decided to spend Thanksgiving with close friends, which was why she had not taken any reservations for the week. He knew Joanne was not planning to come in today, and Danielle typically entered through the kitchen door. *So who just opened the front door?* Walt wondered.

When the ghost of Marlow House reached the entry hall, he found Lily closing the front door. Max, who was no longer racing through the house, sat a few feet from Lily, looking up at her, waiting for a greeting. He let out a meow.

Lily glanced down at Max and smiled. "Well, hello to you too. Do you know where Walt is? I need to talk to him." Lily reached down to pet Max's shoulder.

Walt glanced around, looking for a way to get Lily's attention and let her know he was nearby. His gaze settled on Max, who was now purring and leaning into Lily's hand. With a smirk, Walt found it hard to resist. In the next moment, Max lifted up from the floor, floating in midair near Lily.

The cat let out an unholy screech, and in the next moment he was on the floor again, his paws desperately trying to gain traction on the slippery wood. In a flash he was racing down the hallway, disappearing into one of the rooms.

Lily chuckled and glanced around. "That wasn't very nice, Walt."

"He about knocked me down the stairs a minute ago. Well...he could have knocked someone down the stairs. Serves him right."

"I wanted to let you know Marie passed away last night," Lily told him.

"Little Marie?" Walt murmured. He had questions, but he knew Lily couldn't hear him. The next moment he sent the parlor door opening and closing.

"You want me to go into the parlor?" Lily asked.

Not waiting for a reply, she started for the room. Once inside, she spied a pen seemingly moving on its own accord across a piece of paper. Stepping closer to the desk, Lily looked down at the paper to see what Walt had just written.

What happened?

"According to Dani, she died in her sleep last night. They found her this morning. I was wondering if you've seen her. But since you asked what happened, I have to assume you didn't know about it, which obviously means you didn't see her."

The pen began writing again.

No, I haven't seen her. Has Danielle?

Lily shook her head. "No. But they took Marie's body to the funeral home before Dani got there this morning, and Dani figures Marie might be there. Or...maybe she's already moved on. I kind of hope not. I think Dani will be pretty upset if she can't say goodbye. And, well...I'd like a chance to say goodbye to her too."

"THAT'S A NICE TRICK," Eva Thorndike murmured when she suddenly appeared in the parlor, perched casually on the sofa's armrest.

Walt turned his attention from Lily to Eva and smiled. The attractive specter wore a gown he hadn't seen before, a pale apricot chiffon, a fitting autumn color. "Good morning, Eva. And what trick is that?"

"I'll see you later, Walt," Lily interrupted. "Well...maybe not see you exactly," Lily muttered as she left the parlor, unaware Eva had just joined them.

His attention on Eva, Walt waited for her answer.

"Communicating with the living by way of a pen and paper." With a wave of her hand, Eva sent golden glitter swirling into the air.

With mock seriousness Walt said, "I really wish you wouldn't get that stuff all over the place."

Eva glanced down. The illusion of glitter had vanished before it touched the floor. "Funny," she said with a chuckle.

Walt grinned. "You know, Eva, if you weren't wasting your energy on glitter, maybe you could push a pen around on paper."

"And why would I want to do that?" Eva shrugged. "I was never much for letter writing. Yet it is a nice trick. So who is this newly departed person Lily spoke of?"

"Do you remember George Hemming?" Walt asked.

"George Hemming? Didn't he live across the street from you?" Eva glanced to the window facing the street and the Hemming house.

"Yes. George wasn't married when you knew him. But he and his wife had a daughter—Marie. Lily just told me she died."

"Ahh, and joined our side?" Eva smiled.

"Danielle was very close to Marie. I imagine it'll be hard on her."

"Why? It's not like Danielle won't be able to see or talk to her."

"You have to remember, we are the exception, Eva. I imagine Marie will be moving on."

"I don't know why she would," Eva said as she stood up straight. "I find there is too much for me to see and hear on this realm to move on to the next just yet. But I suppose eventually I will. What about you, Walt? I can't imagine being cooped up in one place like this." Eva glanced around and shivered. "It's enough to make a spirit move on."

"I'm comfortable here," Walt told her.

"Yes, we all know why you're so comfortable," Eva smirked.

"Why are you here, Eva? Just stopped to say hi?"

Eva smiled at Walt as she adjusted her gown's skirt. "I was in the neighborhood. I stopped by Chris's house, but he wasn't there." Eva let out a disappointed sigh. "So I thought I'd drop by to see you. I know you never go anywhere."

"Ahh, Chris." Walt chuckled. "You'll have to come back next week. Chris is off on some charity fundraiser. Chicago...or was it Paris?"

"You know, that man is still quite smitten with your Danielle," Eva told him.

"She's not exactly *my Danielle*."

Eva arched her brows. "Oh, she isn't?"

"And while he does annoy me, Chris is not a bad fellow," Walt begrudgingly admitted.

With a sigh, Eva sat back on the arm of the sofa. "You know, Walt, imagine how wonderful it would have been had Danielle and Chris been alive in our time? The four of us, we could have become such grand friends...me and Chris together, you and Danielle. I can even imagine Chris on the stage with me. Fans would have adored us!"

Walt smiled sadly at Eva. "Fans did adore you, Eva. So did I. But it's not our time anymore. We're simply observers now."

Eva stood again. "I wouldn't call you an observer exactly. From what I understand, you haven't exactly sat back and let things just happen. I suspect Danielle would be on our side by now if you hadn't interfered a few times."

Walt shrugged at the observation.

"So tell me about this Marie who has passed over."

Walt gave her a brief synopsis of Marie, including where she had been when she died.

"Ahh! I remember her now!" Eva squealed.

"How could you?" Walt frowned.

Eva smiled. "You forget, I often visited you—up until your death. I remember the baby across the street. Such a sweet thing. And you know, I do believe she could see me."

"What do you mean? Marie can't see spirits."

"Don't you know, Walt…" Eva paused a moment and then let out a sigh. "I suppose you don't, considering you've been trapped in this house for almost a century. But it's not uncommon for babies—or very young children—to see and hear us. I don't mean someone like Evan, who has a special gift like Danielle and Chris. I mean all babies."

"Actually, I've heard that—about babies seeing spirits. Yet I would imagine that could terrify a poor child." Walt cringed.

Eva waved her hand dismissively, sending blue glitter swirling. "I've never scared a child in my life—or—should I say my death. I used to sing to little Marie."

"Sing to her?"

Eva smiled at the memory. "You know, I never really thought about having children of my own. I was so focused on my career, and I will confess, during my brief marriage, I was a bit terrified of the prospect. But after my death…well, I began to wonder what kind of mother I might have been. What a child of mine might look like." Eva sighed wistfully.

"You're not alone. I've wondered that about myself. What kind of father would I have been?"

"A loving father, I imagine, considering how you took care of me during the end." She then continued with her story. "One day, when I was checking on you, I heard a baby crying. The sound was coming from one of the open windows in the house across the street. I went to investigate."

"It was Marie?"

Eva nodded. "She was alone in her room, crying her little heart out. Her mother was in the kitchen. I suspect she had just put the child down in the crib for a nap. But that baby was not having any of it."

"Did Marie see you?"

"Oh yes. She looked quite startled when I showed up by her crib, looking in at her. She stopped crying for a moment, and then her little face puckered up again, and I knew she was going to start wailing even louder than before. So I started singing."

"Singing?"

"Yes. A lullaby my mother used to sing to me. And right away, her little face unpuckered, and she made this adorable cooing sound. It became something of a ritual—for me and little Marie. Yet, until you just mentioned it, I had forgotten that was her name. I was rarely around when her parents were in the room, so I only heard them say it maybe once or twice."

"So you did know little Marie?"

"In a manner of speaking. I'd sing lullabies to her during nap time. And then she moved away, and I didn't see her again."

"They moved after I died. Her father is the one who found me hanging in the attic."

Eva cringed. "Not a pleasant sight."

"I wonder if Marie has moved on?" Walt murmured.

"Danielle is out looking for her?" Eva asked.

"The impression I got from Lily was that she'd like to find her, at least to say goodbye."

"I remember Marie's father, George Hemming. He was rather shy, as I recall. Sweet man. He would come with you to the theater sometimes, but I don't think he ever said two words to me."

"After George was married, his bride moved into his parents' house with him. Marie was their only child. She was just a baby when I died."

Eva stood up. "I think I'll go help Danielle look for her. I'd like to see how she turned out."

Walt chuckled. "The last time I saw her, she was a ninety-one-year-old woman."

SEVEN

"They're not coming," Adam told Danielle when he stepped out of Sunny's office.

"Why not?" Danielle asked.

"Dad said there was no reason to come down here, since they've already taken Grandma's body."

Danielle frowned. "He didn't have any questions? I mean, doesn't he want to talk to someone and find out more about what happened?"

Adam shrugged and started down the hall, toward Marie's room. "I guess not."

Danielle trailed alongside Adam. "What are you going to do now?"

"Dad told me to stop by her room and pick up Grandma's purse. I asked him about her other things—like her clothes she has here. He told me the home could just clean out her room, get rid of her other stuff. Said we'd just get rid of it anyway." Adam stared blankly ahead as he walked with Danielle down the corridor.

"You're just going to leave her stuff here?" Danielle asked incredulously.

Adam let out a harsh laugh. "Hardly. Grandma would haunt me if I left her things here. She'd expect me to pack up her stuff, take it back to her house, and then decide what to do with it there."

"Want some help?" Danielle asked softly.

"I'd appreciate it. I imagine Grandma would rather you go through her personal things than anyone else."

"I'd be happy to help."

"Sunny said they'd pack up Grandma's stuff for me, and we could pick it up later. But I'd rather do it now."

They walked for a few moments in silence.

Finally, Danielle asked, "Did you call Melony yet?"

Adam shook his head. "No. I just called my dad. Did you call Lily?"

"Yes. Oh…and the chief called me, I told him."

"The chief called you? This early?" Adam glanced at Danielle.

She shrugged.

Adam chuckled. "Ahh, so it's you and the chief now."

Danielle rolled her eyes at Adam. "No. There is nothing between the chief and me. We're just friends."

"Yeah, right."

"No, seriously. We're just good friends." Danielle looked at Adam and smiled. She wrapped her arm around his. "Kinda like us."

Not pulling his arm from Danielle, Adam glanced down to her as he continued to walk down the hallway. "We're good friends?"

Danielle let out a sigh and shrugged. "Yeah, I guess we are."

"I thought you used to hate me," Adam said, only half teasing.

"Well, you did break into my house."

"God, that again? Are you going to be throwing that up in my face forever?"

"Probably," Danielle said with a grin.

"I just thought you were a ditzy broad." Adam chuckled.

Danielle squeezed his arm and gave it a little pinch. "Ditzy?"

"Ouch!"

"You just called me ditzy!"

"It was all that feng shui crap. And not wanting to offend Walt Marlow's ghost," he said with a snort.

"Says the man who is cleaning out his grandmother's room so she doesn't haunt him."

"True. I just figure if there was anyone who could come over from the other side and give me a smack for not doing what she wants, it's Grandma."

"I'm going to miss her," Danielle whispered, giving Adam's arm a gentle squeeze.

Adam patted Danielle's hand. "You and me both…so, I guess we must be friends now."

"We weren't before?" Danielle asked.

Adam shrugged. "Never was completely sure if you were just playing nice for Grandma's sake."

"Don't be silly. Of course we're friends." Danielle gave his arm another little squeeze and said, "Adam, it's kind of hard to dislike a guy who was so good to his grandmother. And you were good to Marie. She adored you, you know."

Adam smiled sadly. "I never doubted her love."

"And I figured, if Marie liked you so much, you really couldn't be all that bad."

ADAM PULLED his grandmother's suitcase from the closet and tossed it on the sheet-less bed. He took a seat on the lone chair in the room and watched as Danielle packed the suitcase. She opened one dresser drawer after another, emptying the contents before neatly stacking the items in the suitcase. Adam didn't offer to help. Instead, he sat quietly, lost in his own private thoughts.

Danielle had just finished emptying the last drawer when Adam noticed the way in which she kept glancing around the room.

"Are you looking for something?" Adam asked.

Danielle paused and looked over to Adam. "What?"

"The way you keep looking around the room, as if you're looking for something."

"Umm…no…I was just seeing what else we need to pack."

"According to Sunny, they probably have some laundry of Grandma's. I'll have to pick that up later. But I don't even know if I'll bother. Her clothes will probably go to the thrift store anyway." Adam glanced upward. "Would that be okay, Grandma?"

"I don't think she'll have a problem with that." Danielle closed the suitcase and latched it.

With a heavy sigh, Adam stood up and walked to the washbasin. He began gathering up Marie's toiletry items.

"Adam, I really don't think Marie would get upset with you if you threw that stuff in the trash."

"I suspect you're right," Adam said as he tossed Marie's toothbrush in the trash can.

Danielle sat down on the edge of the bed, facing Adam. "I had to do this with my parents. It was awful. I couldn't bring myself to just shove their clothes into bags for the thrift store. I kept remembering how my mother always folded anything she donated, stacking them neatly in a box. I used to tell her they probably just dumped the stuff out anyway after we dropped them off. But when I had to do it after they died, I ended up folding everything—just like Mom used to do."

"That's right, you lost both of your parents. It must have been hard." Adam stood by the basin, emptying the drawers. He kept some items and tossed others.

"Yeah. But it's been a long time now." Danielle sighed.

"So you got used to it?"

Danielle continued to watch Adam. "I still miss them. Sometimes even more than right after it happened."

"Because now you realize how permanent that loss is?" Adam suggested.

"Probably."

"I'm not very close to my parents," Adam told her.

"Yeah, I sort of got that. Marie mentioned once there was some sort of falling-out, and she took your side."

"Did she tell you what it was about?" Adam turned from the basin and faced Danielle.

She shook her head. "No. I didn't ask. I figured it was none of my business."

"My dad owns a machine shop," Adam began.

"I believe Marie mentioned that once."

"Back in high school I was sort of a screwup. There was that little thing about me and Melony running away." Adam walked over to a chair and sat down. He leaned back, stretching his legs and crossing them at the ankle.

"Is that what the falling-out was about?" Danielle asked.

"I thought you said it was none of your business?" Adam teased.

"I didn't say I wasn't curious."

Adam smiled. "Nah, that was just one of the many ways I disappointed my folks. I admit, I liked to party. My grades were mediocre, and my younger brother had the patent on brownnosing."

"He was the good son?"

"Ohhhh yes. Always on the honor roll. Never got in trouble.

Anyway, I worked after school at my dad's machine shop. I hated it. Seriously. I hated it."

"Did your brother work there, too?"

Adam shook his head. "No. He never had a job in high school. Dad said as long as he got straight As, he didn't have to work. I suppose I could have gotten the same deal, but I was having too much fun and wasn't willing to settle down at school."

"So what happened?"

"After high school graduation I wasn't sure what I wanted to do. My grades sucked, so anything more than the community college was out of the question. And since I didn't know what I wanted to do, it seemed like a waste to go to school at that point. I started working full time for my dad and hated it. Just doing it because I didn't know what else to do. I was also taking care of my grandma's rental properties. You know, fixing things that broke, keeping up the yards, that sort of stuff."

"Sounds like you were a hard worker."

Adam shrugged. "Well, Dad got an opportunity to move his machine shop down to California. He was approached by a large company to relocate the business. He thought he was going to make a fortune. Dad expected me to go with him and work in his shop. But I refused."

"Was that the falling-out?"

Adam nodded. "Yes. I was living at home at the time. Dad asked me what I thought I was going to do since they'd be selling the house, and I wouldn't have a job. That's when Grandma stepped in. She told me I could live with her, keep taking care of her properties, until I figured out what I wanted to do."

"Was your dad mad?"

"Both my parents were. It's not like Dad was sorry to lose his oldest son, but I was a cheap, underpaid employee that knew the business. I screwed up his plans. Now he would need to hire someone to replace me. Someone who would expect to get paid more than what my dad was paying me. Dad used to tell me that as long as I was living at home, I couldn't expect to get paid as much as a regular employee. I suppose he was right. But the one time I decided to move out and rent a room with a friend, he told me not to expect a raise. He said it was my choice to leave home. And that as long as he was willing to let me stay there, I shouldn't expect to get paid more if I decided to move out."

"Wow. Kind of reminds me of the old company store."

Adam frowned. "Company store?"

"Yeah, where the only store the laborers had access to was owned by their boss."

"Pretty much."

"So you stayed here and went into real estate?"

"I didn't go into real estate right away. I worked a little bit with Bill, doing some repairs for people. But then I decided there were better ways to make a living, and I eventually got my real estate license, opened the vacation rental business, and got a place of my own."

"I would think your parents would be proud of what you've accomplished."

"You would, wouldn't you?"

EIGHT

After Danielle helped Adam pack up the rest of his grandmother's room, she walked with him to the back parking lot. They each carried a portion of Marie's belongings—her suitcase, pillow, purse, and a plastic bag full of miscellaneous items.

Overhead, dark clouds blocked much of the morning sun. Danielle glanced over to her locked car, momentarily regretting leaving her jacket inside the vehicle. She stood between her car and Adam's while he tossed Marie's suitcase and pillow into his trunk.

It started to drizzle. Quickly taking the remainder of the items from Danielle, Adam shoved them into his trunk and slammed it shut before the rain started falling in full force. Danielle reached up and gave Adam a quick kiss on the cheek, telling him she would call later. He gave her a little nod and hurried into his car as she got into hers.

Danielle sat in her red Ford Flex a moment and watched as Adam pulled out of the parking lot. Yet, instead of turning on her ignition, she grabbed her jacket off the passenger seat, slipped it on, and then exited the vehicle as soon as Adam's car disappeared from sight.

Rushing to the rear door of the care facility—the rain still just a light drizzle—Danielle hurriedly entered the password to open the back door, hoping they hadn't changed it since she had last visited Marie. When Adam had entered the password earlier that morning, she hadn't watched to see if it was the one she knew. The door unlocked.

The rear door of the facility opened to a lounge area consisting of a leather couch facing a coffee table and two easy chairs, and several side tables. It was in this area where Danielle had spent most of her care home visits with Marie. There was a similar lounge at the front of the facility, yet that was normally occupied by the permanent residents and their visitors.

During Danielle's visits, she rarely found the rear lounge occupied save for an occasional permanent-care resident who had wandered to the area, attempting to escape out the back door. Since some residents weren't privy to the password, the chance of escape was minimal unless a visitor allowed one of the patients to slip out the door while it was opening or closing.

"If Marie was at the police station earlier, then she probably isn't at the funeral home. It's possible she'll come back here first before moving on," Danielle muttered to herself.

She walked across the lounge. Straight ahead led down the long hallway to the front entrance and the main nurses' station. Midway, from the rear of the building to its front entrance, was the kitchen and dining room, its doorway situated to the right of the hallway. Closed doors leading to other patient rooms lined the hall.

A second hallway ran perpendicular to the main one. Stepping out of the lounge and turning left would take Danielle down the corridor leading to the room Marie had died in. It was in this rear section of the complex that the temporary rehab patients resided. However, since first coming to visit Marie, Danielle had never noticed any of the other rooms in this area being occupied.

Danielle stood along the edge of the rear lounge for a moment, wondering if she should continue down to the main nurses' station and look for Marie's spirit there, or perhaps take a left and see if her spirit had returned to her room.

Deciding to check Marie's room first, Danielle turned left and started down the empty corridor. She was reminded of the times Marie had commented on the eeriness of her hallway during the evenings, which had always seemed vacant. Even the rear nurses' station remained unmanned.

Just as Danielle passed the first doorway along the rear hallway, she heard a female voice call out, "Your friend's no longer here."

Pausing a moment, Danielle turned around, looking back from

45

where she had just come. There, standing by an open doorway, was an elderly woman wearing a blue-rose-patterned nightgown. When Danielle had walked by that room earlier—twice with Adam, and now just by herself, she had noticed the open door, yet she assumed the room was unoccupied.

Danielle recognized the woman. She had seen her several times when she had visited Marie. Those times the woman had been walking down the main hallway, yet the two had never spoken.

With a frown, Danielle glanced from the woman to the open doorway. "Is that your room?"

The woman smiled. "Yes."

"I've seen you here before, but I didn't realize you were staying in this section. I thought all the rooms were empty along this corridor."

"Please, I certainly don't belong on the other side!" The woman gasped. "Most of those poor souls can't even remember their names."

Danielle smiled weakly and then glanced down the hallway to Marie's room. She wondered what she would do if Marie's spirit suddenly appeared. If she called out to Marie while the woman was in earshot, Danielle wondered if the elderly patient would rush to get a nurse and have her committed. She smiled at the idea.

"Was she your grandmother?" the woman asked.

Danielle frowned. "Excuse me?"

"I called her your friend, but I just realized she might have been your grandmother."

"No, she was a dear friend," Danielle explained. "We weren't related."

"The way she rushed out of here, I don't think she's coming back," the woman said.

"Excuse me?"

"Ms. Boatman!" came a second voice.

Danielle turned to where she had just come from and spied Sunny Hartman rushing in her direction. When Danielle glanced back to the elderly woman, she was gone.

"Ms. Boatman, I thought that was you!" Sunny said, slightly out of breath when she reached her. "I saw you leave with Mr. Nichols, and then a few minutes later I noticed you going down this hall."

"I thought I left something in Marie's room," Danielle lied.

"You didn't leave it in Marie's room. It's in my office." Sunny smiled.

Confused, Danielle stared at Sunny.

"Your sack? I assumed that's what you were talking about."

The cinnamon rolls! Danielle told herself. She had forgotten all about the cinnamon rolls she had brought to share with Marie. She must have left them in Sunny's office when she and Adam had gone in there earlier.

"It's still in my office. I would have brought it with me, but I was going into the dining room when I noticed you coming back into the building and heading to Marie's room. I wanted to catch you before you left again."

"Is it alright if I walk down there and get it?" Normally Danielle would have told Sunny to keep the cinnamon rolls, considering the situation, yet since she needed an excuse to have a look around the facility, she decided this was not the time to be pastry generous.

"Certainly. My office is locked, but I'd be happy to walk down with you." Sunny smiled.

"Is it okay if I meet you there in a minute? I mean your office. I wanted to check Marie's room one more time, see if Adam and I forgot anything. Since I'm being so forgetful today, I just figure it would be best to check." Danielle forced a smile.

"Why, certainly. I need to stop in the dining room for a minute anyway. And then I'll meet you back at my office."

Danielle flashed Sunny another smile.

Sunny started to turn away and head back down the hall when she paused and looked back at Danielle. "By the way, who were you talking to a minute ago?"

"The woman staying in that room." Danielle pointed to the nearby open door.

Sunny frowned. "No one's staying in that room."

Danielle glanced nervously from Sunny to the open doorway leading to the room she had thought belonged to the elderly woman in the nightgown. It then dawned on her. The woman was a spirit, most likely someone who had died in that room. Danielle cursed herself for not realizing something was off when the woman claimed to have seen Marie leaving the building. *A spirit will see another spirit, but less likely a living patient will. And if the woman actually saw Marie leaving, it had to have been Marie's spirit she saw,* Danielle thought.

"I was just embarrassed to admit—I—I was talking to Marie," Danielle lied.

Sunny's expression softened. "I understand. I still talk to my mother, and she has been gone for three years now."

Danielle awkwardly excused herself, promising to meet Sunny in her office in a few minutes. As she made her way down the hallway to Marie's room, she muttered under her breath, "Walt is right. I've honed the ability to lie on a dime."

When Danielle reached the entrance to Marie's room, she glanced back down the hallway. Sunny was no longer in sight, and she didn't see the woman in the nightgown. She once again entered Marie's room.

"Marie?" Danielle called out. "Any chance you're here?"

Nothing.

With a deep breath, Danielle headed back down the hallway. She paused at the open doorway leading to the room Sunny claimed had no occupant. Looking into the room, she noticed there were no sheets on the bed, and no sign anyone was using the room.

Just as Danielle turned back into the hall, the woman's voice called out, "Did you come to visit me?"

Danielle looked back into the room again. She found the elderly nightgown-clad woman sitting on the edge of the unmade mattress.

"Hello," Danielle whispered as she stepped into the room. "You mentioned you saw my friend leaving?"

"I asked her where she was going."

"Did she say?" Danielle asked.

The woman shook her head. "No. But she wanted to know if I saw someone running down the hallway. I told her they ran out the back door. She followed them."

"Who did my friend follow?"

"The same person who ran out of her room."

Before Danielle could ask another question, the woman vanished.

"Please, please come back!" Danielle called out. There was no response.

BY THE TIME Danielle reached Sunny's office, she was convinced Marie's spirit had not returned to the nursing home since Evan had seen her at the police station. And the more Danielle thought about it, the more it made sense. Why would Marie return to the nursing home, a place she loathed? It was more likely she would go to her own house or perhaps show up at her funeral before moving on. One thing Danielle knew about spirits—spirits of the newly departed elderly tended to adjust more quickly to their death and grasp their new reality far better than a premature or unexpected death.

When Danielle arrived back at the office, Sunny was already inside waiting for her.

"Here it is." Sunny handed Danielle the bakery sack. "It smells awful good."

"It's cinnamon rolls from Old Salts Bakery." Danielle paused a moment and then offered the sack to Sunny. "Would you like one?"

Sunny gently nudged the sack back to Danielle. "I appreciate the offer. Unfortunately, I can't do sugar this early in the day. But they do smell good. You brought them for Marie, didn't you?"

"Yes. Marie loved cinnamon rolls." The reality of Marie's death now settling in, Danielle added, "I'm going to miss Marie."

NINE

A sack of cinnamon rolls in one hand, her purse's strap slung over a shoulder, Danielle made her way from Sunny's office, past the front nurses' station, and through the main lobby. Unlike the nurses' station in Marie's area, the front one was a hub of activity as staff members dealt with the needs of its patients and questions from visiting family members.

As Danielle headed toward the rear of the building, where she had parked her car, she made her way through the main lounge area. On her right was a row of five recliners, each occupied by an elderly resident. Several of the residents were hooked to portable oxygen tanks, one was reading a book, and two napped. Ahead was a game table where a staff member sat with two of the residents playing a board game. Danielle spied an elderly man making his way to the dining room with his walker, while several people sat quietly in wheelchairs in random spots along the perimeter, either napping or people watching.

Danielle was about halfway through the lounge area when one elderly woman reached out to her from a wheelchair. She grabbed hold of Danielle's paper sack.

"Old Salts! It's from Old Salts!" the woman cried out, clutching the sack and refusing to let go.

Danielle, who had come to an abrupt halt, looked down at the woman who was now clutching the bag. It was obvious to her the woman had spied the bakery's logo on the sack, and by her reaction, she was a fan of the bakery.

As quickly as she had grabbed the paper sack, the woman released her hold and slunk back guiltily in her wheelchair. She looked up at Danielle and blushed. "I'm sorry."

Danielle smiled down at the woman. "You're familiar with Old Salts Bakery?"

"Every Saturday, my husband would bring me one of their cinnamon rolls."

"Does he still?" Danielle asked.

The woman, now clutching the quilted throw draped over her lap, shook her head. "Gene died this past year. No one brings me cinnamon rolls anymore."

Glancing over to a nearby empty chair, Danielle impulsively reached over and pulled it next to the wheelchair and sat down. She opened the sack and grabbed a cinnamon roll. "Would you like one now?"

"Oh no, I can't take your cinnamon roll! I didn't mean for you to give me one." The woman sounded embarrassed. "But when I saw the bag…and I thought of Gene…" She teared up.

"Please, if you would like one." Pulling a napkin from the sack, Danielle tucked it under the cinnamon roll and handed it to the woman. "I brought these for my friend. She loved cinnamon rolls. But…she's not here anymore."

Licking her lips, the woman accepted the roll. After taking a bite, she gave a little moan.

Danielle smiled. "They are good, aren't they?"

"Aren't you going to have one?"

"Now that you mention it…yes, I am." Danielle removed a second roll from the sack and took a bite.

"Is your friend the one who died last night?" the woman asked a moment later.

"How did you know?" Danielle asked.

"You said she loved cinnamon rolls, past tense. And I saw you earlier, walking with that young man. Someone said he was her grandson."

"Yes." Danielle took another bite of the roll.

"She used to visit me in my room."

"Marie visited you?" Danielle asked.

"Well…I'm not sure she ever told me her name. And if she did, well, I'm not very good at names. But I know she was only staying for a few weeks, until she got better from her surgery. They keep those patients in the back." The woman took another bite of her cinnamon roll.

"I didn't realize Marie ever visited any of the residents here."

"I don't think she wanted anyone to know. She would sneak in my room late at night, when everyone was asleep. She would tell me secrets."

"Secrets?"

The woman nodded. "And when I heard that the woman died—and they said she was the only one staying on that wing—I knew it was her."

"What did you mean Marie told you secrets?" Danielle asked.

"Oh, I can't tell you that," the woman whispered. "Can't tell secrets." She popped the last bite of cinnamon roll in her mouth and quickly licked her fingers.

"Okay, Mabel, time for physical therapy," a male voice announced.

Danielle looked up to a thirtysomething man dressed in white slacks and shirt.

"Do I have to?" the elderly woman moaned.

"I'm afraid so," the man said, flashing Danielle a friendly smile.

"Thank you for the cinnamon roll," the woman called out to Danielle as the man pushed her away in the wheelchair.

Just as Danielle stood up, she turned to find Sunny standing behind her.

"I see you met Mabel," Sunny said with a smile.

"I hope it's okay, I gave her one of the cinnamon rolls…I suppose I should have asked someone first," Danielle said guiltily.

"Oh no, that's fine. Mabel's husband used to bring her cinnamon rolls every week."

"She mentioned he died."

Clipboard in hand, Sunny nodded. "Yes. Mabel has been with us a couple of years now. Her husband wasn't able to care for her anymore, but he faithfully visited her every day. He had a heart attack about six months ago. Poor thing, she has been alone since then. They didn't have any children, and other than her late husband, she's never had any other visitors."

"That's so sad." Danielle glanced over to Mabel, who was just being wheeled into the therapy room off the main lobby.

Sunny nodded. "Yes, it is."

"I understand she made friends with Marie."

Sunny frowned. "With Marie?"

"She told me Marie used to visit her at night."

Sunny let out a sigh. "No, she's wrong. It's possible they talked in the dining room, but Marie never visited Mabel's room."

"She did say it was late at night—that Marie snuck over," Danielle explained.

Sunny shook her head. "No. Poor Mabel lives in her own little world. She tends to make up stories—talks about imaginary visitors. I think she believes her stories. But most of them are simply products of her imagination. I think she's just lonely. These pretend friends comfort her."

"That really is sad…"

Sunny glanced down at her clipboard and then looked up at Danielle and smiled. "I really need to be going. I've rounds to make. I imagine you're heading home?"

"Yes. I was on my way to the rear parking lot."

Sunny reached out and briefly touched Danielle's elbow. "I want you to know I'm very sorry about your friend. I had a great deal of respect for her. She never complained about her physical therapy— she was determined to do whatever the therapist asked of her so she could go home. I wish all of our patients were like that."

"Unfortunately, she didn't make it home."

"True. But I don't think it had anything to do with her surgery. Not directly, anyway."

"What do you mean not directly?" Danielle frowned.

"She was ninety-one. Surgery taxes anyone's body—but for a woman her age—well, sometimes our bodies just give out. I sincerely believe it was simply Marie's time to go."

Danielle chatted with Sunny a few moments longer, and then the two parted, Sunny heading off to a patient's room, and Danielle to the main corridor leading to the back lobby.

Thirsty from the cinnamon roll, Danielle stopped along the way at a water cooler and began filling a paper cup with cold water. She spied the nurse who had told Adam and her about his grandmother's death, SeAnne. The nurse was talking to a man in a wheelchair about six feet away. The man seemed angry.

"You have to give me something!" the man shouted.

SeAnne glanced down at the clipboard she was holding and

then looked up at the man. "I'm sorry, Mr. Sharpe. But you had your pain medication two hours ago. I can't give you another pill for another two hours."

"It's not working. I swear, my leg hurts more than it did before I took the damn pill!"

"Let me see what I can do," she said calmly.

"That's what you told me yesterday!" he snapped.

"I promise. I will talk to your doctor and see if he can prescribe something else."

Several minutes later, Danielle found herself walking down the hallway with the young nurse.

"He seemed awful upset," Danielle noted.

"They just don't understand. We have to monitor the pain medications so closely. It's not like candy that we can just hand out when they want it."

"I understand pain meds can be pretty addictive," Danielle said.

"Unfortunately. And some patients believe since they're living here full time, then there should be no problem with us giving them more pills."

"Ironically, Marie always complained about having to take too many pills here," Danielle said.

SeAnne smiled. "I don't know about that. But I do know Marie never asked for additional pain medication."

"Well, some people have a higher tolerance for pain than others."

"True." SeAnne readjusted the clipboard in her arm as she walked down the hallway with Danielle. "I noticed you visiting with Mabel."

"Yes. I gave her one of the cinnamon rolls I'd brought for Marie."

"That's nice. I seem to remember her husband used to bring her those."

Danielle glanced over to the nurse. "She told me Marie used to visit her at night, but Sunny said that wasn't true."

SeAnne smiled. "Mabel does have an active imagination. She was sitting in the back lobby this morning when the funeral home picked up Mrs. Nichols. She didn't actually see them take her away, but she knew why they were here. After she found out the patient staying in the rehab center was the one who had died, she got it into her head that it was her friend staying in rehab."

Now near the rear nurses' station, Danielle and the nurse stopped walking.

"There's no one else staying in the rehab right now, is there?"

"If you mean someone aside from one of the permanent residents, no. The last month has been oddly quiet. I don't ever remember having just one patient in rehab before. But I suppose that's a good thing."

"True."

"Working in a place like this, we know our full-time residents will probably die here. That's a given. But when one of our patients like Mrs. Nichols—someone who is only supposed to be here for rehabilitation—dies, well, I have to admit it bothers me more than the other deaths."

"Does it happen very often?" Danielle asked. "When one of your temporary guests dies here?"

SeAnne shrugged. "Not really. Since I've been here, the only one I know of was Doris Price. It was two months ago. Heart attack. Right in the dining room."

"Was she staying in the room on Marie's corridor, the one facing the rear lobby?"

"Why yes. How did you know that?" SeAnne asked.

"Umm...I must have heard someone talking about her," Danielle lied.

"She was a nice woman—yet a bit of a busybody. She loved to hang out by the front nurses' station and check out all the action. Used to drive poor Sunny crazy. But I have to give her credit, she was always very kind to the woman." The nurse smiled. "She was here recovering from a knee replacement."

"Sunny seems nice," Danielle noted.

SeAnne nodded. "Yes, and she really cares about the residents here."

TEN

Disgusted with the treatment she had received at the Frederickport Police Department, Marie marched angrily toward her house. She might as well go there, she thought. Chances were Edward had already called her son or another family member about her being at the police station. They were probably out looking for her now. She was infuriated that the chief had refused to acknowledge her concerns over the attack at the care home. Instead, Chief MacDonald had just stood there like an idiot, staring blankly at her, listening to her recount what had happened, before making an abrupt turn and going back to his office. *Back to his office to call someone about me leaving the home,* she thought. Or at least, that was what she had assumed. Marie hadn't waited around to find out. Instead she had left the police station, fuming.

"That's why I didn't want to stay at that place," Marie muttered. "Once you go into one of those old folks' homes, everyone just assumes you're now a doddering idiot not capable of making any decisions for yourself or being able to see what's clearly going on right before your eyes!"

She turned onto her street. One of her neighbors, just two doors down from her house, had just stepped outside, onto his front porch.

ADAM HAD COME to Marie's house to see his parents, yet he couldn't bring himself to go inside just yet. Instead, he sat on the side porch, on his grandmother's rocking chair—the one that had belonged to Emma Jackson. Now Marie, like Emma, was gone. Neither death should have surprised Adam. Emma had been over a hundred when she passed, and his grandmother had surpassed the ninety marker. Yet he couldn't quite believe Marie was really gone.

As Adam rocked gently in the chair, the toe of his right shoe pushing against the porch, his stomach growled. He hadn't had breakfast yet. Adam then remembered the cinnamon rolls Danielle had brought his grandmother. He wondered briefly what had happened to them.

Sound from the street caught his attention, and he looked up. It was the car of the man who lived two doors down. Adam guessed he was probably on his way to work. *He has no idea his neighbor is dead,* Adam thought.

MARIE SPIED Adam the moment she stepped onto her lawn. He sat rocking in her chair on the side porch. She called out to him. Since he didn't look up, she assumed he couldn't hear her. Walking to the wooden stairs leading up to the porch, she called his name again. Behind her, the neighbor she had seen leaving his house drove by in his car.

Adam looked up.

"You don't seem surprised to see me," Marie snapped, her eyes looking into his.

Adam didn't reply.

Marie shook her head and then made her way up the stairs. Surprisingly it didn't take the normal effort it usually did. In fact, it didn't take any effort at all.

"It must be that therapy," Marie muttered. "Amazing."

When Marie reached the top step, Adam was no longer looking in her direction. Instead, he was staring down at his lap.

"Oh, stop pouting," Marie told him. "You can't really blame me for leaving that place."

Adam looked up and glanced over his shoulder, looking at the house. The sound of his father's voice drifted out through the open window. He looked back in Marie's direction.

"Oh, I understand now," Marie whispered. "You don't want him to hear us."

Marie took a seat on a chair next to Adam. "But you can see I'm doing remarkably well, so he and your mother can just go home. Although, I wouldn't mind if your brother stays a while. I'd like to get to know that fiancée of his. I don't think I've heard her say three words since she got here."

Adam glanced back to the house again and the sound of his father's voice. He frowned.

"Oh, he's not going to hear me!" Marie insisted. "You know as well as I do the man needs a hearing aid! And anyway, so what if he does hear me. I'm eventually going to have to let him know I'm out here, and I'm not going back to that place. He'll just have to accept it."

Adam looked out to the yard.

Marie frowned. "Although, I am a little surprised one of you wasn't out looking for me. Did Edward tell you what I told him at the station?"

Adam looked over toward the street.

"I'm not making things up. I know someone was in my room and tried to smother me! They held a pillow on my face! I thought I was going to die! It was probably one of those crazy people staying in the other side of the building. And I think the person went out the back door. Whoever it was is probably wandering around Frederickport unattended. That place doesn't keep a close eye on those people, and then they expect me to sleep with my door unlocked! I don't care what your father says, I am not going back!"

"Adam, is that you out there?" came a voice from inside the house. It was Adam's father.

"Yes, Dad." Adam stood up.

"Don't tell him I'm out here. Not just yet," Marie whispered.

Without saying a word, Adam walked over to the back door leading to the kitchen and went inside his grandmother's house.

Marie got up from her chair and tiptoed over to the open window, quietly eavesdropping on her family.

INSIDE THE KITCHEN, Adam found his parents, brother, and future sister-in-law sitting around the kitchen table, drinking coffee.

"What were you doing outside on the porch?" Warren asked his son.

"I was just thinking." Adam walked to the counter and pulled a coffee mug from one of the overhead cabinets.

"We've been waiting for you. I didn't even realize you were out there until Jason mentioned your car had pulled up about ten minutes ago," Warren said.

Adam filled his cup with coffee. "Why didn't you come down to Seaside Village?"

"Why? Your grandmother wasn't even there."

"That's not the point." Adam leaned back against the counter and sipped his coffee. There was no place for him to sit at the kitchen table. All the seats were taken.

"We need to get this house ready to sell," Adam's mother, Chloe, said, glancing around the room. "It could use some sprucing up. It looks like an old person lives here."

"One did," Jason said.

"Prospective buyers don't need to be reminded of that." Chloe stood up and wandered around the kitchen, quietly inspecting the woodwork, walls, countertops, and cabinets. "This is prime real estate, and with a little work we can maximize our profits."

"Do we really need to talk about that now?" Adam snapped. "Don't you think we should be talking about Grandma?"

"What's to talk about?" his mother asked. "From what I understand, all the arrangements have been made. Nothing more to discuss. This only proves your father and I were right. Your grandmother was in no condition to move back home."

"But you're talking about selling her house—now—so soon—after all, she just…" Adam's voice crackled.

"We're all sorry about my mother. But it's not like any of this comes as a surprise. She was ninety-one. She had a good long life, and she was able to live most of that on her own. Wouldn't we all like to be able to do that? And your mother is right. This place needs some work before we put it on the market. And frankly, we can't stay here indefinitely. We need to get home. I need to get back to my business."

"YOU THINK you're going to sell my home out from under me,

59

stick me back in that horrible place and go home to spend my money? I don't think so!" Marie peered through the screen, wanting desperately to give her only son a good smack.

Just then she heard a car pull up to the house. She turned to see who it was. A red Ford Flex was now parked by the front sidewalk.

"Danielle," Marie said in relief. "At last, someone I can count on!" Marie lingered a few moments longer by the window, listening, before making her way to the patio stairs leading to the yard.

DANIELLE HAD JUST RUNG the doorbell when Marie appeared by her side.

"Danielle! I'm so glad you're here!"

"Oh, Marie!" Danielle's expression broke into a smile. "I've been looking for you!"

"It seems you're the only one," Marie grumbled.

Danielle glanced nervously at the front door, now regretting ringing the bell.

"Please listen to me, Marie. When I leave, come with me. Please, just get in my car and come with me. I'll explain everything—"

The front door opened.

Danielle found herself looking into the unfriendly face of Warren Nichols.

"This is not a good time for a visit," he said rudely.

"Seriously, Dad?" Adam interrupted. He stepped around his father, taking his place by the open doorway. "Come on in, Danielle."

"Umm...that's okay." Danielle glanced nervously from Adam to Marie. "I understand this is a bad time. I just wanted to see if you were okay."

"Danielle was very close to Grandma. Maybe you don't understand what I'm feeling, but I imagine she does." Adam reached for Danielle's hand and pulled her into the house, unaware of his grandmother's spirit following her inside.

"Oh please, Adam, she was my mother, for heaven's sake."

"You don't seem that upset," Adam snapped as he slammed the door shut.

Feeling awkward, Danielle glanced from Adam to Marie, who stood quietly at her side in the entry hall. A few feet away, Warren glared at his son. Behind Warren and Adam, the rest of their family was filing into the living room and each taking a seat.

Before Danielle could make her exit with Marie, she found Adam pulling her into the living room, clutching her arm. In that moment, Danielle knew what a security blanket must feel like. As much as she wanted to flee and take Marie with her, she didn't feel right ditching Adam when he seemed to need emotional support.

Damn, I should have called Melony on my way over. Let her know what was going on, Danielle told herself.

"Is she being cremated?" Sondra asked Jason when Danielle stepped into the living room. All the family members except Adam and his father were now sitting in the room.

"Is who getting cremated?" Marie asked, hovering in the archway leading from the entry hall to the living room.

"No. Grandma made all her funeral arrangements when my grandfather died," Jason explained. "She has a funeral plot right next to his where she'll be buried."

"You were talking about me?" Marie gasped. "Aren't you people getting a little ahead of yourselves?"

"It's ridiculous, really," Chloe said. "Spending all that money on a casket. I bet they charge a fortune for those things these days."

"You do know I'm standing here, Chloe," Marie snapped.

Danielle glanced wearily from Marie to Adam's mother.

"It would be better for the environment if you had her cremated. You can always bury her urn instead of a casket. I imagine you'll get a refund," Sondra suggested.

Marie glared at Jason's fiancée. "Who are you, missy, to be putting your two cents in?"

"That might be a good idea," Adam's father muttered. "Yes. I'll call the funeral home and talk to them about it."

"Wait a minute!" Adam spoke up. "Grandma made her arrangements. We need to honor her wishes."

Marie looked anxiously from Adam to Danielle. "Why are they talking about cremating me? Why are they all ignoring me?"

"She'll still get a funeral and be buried next to your grandfather. It will just be in an urn, not a casket. Like Sondra said, it is better for the environment." Chloe smiled at her son.

"Since when have you ever cared about the environment?" Marie snapped.

"Will the funeral home refund the difference?" Jason asked.

Marie frowned. She turned to Danielle. "Umm…I'm not getting a good feeling about this."

"Absolutely not! We're going to honor my grandmother's wishes," Adam shouted.

Warren let out a sigh and said, "It's not like your grandmother will even know. She's dead."

ELEVEN

"I think I should go," Danielle said abruptly, clutching her purse. She glanced over to Marie as she inched toward the archway leading to the entry hall.

Adam's family members—most of whom seemed to have forgotten she was standing in the room—looked at her, their expressions blank.

"That's probably for the best," Adam's father said. "I'm sure you can visit with Adam later. But for now, we have some family business we need to discuss."

Adam reached out and grabbed hold of Danielle's forearm. "Danielle, do you think my grandmother would want to be cremated?"

"I don't think we need to involve Ms. Boatman in our personal business," Chloe said primly.

"She is more a daughter to me than you ever were!" Marie snapped. "And why are you all ignoring me!"

"If Marie has already made her final arrangements, and it didn't include cremation, then I would have to assume it was not something she wanted," Danielle told Adam.

"Danielle's right!" Marie agreed.

"While we should consider Marie's wishes when making these types of decisions," Chloe began.

"Damn right!" Marie shouted.

"When it comes right down to it, we ultimately have to do what is best for everyone. For example, Marie might be dead set against us ever selling this house, but that would obviously not stop us from listing it as soon as possible. It's the right thing to do. As for cremation, if it ends up costing less than what Marie arranged, while being better for the environment, isn't it something we should seriously consider?" Chloe asked.

"Would you please stop talking like I'm not here! You have no business trying to dictate my life!"

"I really do need to go. Adam, I'll talk to you later." Danielle turned from Adam, her back now to him, and looked at Marie. In a whisper, she said, "Marie, come with me."

"DID that woman just say *Marie, come with me?*" Jason asked while looking out the living room window. He watched Danielle making her way down the front walkway—*talking to herself.*

"I didn't hear anything," Adam said, flopping down onto one of the empty chairs in the room.

"I heard her," Sondra said. "She seems like an odd one."

"Danielle's just a little…well, spiritual." Adam suggested.

"Spiritual?" his mother asked with a frown.

Adam shrugged. "I'm not sure what to call it. But I remember when she moved into Marlow House, she didn't want to upset Walt Marlow's spirit."

"Walt Marlow's spirit? Isn't that the guy who hanged himself in the attic at Marlow House? The one my grandfather found?" Warren asked.

"Yes," Adam grumbled as he sank down into the chair and crossed one leg over the opposing knee. "But he didn't kill himself. Danielle found out he was murdered. I think she believed Walt Marlow's spirit might still be in the house, and she didn't want to upset him."

Adam's father chuckled. He sat down on the edge of the fireplace hearth. "Then I have to agree with Sondra, she is odd."

"There are a lot of people who think Marlow House is haunted," Adam said.

"That's just silly," his mother snapped.

"What did she think? That Grandma's ghost was hanging

around in the living room?" Jason asked as he turned from the window.

"I didn't hear what she said. But maybe Grandma's ghost is here, listening to us. And I don't imagine she would appreciate how you're all talking. Do any of you even care that she died?" Adam asked.

"First, there are no such things as ghosts," Chloe said. "When a person dies, they are simply dead—no more."

Jason glanced to his fiancée and explained, "Mother doesn't believe in a heaven or hell. She thinks it's all a big sleep when we die."

"Which is why it's silly to get all worked up trying to honor Marie's wishes, when some of the things she wanted don't make sense. After all, it's not like she'll ever know," Chloe huffed.

Jason glanced back out the window. "She's just sitting there in her car. It looks like she's talking to herself."

"I DON'T UNDERSTAND," Marie grumbled. She sat next to Danielle in the passenger seat. "Even Adam seemed to be ignoring me." Crossing her arms angrily across her chest, Marie slumped back in the seat and stared out the window.

"Marie," Danielle said in a calm voice, "I'd like to tell you something about myself."

Marie glanced over to Danielle. "Dear, I would normally love for you to share some story about yourself, but at the moment, I have more pressing matters. My family is plotting to sell my home right out from under me. They refuse to talk to me, I assume because they know there's nothing they can say that will convince me they're doing the right thing. And frankly, I'm surprised my son hasn't forced me into his car and made me go back to that awful place."

Clutching the steering wheel, Danielle took a deep calming breath while looking out the front windshield.

Narrowing her eyes, Marie stared at Danielle. "Please don't tell me my son has convinced you to take me back there. No, Danielle, please, you can't be the Judas!"

"No, Marie. I'm taking you to Marlow House. You never have to go back to Seaside Village ever again."

Marie let out a sigh and smiled over at Danielle. "Dear, I know what you're doing. You think if you have me live at Marlow House, that my son won't try to force me back into the care home. But you don't have to do that. I'm still very capable of taking care of myself. But it is very sweet of you."

"Marie, when I was a child, I saw my grandmother's ghost."

Marie frowned. "Excuse me?"

"I suppose some might call it her spirit. It was at her funeral. She came to say goodbye to me."

"I believe I saw my mother after she died, but I'm not really sure what that has to do with our current conversation."

"My grandmother is not the only spirit I ever saw. You see, I have a gift. Although, there have been times I've thought it a curse. I can see spirits, Marie. After a person dies, before their spirit moves on to the next realm, well, I can see them sometimes."

"You mean...like that Long Island Medium?" Marie frowned.

Danielle glanced over to Marie and smiled. "Something like that."

"Why haven't you ever mentioned it before?"

"It's not really something I like talking about. People will think I'm crazy."

"Why are you telling me now?"

"The chief's youngest son, Evan, he's like me."

Marie moved restlessly in her seat. "What do you mean?"

"He can see spirits too."

"I...I still don't understand why you're telling me all this...I mean now..."

"When we were in your house a minute ago, didn't you hear what your daughter-in-law said, right after she said you wouldn't know if they didn't follow your wishes?"

Marie stared blankly at Danielle. They sat in silence for a few moments.

"Marie, what are you wearing right now?"

Marie glanced down at her lap and then looked back to Danielle. "My nightgown."

"Do you have any shoes on?" Danielle asked.

Marie looked down at her bare feet and wiggled her toes. "No. That place tried to get me to sleep in those bulky hospital socks. But I've never liked to sleep with socks on my feet."

"Don't you find that a little odd? Walking all over town in your bare feet and nightgown?"

"Well...when I left this morning, I didn't stop to change my clothes."

"And your feet don't hurt? Walking all over town barefooted?"

Marie frowned and looked back down at her feet. "No. Until you mentioned it, I didn't even notice I had bare feet."

"And you're walking pretty well for someone who just broke her hip and had surgery. All the way from the care home to the police station—and then here."

Marie looked quickly to Danielle, confusion wrinkling her forehead. "How did you know I went down to the police station first?"

"The chief called me."

Marie let out a little grunt and said, "And I have a few choice words to say to him. I go down there for help, and what does he do? He totally ignores me!"

"Don't blame the chief. He couldn't see you," Danielle said softly.

"Don't be ridiculous. He was looking right at me," Marie snapped. "Ask Evan, he knows I was there."

"Yes, I know. Evan told his father."

"Danielle, you are not making any sense!"

"Marie, please. Think. What was it your daughter-in-law said? You didn't answer my question a moment ago." Danielle glanced to the house. Standing at the window were Jason and his fiancée, staring at her.

"If you have something to say, Danielle. Just say it!"

"I think we need to go. Your grandson is going to think I'm crazy, sitting in my car talking to myself."

"You're not by yourself. I'm here!"

Danielle slipped her car key into the ignition and turned it on. "True. But he can't see you."

Marie sat quietly in the passenger seat as Danielle drove the car down the street, away from Marie's house.

After a few moments of silence, Marie blurted, "Holy hell, I'm dead!"

Danielle glanced quickly over at Marie. She was relieved to see her friend did not seem particularly upset with the realization; in fact, by her expression, she seemed more curious than concerned.

Letting out a sigh of relief, Danielle relaxed as she drove toward Marlow House.

Marie stared at her own hands, turning them from right to left. She then extended her right hand, sending it through the closed window of the passenger door. Marie watched in fascination as she wiggled the fingers on the hand now on the outside of the car—the closed window a penetrable barrier.

"Does this mean I'm a ghost?" Marie pulled her hand back inside the car and turned to face Danielle. She seemed rather excited at the prospect.

"Just so you know, some spirits don't like being called ghosts." Danielle chuckled.

"I've never really been afraid of dying. But I have to say, I never quite imagined that when I did, I would be driving around in your car with you, discussing my death. I just figured I would go to heaven...I never thought I did anything bad enough to go to hell. Does this mean there is no heaven or hell?"

Danielle shrugged. "I'm not sure exactly what happens. But spirits move on after they die—to another realm. Maybe it's heaven. I'm pretty sure when you go there, you'll see all your loved ones and friends who have passed on.

"Sometimes, after a person dies, their spirit stays on this plane for a while. I suspect you'll move on fairly quickly now that you've figured it out. But I have to say, I'm really glad you didn't move on right away. Because I'm really going to miss you, Marie. You have no idea how much you've meant to me." Tears began slipping down Danielle's face.

"Oh, my dear..." Marie reached out to touch Danielle's arm, yet her hand slipped through it, as it had through the closed window. Abruptly pulling her hand back, Marie stared at it for a moment and muttered, "I guess I really am dead."

Wiping the tears from her face with the back of her sleeve, Danielle sniffled. "I'm going to miss you."

Marie settled back in the car seat and smiled. "Don't be silly, dear. I'm not going anywhere."

TWELVE

"So, you're telling me Walt Marlow's ghost has been haunting Marlow House since he died? And you can see him? Talk to him?" Marie asked incredulously.

Danielle pulled the Ford Flex into her driveway. "Pretty much. But don't call him a ghost. Walt hates that." She parked the car and turned off the ignition. Danielle made no attempt to get out of the vehicle. Sitting in the driver's seat, her hands gripping the steering wheel, she glanced from Marie to Marlow House and back to Marie, who continued to sit in the passenger seat.

"And you never told me?"

Danielle smiled over to Marie. She removed the key from the ignition and reached for her door's handle. "Would you have believed me?"

Marie considered the question a moment. "Probably not. While I've never dismissed the possibility of such things—after all, I did see my mother—I have to admit when people claim to have actually communicated with someone who has died, I usually think they're a little nutty."

"Pretty common assumption." Just as Danielle got out of the car and slammed its door shut, she heard someone call her name. She glanced toward the open gate. It was Lily, running in her direction.

Marie, who had just gotten out of the car, stood between Danielle and Lily. She turned to Lily and started to greet her, yet was stopped abruptly when Lily ran through her body. Letting out a surprised gasp, Marie looked down—still clad in her dressing gown, her feet bare—Marie's eyes widened at the unexpected intrusion. She twirled around to face the backside of Lily, who now stood a few feet from her, slightly out of breath.

"Any news of Marie?" Lily asked. "Do you think she's moved on?"

Danielle pointed over Lily's shoulder.

Lily cringed and then turned around slowly. "Oh no…did I run through Marie?"

"I assume Lily can't see me?" Marie asked.

"No. But she knows I can see spirits."

Marie chuckled. "Well, this is all very interesting."

"I'm so sorry, Marie. Not just because I plowed through you, but because…well…because you died." Lily began to cry.

"Well, dear, we knew it was going to happen eventually, and I've lived a very long life. Plus, I have to admit, this is all very thrilling. I haven't had this much excitement since…well, I'm not sure when!" Marie reached out to touch Lily's arm. When her hand moved through the young woman with no reaction from Lily, Marie arched her brows curiously and then took back her hand, inspecting it.

"It's okay, Lily. Marie's not upset," Danielle said.

After a few minutes, Lily stopped crying. With a sniffle, she wiped her tears with the back of her hand. "I'm glad she hasn't moved on yet. I really wanted to tell her goodbye."

"Oh, don't be silly, dear. I'm not going anywhere," Marie said cheerfully. She then marched into Marlow House, moving through the kitchen door as effortlessly as Lily had moved through her.

Danielle stared at the door for a moment, not following Marie inside.

"Marie, I just want you to—"

"She isn't here," Danielle interrupted. "She just went into the house."

"Ugh…why do they always do that to me?" Lily groaned. "Well, I guess I can tell her inside how much I'm going to miss her."

"According to Marie, she isn't going anywhere just yet," Danielle said as she unlocked the back door.

WALT WAS SITTING at the kitchen table when Marie stormed through the wall. She stopped abruptly when she saw him, her eyes wide.

"It really is you!" Marie gasped.

"Hello, Marie. It's been a long time." The chair next to Walt moved out from the table. He nodded toward it, silently suggesting she sit down.

Accepting the invitation, her eyes never leaving him, she studied his face. "I believe I would recognize you anywhere. You look remarkably like your portrait."

"So I've been told." Walt smiled.

Marie continued to study him, her head cocking slightly to one side. "You know, I dreamt about you not long ago. I swear, your voice sounded just like it does in real life."

"Real *life*?" Walt chuckled.

Marie shrugged and glanced around. "Or whatever this is."

The back door opened.

"I suspect the reason you recognized my voice, I did visit you in your dream. That was my real voice."

Danielle walked into the kitchen, followed by Lily, who shut the door after them.

"Really?" Marie perked up. "We can do that? Visit people's dreams?"

Walt smiled. "Yes."

"Wonderful!" Marie was practically giddy. "This is much more interesting than I imagined it would be."

"Hello, Walt," Danielle greeted him, taking a seat at the kitchen table.

"Hey, Walt," Lily added, still standing. She glanced to the seemingly empty chairs at the table.

Walt smiled. "Ladies…"

Lily let out a sigh. "I imagine you three have a lot to discuss. I'll take off so you can do that. One-sided conversations drive me insane. But before I leave, I want to say, Marie…" Lily glanced around, trying to figure out where Marie was in the room.

Danielle pointed to one of the seemingly empty chairs at the table.

Lily looked to the chair and smiled. "Before I go, I want you to know, Marie, I'm so grateful you were part of my life. While I know you'll still be around—either in this realm or wherever it is you move on to on your next leg of your journey, I'm going to miss you. Unlike Dani, I won't be able to see or hear you." She then smiled and added, "Unless, of course, Walt teaches you to dream hop and you pop in to say hi."

"Dream hop?" Marie frowned.

"What I was talking about," Walt told her.

Lily blew a kiss at the table and then dashed out the back door, tears glistening in her eyes.

"She's a sweet girl," Marie mused. She then glanced down and frowned.

"What is it?" Danielle asked.

"Do I have to spend eternity in my dressing gown?"

"Not necessarily," Walt said with a smile. In the next moment, his suit changed from a gray pinstripe to a blue one.

"How did you do that?" Marie asked.

"It takes a little practice, but I can show you later."

"Marie, don't you want to move on?" Danielle asked. "I can see you've accepted your death, which usually means a spirit is ready to continue on in her journey."

Marie looked at Walt. "Does this mean Walt hasn't accepted his death?"

"I'm just not ready to move on," Walt explained. He waved his hand and a lit cigar appeared. He took a puff.

Marie broke into a smile. "Aha! That explains the cigar smell I used to notice over here!"

Before anyone could respond, the back door flew open, and Heather Donovan rushed into the house, her silky black ponytail bouncing atop her head. She had been jogging earlier that morning and still wore her purple jogging suit.

"Oh my god! Marie really is here!" Heather said, trying to catch her breath.

"You can see me?" Marie asked.

"Of course I can see you." Heather sat down at the table. "I ran into Lily on the street, and she told me about Marie, and that she was here." Impulsively, Heather reached forward and poked a finger through Marie's face.

With a frown, Marie leaned back, away from Heather. "What was that for?"

Heather shrugged. "I needed to make sure Lily wasn't messing with me, and you're really dead."

"Hardly something Lily would joke about," Danielle said.

"It's a good thing she was telling the truth or you would have just poked my eye out!" Marie snapped.

With a guilty blush, Heather slumped back in her chair and mumbled, "Sorry."

With a shake of her head, Marie sat up straighter in the chair, her brow drawn into a frown. "So you're telling me Danielle, Evan, and now Heather can see ghosts?"

"Spirits," Walt corrected.

"And Chris," Heather added.

"Chris too?" Marie asked.

"Yes," Danielle said with a nod. "Chris is like me and Evan, he has seen spirits all his life. Heather here, well, she had a little ability when she first moved to Frederickport—most people have some, like the way you could smell Walt's cigar. But over time, her abilities increased, so she's almost as sensitive as I am."

Marie slumped back in the chair and folded her arms across her chest. "So you're saying this has been going on around me, and I had no idea? The four of you have been consorting with dead people?"

Walt cringed. "I have to say, dead people sounds worse than ghosts."

"Makes me think of zombies," Heather added.

"I see you found little Marie!" Eva said as she abruptly appeared in the kitchen.

Marie looked to the new apparition, her eyes widening. "Eva Thorndike?" she stammered.

"Wonderful, you recognized me!" Eva punctuated her comment with a wave of her hand and a flutter of gold glitter. The glitter vanished before it hit the floor.

Since there were no empty seats in the kitchen, Eva sat down on an imaginary barstool, her body seemingly floating in midair—in a sitting position, her legs crossed under the long satin gown she wore.

"This is amazing," Marie murmured. "Are my parents here somewhere? My husband?" She glanced around the room as if expecting more spirits to pop into the kitchen.

"I suspect they've moved on," Danielle told her. "Like I explained in the car, most spirits do. But there are a few, like Walt and Eva, who, for their own reasons, linger on this plane."

"So we don't have to move on?" Marie asked.

"Well…some do." Danielle thought of Felicia and Tagg, who were not given the option to linger. It gave her chills to imagine where they might have ended up.

Marie started to say something, and then she paused and focused her attention on Eva. "You know, that portrait at the museum does not do you justice. I always thought the artist tried too hard to make the comparison between you and the Gibson Girl. You are really much more beautiful."

"You're very sweet," Eva said.

"My father told me…" Marie paused and then looked from Eva to Walt. "Of course! Now I understand! This is rather romantic!"

Heather frowned. "Romantic?"

"Of course, dear. Everyone knows how much in love Walt was with Eva. It's obvious she returned that love, and they were reunited after his death!"

"About a hundred years later," Heather said with a snort.

Marie frowned. "I don't understand?"

"Eva and I are just dear friends," Walt explained. "It's true, when I was a young man, I believed I was in love with her. But the truth is, it wasn't until Lily's wedding that I saw Eva again."

"Really?" Marie asked.

"I told you, Marie, Walt is confined to this house. He hasn't been anywhere else," Danielle reminded her.

"But Eva is free to come here, isn't she?" Marie asked.

"Yes. But I chose to stay away, for my own reasons," Eva said.

"Hmm…" Marie glanced from Eva to Walt. "The afterlife seems like a bit of a soap opera."

"I suppose it does." Danielle chuckled. "While Eva and Walt have their own reasons for staying, you probably want to move on. It's what spirits normally do—especially those like you who've come to terms with their death."

"Who said I've come to terms with my death?" Marie asked.

Danielle shrugged. "You didn't seem that upset when I explained—and I just assumed you would be anxious to reunite with your husband, your parents, those who've already moved on."

Unfolding her arms, Marie leaned forward, resting her elbows on the table. "You know, one would assume I'd be anxious to see them. I'm a little surprised I'm not more eager to move on. It's not as if I haven't been aware of the fact I could go at any time. Heavens, I recently celebrated my ninety-first birthday."

"Is it because of Adam?" Danielle asked. "You mentioned you wanted to see him married first before you move on."

Marie considered the question a moment and then shook her head. "No. I suspect the true reason is a little more self-centered."

"Self-centered?" Danielle asked.

"Yes. I'd first like to figure out who murdered me."

THIRTEEN

"M urdered? What are you talking about?" Heather asked.
"Marie, you weren't murdered. You died in your sleep,"
Danielle told her.

Sitting up straight in her chair, Marie stubbornly shook her head. "No. I was murdered."

"Why do you think that?" Walt asked.

"It was the food, wasn't it?" Heather suggested. "I used to visit my grandfather in one of those places, and the food was hideous. There were a couple of times I caught them serving food that had spoiled. It was one of the ways they cut corners to save money. Of course, that isn't murder exactly, more like negligent homicide."

"No. It wasn't the food," Marie told her.

"How can you be so sure?" Heather asked.

"Because I remember the pillow!"

Danielle frowned. "Pillow?"

Marie nodded. "Yes. The pillow someone used to smother me."

"What are you talking about, Marie?" Danielle asked.

"I have to admit, at first I thought I was just attacked. That's why I went to the police station. But if I'm really dead—well, it must mean my attacker was more successful than I realized! I was murdered!"

"What happened?" Heather asked.

"I remember I couldn't sleep. I looked over to the clock on the nightstand and saw that it was a few minutes past three. And then I heard it. Footsteps coming down the hall."

"Who was it?" Danielle asked.

Marie shrugged. "I don't know. It was pretty dark. I didn't have my glasses on." Marie paused a moment and tried touching her face. "Do I have glasses on now?"

"No," Danielle told her.

Marie smiled. "It's amazing. I can see beautifully without any glasses!"

"You are dead," Walt reminded her. "Eyeglasses aren't really necessary on this side."

"This just keeps getting better!" Marie continued to smile for a few moments, but then the smile faded when she considered the recent turn of events. "Although I'm not particularly thrilled about the murder thing. While this side seems quite interesting, I wasn't quite ready to make the move, and frankly I'm annoyed someone killed me!"

"Marie, please finish your story. You said you heard footsteps," Danielle urged.

"Oh yes…umm…well, I heard someone coming down the hall. And then I saw them at my doorway. Like I said, I didn't have my glasses on, and it was pretty dark. I assumed it was one of the nurses making rounds, so I closed my eyes and pretended to sleep."

"Why pretend?" Walt asked.

"Because if they knew I was awake, they would push another pill on me. Places like that want to keep everyone drugged up. It makes it easier for them."

"I have to agree with that," Heather said. "They had my grandfather on a ton of pills."

"I wasn't going to let them overmedicate me! In fact, the pain pill they gave me last night before I went to bed, I pretended to swallow, and then hid it in my pocket when they weren't looking." Marie tucked her hand in the pocket of her dressing gown and then pulled it out. Her hand was empty. She shrugged and said, "I guess it's still in the pocket of my other dressing gown—the one on my poor body."

"Then what happened?" Eva asked.

"Whoever had come into my room was still there, but I wasn't sure. It had gotten very quiet, and I finally opened my eyes. But when I did, I found myself looking up at a pillow, and the next thing

I knew, whoever was holding the pillow tried to smother me. It was quite horrible, actually." Marie shivered at the thought.

"Afterwards, you didn't see who it was?" Danielle asked.

"To be honest, afterwards I thought I was still alive. I figured whoever had tried to smother me had given up and run out of the room. I followed them out into the hall, and one of the other patients in my wing saw them run out the back door."

"Who was this other patient?" Heather asked.

Marie shrugged. "I have no idea. She must have moved into that room that morning, because the room was empty the day before. It's the room on the end of that corridor, near the rear nurses' station, facing the back door."

"Wait a minute." Heather spoke up. "How did you know this other patient saw your attacker run out of the building?"

"She told me, of course."

Danielle and Heather exchanged glances.

"Marie, I talked to the woman who saw you leave the building," Danielle told her. "But she wasn't a patient there—at least not a current one. She was a spirit."

Marie frowned. "Are you sure?"

"I saw the woman this morning; I talked to her. She told me she saw you run out of the building, and then I learned there were no other patients staying in your wing. She has to be a spirit."

"Perhaps it was a patient from the other section," Marie suggested. "After all, those patients often get confused."

"Because she saw you," Eva reminded her, "it is obvious it was your spirit that left that room, which means the only ones who could see or hear you would be other spirits or someone with a gift. Considering where you were, it's more likely it was another spirit. I imagine there are other ones there."

"Plus, she vanished right before my eyes," Danielle said. "That sorta cinched it for me."

"Why would anyone hang around in a place like that after they died?" Marie asked. "Gracious, at my first opportunity, I would be out of there! Now that I think about it, that's exactly what I did."

"I suspect that spirit may not understand she's dead," Danielle suggested.

"Marie," Heather began, "I've been doing a lot of studying on this subject. From what I've managed to piece together, houses that are supposedly haunted are—at least the ones that really are haunted and not some scam—are typically inhabited by a ghost who is conflicted, confused. Like a murder victim."

"I was a murder victim, and I didn't stick around," Marie said.

"We are all individuals," Walt reminded her. "Not all spirits react in the same way. But Heather's theory has merit. People whose death resulted from violence tend to be more confused after death. I speak from experience."

"If this is true—that someone smothered you—I need to tell the chief. He has to order an autopsy before the funeral. As it stands right now, everyone believes you died of natural causes," Danielle said.

"And just like that, Edward will order my autopsy? I wish he would, but I can't imagine what you could say to make him do that."

"Just tell him the truth," Danielle said.

"What, that my ghost told you I was murdered?"

"You forget, the chief's youngest son is like me."

Marie frowned. She studied Danielle a moment. "So you're telling me Edward knows about all this? He believes his son can see ghosts?"

"Yes," Danielle said. "Lily isn't the only one who knows. Aside from Lily, both the chief and Ian know. And I suspect Brian Henderson believes Marlow House is haunted."

"Interesting...and to think all of this was going on around me when I was alive, and I never suspected a thing," Marie mused.

Before Danielle could respond, her stomach growled. Everyone looked at her and chuckled.

Danielle shrugged. "I did miss breakfast this morning." She stood up. "I'm going to make myself a sandwich. Heather, you want one?"

DANIELLE MADE sandwiches for Heather and herself and suggested they all go into the dining room. There were enough chairs for everyone around the dining room table, and she found having Eva lounging in midair in the kitchen too much of a distraction. It was bad enough trying to ignore the occasional burst of sparkling glitter.

"I suppose we might want to figure out who killed Marie, before

Danielle calls the chief," Heather suggested just before taking a bite of her sandwich.

"I've been giving that some thought," Marie said. "It has to be Crazy Earl."

"Crazy Earl?" Heather frowned. "Isn't that the town drunk from *Hart of Dixie*?"

"I have no idea what *Hart of Dixie* is," Marie said. "Crazy Earl is a resident of Seaside Village who used to hang out by the back door, trying to escape."

"Earl Sharpe," Danielle clarified. "The elderly man you talked to Sunny about?"

"Everyone is elderly at Seaside Village," Marie said. "Except, of course, the staff. But yes, that Earl. Although everyone at that place calls him Crazy Earl because he's always trying to escape."

"Why would he want to kill you?" Heather asked.

"I suspect because I told Sunny what he was up to, why he kept hanging out on our side of the building. Of course, they should have known that without me having to tell them. But of course, no one over there ever pays attention to what's going on in that place."

"If they just let the patients wander around unattended, it mustn't be that difficult for them to escape. Can't they just walk out of the building?" Eva asked.

"All the exterior doors are locked," Marie explained. "The back door has a password keypad, so staff and visitors—at least the visitors who have been given the password—can come and go from the building without using a key. Crazy Earl would wait by the back door, hoping someone would open it for him."

"Marie, didn't you tell us your attacker left out the back door?" Walt asked.

"Yes, so?" She frowned.

"Then that would mean your attacker knew the password, which would mean it was clearly not this Earl fellow."

"Maybe someone finally told him what it was." Marie paused a moment and frowned.

"What?" Danielle asked.

"Now that I think about it, I don't recall keying in the password when I left the building last night."

Walt chuckled. "Because you probably didn't. I imagine you moved through the wall to get outside."

"Why didn't I find that odd? Heavens, I still thought I was alive at that point."

"It's pretty common for a spirit to be confused immediately after death. Things you would normally notice when alive, you might overlook—at least until you come to accept your death," Danielle explained.

"Shouldn't we be asking who had a motive to kill Marie?" Heather asked.

"I just told you. Crazy Earl. He was mad at me for talking to Sunny."

"I don't believe he's our killer. When I've seen him, he's been in a wheelchair. So, he couldn't have run out the back door even if he had the password. Who else has a motive?" Danielle asked.

"Money is always a motive." Heather looked at Marie. "Who stands to inherit your estate?"

"Don't be silly, no one from my family would kill me," Marie scoffed. "If it wasn't Crazy Earl, it has to be one of the other residents. They're free to roam that place, and since we aren't allowed to lock our bedroom doors, anyone can enter any of the bedrooms during the night. It was probably some homicidal maniac they have living there. Since that first night in that place, when they wouldn't let me lock my door, I was afraid something like this would happen!"

"Why waste time debating motive?" Eva asked. "Wouldn't it simply be easier to talk to the witness?"

"Witness? You mean the woman who saw the attacker leave the building?" Heather asked.

Waving her hand to release more glitter, Eva said, "Obviously."

"I hate going back over there, but I suppose I could," Marie said with a sigh. "It would make things easier if we could simply tell Edward who killed me. Of course, he'll still have to find some way to prove it. I don't imagine my word on the killer's identity is going to help much."

Danielle stood up. "I think the first thing we need to do is tell the chief there's been a murder so he can order an autopsy. And I just remembered something…"

"What's that?" Walt asked.

"When I was at Marie's earlier, her family was talking about having her body cremated."

"But they can't do that," Marie insisted. "I've already made my arrangements."

"Maybe they can't. But if they manage to have you cremated instead of buried—and they do it before an autopsy is ordered, it will be virtually impossible to prove you were murdered," Danielle explained.

FOURTEEN

Officer Brian Henderson greeted Danielle when she walked into the police station that afternoon. He was standing by Holly's desk, manning the phones while the dispatcher was in the bathroom.

"Hello, Danielle. I'm sorry to hear about Marie Nichols." He reached out and briefly touched her right elbow.

Looking into Brian's face, Danielle couldn't help but remember all those times she had been at odds with the older officer. On more than one occasion he had been more than willing to see her tried for murder. Yet their relationship had evolved over time, and while she wouldn't call him a close friend, they had entered a truce, and at moments like this, he behaved like a friend. By his expression, she could tell his sentiment was sincere.

"Yeah, me too." Danielle smiled sadly.

"One consolation, she lived a long life, and from what I understand, she went peacefully in her sleep."

"I suppose, but I'm still going to miss her."

Brian reached out again and touched her arm. "I imagine you are. She was like family to you, wasn't she?"

"She was."

"Do you know if they're having the funeral before Thanksgiving or afterwards?"

"That would mean they'd have to have the funeral tomorrow,

considering the next day is Thanksgiving. I don't see how that's possible."

"You're probably right. Wonder if they'll have it over the weekend?"

Danielle considered the complications of a murder investigation, which would mean an autopsy. She couldn't imagine Marie's body would be ready for burial until next week. "I kind of doubt it."

"So what are you doing here?"

"I need to talk to the chief. Is he in his office?"

"He is."

Several minutes later, after exchanging a few final words with Brian, Danielle made her way alone to the chief's office. She found the door open and the chief working at his desk.

"I know why Marie was here this morning," Danielle announced when she walked into the office.

MacDonald glanced up. He set the pen he had been holding on his desktop and leaned back in his chair, studying Danielle. "You've seen her?"

Danielle closed the office door and took a seat facing the desk. "Yes. She was murdered, Chief. She was coming to you for help... although at the time, she thought she was alive and just reporting an assault."

He leaned forward, resting his elbows on the desktop. "What do you mean murdered? Murdered how? By who?"

"She was smothered."

He sat up straight in the office chair. "Smothered?"

"With her pillow." Danielle then went on to recount Marie's story, beginning with the time she was killed.

When she was done, the chief asked, "And she has no idea who did it?"

"No. But she went over to the Seaside Village to see if she can find that witness."

"Oh brother." MacDonald groaned, leaning back in the chair.

"I was a little concerned about letting her go over there alone. Spirits can get a little disoriented at first until they figure everything out. So Eva went with her," Danielle explained.

"Eva? As in Eva Thorndike?"

"Yes."

MacDonald groaned again. Leaning forward, he placed his

elbows on the desktop, rested his forehead on his open palms, and rocked his head back and forth while muttering, "*This is too weird.*"

"No weirder than normal."

He lifted his head and peered at Danielle. "Normal? What's that?"

Danielle glanced up at the wall clock. "I wonder if Marie has found out anything."

"Even if she tells us who did it, we'll have to prove it," the chief reminded her.

"I know." Danielle shifted in her chair to get comfortable.

MacDonald sat up straight and grabbed a notepad and pen to take notes. "Obvious suspects, whoever benefits from Marie's death, which would mean her family."

"Marie insists no one in her family was involved."

"I'm sure she wants to believe that, but I know Marie's estate is worth a couple of million at least. She just sold the Beach Drive house, and I know oceanfront houses along that stretch go for over a million. And that doesn't even count her other properties. She owns a lot of real estate in this town."

"Come on, we know Adam would never hurt his grandmother," Danielle scoffed.

"He's not the only family member. She has a son she's been estranged from, another grandson that never sees her. Do you have any idea how she has her estate set up?" the chief asked.

"According to Adam, half of her estate goes to his father, and the other half is divided between him and his brother."

"I'm not really surprised Marie didn't leave it all to her son. But I am surprised she equally divided the half between Adam and his brother, considering Adam is the one who looked after her all these years."

Danielle shrugged. "From what Adam told me, the estate was originally to go to his father. But after his father and Marie had a falling-out, she changed her will. She didn't cut her son out completely, she left half to him and divided the other half between her grandsons."

"This gives all the family members a motive. Even twenty-five percent of the estate, that's a lot of money."

"Why kill a ninety-one-year-old woman for an inheritance? Why risk it? Why not just wait for her to die?"

"Agatha was killed by her grandson, and considering her age and health, she could have easily died at any time."

"But that was different," Danielle reminded him. "That wasn't premeditated. It was a crime of opportunity—spur of the moment. Someone planned this. They came into her room in the middle of the night and smothered her."

"If not a family member, why else would anyone want to hurt Marie?" the chief asked.

"Marie seems to think it was one of the other patients."

"But why?"

Danielle shrugged. "She thinks some of them are...well, a little crazy...and unsupervised."

"I find it hard to believe those patients—the ones who may no longer be fully competent—are wandering the halls at night unsupervised. I can't imagine Sunny allowing that."

"Sunny? Sunny Hartman? You know her?"

"Sure. She was a friend of Carol Ann's."

Danielle arched her brow.

"Don't hold it against Sunny. None of us realized what Carol Ann was really like. The two went to nursing school together. Sunny was as surprised as I was over what Carol Ann had done."

Carol Ann had been the chief's girlfriend. She had conspired with her brother in an elaborate kidnapping scheme and was currently serving time in prison.

"Carol Ann had me fooled too. Were the two close friends?" Danielle asked.

"I think Sunny thought they were. They went to nursing school together, and after graduation they both got a job at the hospital, but then Sunny was in a bad car accident and was off work for almost six months. I didn't know either of them back then. That's just what Carol Ann told me when I first met Sunny. By that time, Sunny was working at Seaside Village. But she always struck me as someone who was very dedicated to her job. She took it seriously and wanted what was best for the patients under her care."

"From what I understand, Sunny doesn't work nights. So she really doesn't know what goes on in that place when she leaves work," Danielle reminded him.

"You have a point. But before we can investigate this as a murder, we really need to have an autopsy."

"IT'S NOT as simple as just ordering an autopsy," the chief said after he hung up the telephone twenty minutes later.

"I thought that's who you were calling?" Danielle asked.

"No, you heard me on the phone. I asked if there was anything suspicious that might warrant an autopsy."

"Can't you say you got a tip from a witness who saw someone leaving her room late at night? Or just that they know she was murdered? We've stretched the truth before."

"You mean lie, Danielle."

"I suppose you could call it a lie. I call it a little white lie."

"White lies don't hurt people."

"How could this white lie hurt someone?"

"Because if Marie is right and someone murdered her, and if the killer hears someone called in claiming to have seen him or her —that could put others at the home in danger."

Danielle groaned and slumped back in her chair. "I see what you mean. They might kill off someone who they think is the witness."

"I can't be responsible for putting others in danger."

"What are we going to do?" Danielle asked. "We can't let the killer get away."

"We're going to have to get someone in her family to request an autopsy."

"What if one of her family members is the killer?" Danielle asked. "They sure aren't going to want an autopsy."

"I thought you said you didn't believe the killer was a family member," he reminded her.

"I don't believe Adam would hurt Marie. As for the rest of the family? Maybe Marie doesn't want to consider the possibility, but her son is already talking about going against her wishes and having her cremated."

"Cremated?" the chief asked.

"Marie had already made her final arrangements before she ever broke her hip. She's supposed to be buried next to her husband. But her son wants to have her cremated."

"That's interesting," the chief murmured.

"In all fairness, he didn't come up with the idea. It was actually the brother's fiancée. She mentioned cremation, something about it being better for the environment, and then Adam's father and mother thought it was a great idea."

"What did Adam think?" the chief asked.

"He got angry. Told them they were going to honor Marie's wishes. That she wasn't going to be cremated."

"I'm certain Adam is the one with Marie's power of attorney. He's been looking after her for years. He's the one who has the power to order an autopsy—and he may be the only family member willing to demand one."

Danielle cringed. "I don't know. Not sure Adam will be willing to have them cut on his grandmother—not if he believes she died of natural causes. People are funny about that."

"Then you better come up with some good story to convince Adam to get an autopsy."

"Me? Why me?"

"I can't be making up lies, and we all know you've become pretty good at twisting the truth to get what you want."

"Now you sound like Walt," Danielle grumbled.

"How's that?"

Danielle slumped down in the chair. "He's always telling me I've become adept at lying on the spur of the moment. But that really isn't fair. I'm usually making up stories to cover for something he did!"

"It's a good thing you're good at it." The chief smiled. "Plus, it's better if you talk to Adam than me. Not only are you a better liar, you were close to Marie."

"You call me a liar like it's a good thing."

"Sometimes it is."

With a sigh, Danielle pulled her cellphone out of her pocket and dialed Adam. When he answered, she said, "Adam, this is Danielle. I need to talk to you, alone. Can you meet me at Pier Café? Thirty minutes? Okay, see you there."

"Now what?" the chief asked after Danielle ended her phone call.

"Now I have thirty minutes to come up with a lie that will convince Adam it's a good idea to request an autopsy."

FIFTEEN

Danielle arrived at Pier Café before Adam. However, she wasn't alone for long. Just as she picked up the menu to browse through the dessert section, Eva appeared in the seat across from her in the booth. Eva wasn't alone. To her right was an attractive thirtysomething spirit wearing a brightly colored flowered house-dress. Danielle wondered who it was, and where was Marie?

"I told Marie that was you coming in here," Eva said brightly. "We were on the way back to Marlow House when I saw you going on the pier."

"Did Marie go back to the house?" Danielle asked, flashing the woman next to Eva a smile and waiting for an introduction.

"You don't recognize me!" The woman laughed.

Danielle narrowed her eyes and leaned forward, studying the woman. "Marie? Is that you?"

"Of course, who did you think it was?" Marie laughed again.

Confused, Danielle shook her head and looked from a much younger Marie to Eva. "Wow, you look great. Did you find the witness?"

Marie shook her head. "No. We started in the room where I initially saw her. She wasn't there. We looked through every room in that place, but we couldn't find her."

"It's possible she's moved on," Eva suggested.

"Perhaps." Danielle studied Marie a moment and then asked, "So what is this all about?"

Eva grinned and then said, "On our way to the nursing home, I started teaching Marie about costume changes. After all, one can't walk through eternity barefoot and in a nightgown. Once she mastered that, it was easy for her to bring forward a younger version of herself."

"While I can appreciate the desire to…well, turn back the clock…and you do look beautiful…but I have to say, it feels a little odd. You don't seem like *my* Marie."

Marie flashed Danielle a smile and in the next moment transformed into the image of a much older woman—the ninety-one-year-old version—one wearing a floral housedress instead of a nightgown.

"Oh, that's okay. I mean, I understand…you don't have to change back for me," Danielle told her.

Marie shrugged. "Truth is, dear, it's not like I can see my younger version. I asked Eva if we could stop somewhere so I could look in a mirror and see myself, but she told me I wouldn't have a reflection. So if you feel more comfortable seeing me as you knew me, then there's no reason I can't go back to how you remember me. I'm just happy not to be traipsing around town in my nightgown."

"Later, I can show Marie how she can automatically alter her appearance according to who she's talking to," Eva said. "Considering how well she's done, it will be easier for her."

"I don't understand?" Danielle said.

"As a spirit, I no longer have possession of my body; however, I have the ability to create an illusion of it—in all its varying stages. If a spirit was only able to reflect his or her body as it appeared at death, well, that would be unpleasant for many of us. Quite frankly, if I could only conjure up the illusion of my body at the time of my death, well, that would be an unsightly thing." Eva shuddered.

"I understand all that," Danielle said. "But what did you mean, *automatically alter her appearance* depending on who she's talking to?"

"It is possible, for example, for Heather to see Marie as a much younger woman while you see her as an older woman—at the same time. You can both be talking to her, yet you each see something different. Marie can learn to control that," Eva explained.

"Fascinating," Danielle murmured. "I knew about a spirit being able to present as an older or younger version, Walt has tried that. But I didn't realize it was possible to make people see different things at the same time."

"As an actor, I see it as nothing more than a costume change."

"Does that mean it's possible for a spirit to change his or her appearance entirely—I mean, not just an older or younger version of herself? But to take on someone else's appearance?" Danielle asked.

Eva leaned forward, closer to Danielle, while Marie attentively listened to what she had to say.

"I certainly can't," Eva whispered. "In fact, I've never encountered a spirit who could. Although, there are rumblings in my realm of the possibility—yet it's considered taboo."

"Taboo?" Danielle frowned.

"Evil," Eva whispered.

Their conversation was interrupted when a voice asked, "Is everything okay, Danielle?"

Danielle looked up. It was Carla the waitress, holding a pot of coffee, a worried expression on her face. Danielle then remembered —she had been sitting at the booth alone, talking to herself. Or at least that was how it appeared.

"Umm…yes…" Danielle blushed. "I…I'm just upset…and sometimes when something's on my mind, I think out loud." Danielle thought thinking out loud didn't sound as crazy as talking to herself.

"Oh, that's right," Carla said sympathetically, taking a seat on Eva's lap. She set the pot of coffee on the table as she studied Danielle.

Eva jumped from the seat with a curse and then said, "Let's go back to Marlow House, Marie. Danielle clearly won't be able to talk to us now." The next moment both Marie and Eva vanished.

"You're upset about Marie Nichols, aren't you?" Carla asked.

"How did you know?"

The waitress shrugged. "Brian and Joe were in here earlier and mentioned she died. I know you were close to her."

"Yes, I was."

Without asking if Danielle wanted coffee, Carla reached over and turned the empty cup that was upside down on a saucer right side up and filled it with coffee. She pushed it toward Danielle, and then filled the other empty cup on the table. Carla set the pot back onto the table and then picked up her cup and took a sip.

Setting the cup back on the table, Carla said, "Although, I can't say I'm surprised. The moment I heard poor Mrs. Nichols got put in that place, I said, mark my words, she's not long for this world."

"Why did you think that?"

"Whenever someone goes into one of those places, seems like it's checkout time, if you know what I mean. Except for Sam."

"Samuel Hayman?" Danielle asked.

Carla shook her head. "No. The Sam who works over at the Seahorse Motel. He had a knee replacement last year and had to stay at Seaside Village during his rehab. Bitched like hell when he got out, about how painful it all was. But at least he came home, unlike poor Mrs. Nichols."

"I've heard knee replacements can be pretty painful."

"Hey, Carla, can I get some coffee over here?" a customer across the café shouted.

With a sigh, Carla stood up and grabbed the coffee pot. "I'll be back in a minute to take your order."

"No hurry. I'm waiting for Adam."

A few minutes later, Adam Nichols entered the café. He stood in the entrance a moment and glanced around. When he spied Danielle sitting in a booth, he headed in her direction.

"Is someone else joining us?" Adam asked as he took a seat and noticed the half-filled cup of coffee on his side of the booth, bright red lipstick along its rim.

"No." Danielle shoved the cup to the edge of the table. "Carla sat down with me a minute ago and poured herself a cup of coffee.

"Sorry I'm late." Adam slumped back in the booth. "But my father decided to start an argument with me right before I was about to leave Grandma's house."

"I'm sorry," Danielle murmured.

"He wants to have her cremated."

"Cremated? But that's not what she wanted."

"I know, and that's what I told him...*again*."

"Why do you think he wants to have her cremated? Marie already made the arrangements. Everything is already paid for." *Does he want to destroy the evidence?* Danielle wondered. *Is it possible her son is the killer?*

"It's nothing more than a power trip on Dad's part. Very

typical of him. Whatever plans any of us makes, he always—and I mean *always*—has to make some change. He wants to be in control."

"Does this mean he'll get his way?"

Adam shook his head. "Not this time. I'm the only one who has the power to make any kind of changes like that. Grandma gave me power of attorney years ago, and on the contract she has with the funeral home, I'm the only one who can make changes. Grandma knew her son."

Danielle reached across the table and patted his hand. "Marie knew she could trust you to do what was best."

Before Adam could respond, Carla walked up to the booth, no longer carrying the pot of coffee. "I'm so sorry to hear about your grandma, Adam."

Adam smiled at Carla. "Thanks."

"She was such a dear sweet lady. I'll really miss her," Carla gushed. "What can I get you two?"

"I'd just like some apple pie, with ice cream," Danielle said. "And more coffee."

"Me too," Adam said.

With a nod, Carla grabbed the cup she had been using and scurried off to fill the order.

Adam chuckled.

"What's funny?" Danielle asked.

"Carla. *Dear sweet lady?*" Adam laughed.

"Yeah, that is kind of funny. From what I recall, Marie had no patience with Carla and was pretty short with her."

"Find it hard to believe Carla sincerely looked at Grandma that way. Hell, I loved my grandma, but I don't think I would describe her as a *dear sweet lady.*"

A few minutes later their conversation was interrupted again when Carla brought them each a slice of pie and ice cream, a cup of coffee for Adam, and a refill for Danielle.

When the two were alone again, Adam asked, "So why did you want to see me?"

"I know this is going to sound strange, but…you need to request an autopsy."

Pausing mid-bite, Adam frowned at Danielle. He set his forkful of pie and ice cream back on his plate. "Autopsy? Why?"

"I believe Marie may have been murdered."

93

"Murdered? What are you talking about, Danielle? Grandma died in her sleep."

Danielle shook her head. "Maybe she did…but maybe she didn't. I didn't say anything earlier, when we were at the home, but I've been thinking about it all day, and I finally decided I can't keep quiet. It's not fair to Marie. It's not what she would want."

"Danielle, you're not making sense. What purpose would an autopsy serve? Even if they overlooked some infection, she was ninety-one. I doubt the outcome would be much different if they caught something earlier. And I know she wasn't sick. She was feeling great."

"Exactly, she was feeling great."

Adam frowned. "Then why the autopsy? She obviously died of old age. It was her time."

"I'm not suggesting an autopsy because I suspect malpractice. I'm suggesting an autopsy because I believe she may have been murdered."

"Murdered? Who would want to murder my grandmother? That's crazy."

Danielle took a deep breath, trying to keep straight the lie she was about to tell. "Remember I told you I spoke to Marie on the phone last night?"

"Yes."

"Last night, Marie told me she thought someone was trying to kill her. She didn't tell me who or why. She said she couldn't talk to me about it on the phone, afraid someone might overhear. That's the real reason I brought her cinnamon rolls this morning. She was going to tell me what was going on."

Adam sat in silence for a few moments, digesting what Danielle had just told him. He then reached across the table and took hold of one of Danielle's hands, giving it a gentle squeeze.

"I know what she was talking about. Grandma hated staying in that place. From the first night she slept there, she complained about the lack of locks on the doors—and how anyone could walk into her room and do whatever. She'd read articles about abuse in nursing homes."

"Umm…I know she didn't like staying there, but she was talking about something more specific."

Adam shook his head and released Danielle's hand. Picking up his coffee, he took a sip and then set the cup back on the table. "I don't think so. Each day she stayed, it got worse. But then she found out my parents had toured the facility, checking out the rooms for the full-time residents. She knew Dad intended to push to have her stay there. She was panicking. That's what the conversation was about. No one was actually trying to kill Grandma."

"Please, Adam, can't you just request an autopsy? Just to be sure."

"I know you loved my grandmother. But the fact is, I know she abhorred the thought of an autopsy—people cutting on her body. No. I can't allow that. Grandma died in her sleep."

SIXTEEN

W arren Nichols was over arguing with his eldest child. As far as Warren was concerned, he was the head of the family, not Adam. Marie had been his mother, and as her son, it was his right to make the final decisions regarding her funeral and her estate. Annoyed at his mother for leaving half of that estate to his sons—it should have all gone to him and only passed to his sons after his death—he recognized his fifty percent, along with Jason's twenty-five percent, gave him a clear majority over Adam.

His first stop would be the bank. As a signer on his mother's bank account, he didn't believe there would be any problem withdrawing the necessary funds today. He suspected he would need his mother's death certificate to close the account. But he didn't need to close the account, he just needed to withdraw five thousand dollars before his world fell apart. He knew his mother had more than that in the account; he had seen her bank statement in her file drawer.

At the bank he waited patiently in line for his turn to see a teller. When it was his turn, he removed his wallet from his pocket.

"I need to withdraw five thousand dollars from my account." He handed the teller a slip of paper with his mother's checking account number on it, along with his driver's license, which he had just pulled out of the wallet.

"Certainly," the teller said with a smile. She then turned her attention to her computer. After a few moments of searching, she turned to him with a frown. "Um, this isn't your account number."

"Technically, it was my mother's, Marie Nichols. But I'm a signer on the account."

"Umm…just a minute." The teller smiled at Warren and then walked away. She returned a moment later and then pointed to a desk off the main lobby. "You need to speak to Mrs. Mitchell."

A moment later Warren Nichols sat at the desk of Susan Mitchell.

"Marie was your mother?" Susan asked.

"Yes, she was."

"I'm very sorry to hear about Marie. She was one of the first people I met when I moved to town," Susan said with a smile. "I know your son Adam."

"From what I remember about Frederickport, it's a small town. Everyone knows everyone." The way he said it, it didn't sound as if he thought it was a good thing.

"Yes…I suppose it is…Now, how can I help you today?"

"I need to withdraw some money from my mother's bank account."

"I'm afraid that account's in a trust, and only a trustee on the account can remove any funds."

"I'm a signer on the account. Of course I can withdraw money," he argued.

"I'm afraid you aren't."

"I've always been a signer on her account!" he insisted.

Without considering her words, Susan said, "Adam is the trustee. He's the only one who can withdraw any funds from the account."

"Damn!" Warren stood up abruptly. "I don't know what that boy's trying to pull! I'll be talking to my attorney, and then I'll be back." Not waiting for a response, he stomped from the bank.

Fifteen minutes later, Warren Nichols sat in an office of the funeral home, waiting to see the pre-need counselor. He didn't have to wait long.

"Mr. Nichols," the young woman greeted him when she walked into her office and extended her hand to him, "I'm Liz Cramer. I'm so sorry for your loss."

Standing up, he accepted her brief handshake and then sat back down. "Thank you. I wanted to talk to you about my mother's services. I was hoping we could have it right away."

Liz took a seat behind her desk and smiled at Warren. "Your son Adam called earlier and told me he would be in tomorrow so we could discuss the date."

"Yes, well, I am Marie's son; Adam isn't. I don't think we need to wait to schedule her service. And I also want to talk to you about cremation."

"Cremation?" Liz opened one of her desk drawers and pulled out a file. Opening it, she glanced over the pages before looking back at Warren. "Your mother isn't being cremated."

"I understand she arranged for a burial, but Mother tended to do things a certain way because it was the way it had always been done—not because it was the best option. She isn't going to know one way or the other if she is buried or cremated. I see no reason why she can't be cremated, save the ridiculous expense of a casket, and have her ashes buried with my father."

Liz closed the file and set it on her desk. "I'm sorry, but the only person authorized to make any changes is your son Adam."

"That's ridiculous. I'm her only son. It should be my decision, not Adam's."

With a sigh, Liz picked up the file, opened it, pulled out a sheet of paper, and handed it to Warren. As he took it, she pointed to one line.

"As you see, according to the contract, your mother specified the only one authorized to make any changes to her funeral plans is her grandson Adam."

"But I'm her only son! Certainly that means something!"

"I'm sorry. Had your mother put down the name of her gardener instead of her grandson's, the gardener would be the only one with authorization to change her plans—regardless of the fact he's not a relative. You see, these are your mother's arrangements—she made them and paid for them—and only she or whoever she delegated can make any changes. Certainly you can understand."

"No, I can't understand. I suppose this means I have no say in when to have the funeral?"

"I suggest you talk to your son and the rest of your family before Adam comes in tomorrow."

"I was hoping we could have the funeral tomorrow."

"I'm sorry. We already have several funerals planned for tomorrow, and the next day is Thanksgiving. Frankly, even if we didn't have any funerals tomorrow, the soonest we could possibly have your mother's funeral would be Tuesday."

Warren stood abruptly. "Perhaps I'll take your advice and go talk to my son."

WHEN DANIELLE ARRIVED home from Pier Café, she found Marie in the parlor with Walt. The two sat together on the sofa.

"Where's Eva?" Danielle asked as she tossed her purse on the small desk.

"She left," Walt told her. "Said something about attending a theater production opening in Astoria."

"She invited me to go," Marie told Danielle. "I thought that was very sweet of her. She's really nothing like I imagined she would be. Very helpful. And did you know I once could see spirits too!"

"See spirits?" Danielle asked.

Walt chuckled. "She told you about the lullabies, didn't she?"

"Lullabies?" Danielle asked.

"Before Walt died, Eva used to keep an eye on him. Which I can understand," Marie said with a snort.

Walt frowned. "What does that mean?"

"Sorry, Walt, but men can be foolish. Even my dear father was taken in by that manipulative wife of yours. But my mother had her number!"

Walt chuckled. "I suppose you have a point, Marie. I remember your mother was nobody's fool."

"So what is this about lullabies?" Danielle asked.

"When I was a baby, Eva's spirit would visit me in my crib and sing to me—and I saw her! She said I responded to her songs, and you know what?"

"What?" Danielle asked.

"I remember! I always thought it was a dream. But I recall the first time I saw Eva's portrait in the museum, I had this vivid memory of her standing over me, singing the most soothing lullaby. To be honest, I always assumed I was recalling a dream, and since the first time I saw Eva's likeness was her portrait, I naturally assumed that I had dreamt about the Gibson Girl singing to me. Although, when I saw Eva's portrait, it was troubling. My memory wasn't of a caricature like Gibson's drawing, but of a real woman. It was that woman in the portrait. And now I know it was."

"Interesting…" Danielle murmured.

"Eva invited me to go with her this afternoon, but I told her maybe next time. I thought I better stick around here and get my murder squared away."

"When that happens—and I hope it will—don't you think you'll be moving on afterwards?" Danielle asked.

"Are you trying to get rid of me?"

Walt flashed Marie a grin. "Don't feel bad. Danielle believes it's some moral duty of hers to cheer us on to the next leg in our journey."

"I'm not done here!" Marie insisted.

"And I'm not sure we'll be able to prove it was murder. We have a problem." Danielle plopped down on one of the chairs facing the sofa and let out a sigh.

"Didn't you tell the chief about Marie?" Walt asked.

"Yes. But he can't just order an autopsy at this point. Not when the medical examiner thinks she died of natural causes."

"What kind of medical examiner is that?" Marie snapped.

"One that didn't do a complete autopsy. At this point, aside from what you've told me, they've no reason to believe there was foul play. According to the chief, I would need to get Adam to request an autopsy."

"Then do it!" Marie urged.

"I tried." Danielle then recounted her visits with the chief and Adam.

"Oh dear," Marie muttered. "I did carry on once about autopsies. Foolishly told Adam he better never let anyone cut on me unnecessarily."

"I imagine at the time you didn't think you'd be a murder victim," Walt said.

"True. So what do we do now?" Marie asked.

"I suppose we could still try to figure out who killed you. But there won't be much the chief can really do to help us. At least, not on the record." Danielle let out a sigh. "And if we do figure out who killed you, I'm not sure what we can do about it."

"If I could only talk to Adam like I can to you…" Marie groaned.

"Perhaps you can," Walt said with a smile.

Danielle looked at Walt. "A dream hop?"

"It's worth a shot. Maybe Marie can convince him. And considering how quickly Marie caught on to wardrobe changes—as Eva calls it—I'm fairly confident I can guide her in her first dream hop."

SEVENTEEN

R ain began falling late Tuesday afternoon and continued into the evening. Adam stood in front of his microwave oven, waiting for a frozen burrito to finish defrosting, when he heard the doorbell. Glancing at the kitchen wall clock, he saw it was almost half past six. Leaving the microwave running, he went to answer the door.

"I stopped at your office," Warren greeted him the moment Adam opened the front door. Not waiting for a response, he pushed into Adam's house and began taking off his wet overcoat.

"Didn't Mom tell you?" Adam took his father's jacket and hung it on the coat rack. "I told her I'd talk to you all in the morning. It's been a long day; I'm beat."

"Yes, she told me." Warren headed for Adam's kitchen. "I wanted to talk to you now. Have any beer?"

"Yes," Adam said with a grunt as he trailed after his father, following him into the kitchen. Just as he entered the room, the microwave began to buzz.

"What are you cooking?" Warren opened the refrigerator and helped himself to a beer.

"Just a frozen burrito. Want one?"

Warren frowned. "Hell no." He opened the beer and took a swig.

With a shrug, Adam opened the microwave and stabbed the

burrito with the tip of one finger. It wasn't completely thawed yet. He set the timer for another minute. Turning from the microwave, he faced his father, who was now sitting at the breakfast bar. "What did you need to talk to me about that can't wait until tomorrow?"

"I stopped at the bank. They told me I'm no longer on Mother's account."

"That surprises you?" Adam asked. "Grandma changed that a few years ago."

Warren angrily gripped the bottle of beer. "Yes, it surprises me. Why did she do that? And why did you keep it a secret? What are you trying to pull, Adam?"

"What is your problem, Dad? I'm not trying to pull anything. Grandma just decided it wasn't necessary to have you on her account. I was the one managing her properties, taking care of her. And hell, when was the last time you were even here? Three, four years ago?"

"I have a business to run. I can't just take off whenever I feel like it. Was it your idea to remove me from the bank account?"

"I had nothing to do with that! You know Grandma, she was quite capable of making those kinds of decisions on her own. What's the big deal?"

"The big deal, I wanted to take out some cash—after all, this trip is costing us more than we expected. I'd planned to head home the day after Thanksgiving, but now we have a damn funeral to plan. And each day I'm here, it's costing me money."

Adam ignored the buzz of the microwave. "It's not like you have to pay for a hotel. What's the big deal?"

"I have a business to run, and if I'm here, I'm losing money. I have obligations. Something you never quite seemed to understand."

"Excuse me? The last time I noticed, I was the owner of a successful property management company."

"Yes, because of my mother. But she's no longer here."

"What's that supposed to mean?"

"When we liquidate Mother's estate, I can't imagine that'll leave you with many properties in your rental program. Of course, I guess with your share of the proceeds, you can figure out something new to do."

BY THE TIME Danielle reached her bedroom with her cup of hot cocoa, the only evidence of whipped cream in the cup was the swirl of white atop the chocolate. Before heading downstairs to make the drink twenty minutes earlier, she had laid out a fire in her bedroom fireplace. Upon reentering the room, she was happy to find the fire blazing, a fitting companion to the sound of rainfall on the roof.

Curling up on the small sofa, she looked into the dancing flames and took a sip.

"You look comfortable," Marie said as she suddenly appeared, standing between Danielle and the fireplace.

Danielle smiled up at her friend. "Hello, Marie, did you finish your dream hop instructions with Walt?"

"I did." Marie took a seat next to Danielle. "And I now understand why you have such horrible luck with men!"

About to take a sip, Danielle paused and arched her brows. "Excuse me?"

"First it was Adam…"

"Adam?" Danielle took a sip of the cocoa.

"I know you were interested in him," Marie began.

Danielle choked on her cocoa. When she stopped coughing, she looked at Marie. "Me? Interested in Adam?" Danielle remembered there had been a time when Marie had accused her of having an interest in her grandson.

"I assumed it was because of Cheryl—that she got to Adam first. But then I found out you were seeing Joe Morelli. And I realized I might have misread the extent of your interest in Adam."

Danielle smiled and before taking another sip muttered, "Something like that."

"But then you let Kelly snap up Joe right from under your nose," Marie continued.

"Well, in all fairness, I wasn't dating Joe anymore. So he wasn't exactly under my nose at the time."

"No, there was Chris. And I rather like Chris, especially now that I know when he comes back from his trip, he'll be someone I can talk to." Marie smiled.

Danielle resisted the temptation to ask, *Won't you be gone by then? Moved on?*

"But from what Adam told me, you and Chris are no longer an item."

Danielle shrugged. "But we're still good friends."

"Oh poo!" Marie scoffed. "You're a young woman. You need a man in your life. Someone you can start a family with. Not a buddy. And I now know the reason you have such a horrible time maintaining a relationship with a man. It's because of Walt."

"Walt?" Danielle set her half-full mug on the coffee table.

"Certainly." Marie glanced to the ceiling and lowered her voice. "I must say he's even more charming and handsome than I imagined. I can understand why my father was so fond of him, and why my mother felt somewhat protective toward him. Oh, if he were a living breathing man, I would help you plan your wedding!"

"Walt's a ghost!" Danielle reminded her.

"Exactly."

"What are you saying, Marie?"

"I think your feelings for Walt are interfering with your ability to establish a relationship with a man—a man like Chris or Joe. Or even Adam, although I imagine he has his sights on Melony now."

"Not Adam," Danielle muttered under her breath as she picked up her mug. "And never Joe."

"And it certainly doesn't help that Walt returns your feelings."

"Marie, Walt and I are just good friends."

Marie rolled her eyes. "I've seen how he looks at you."

"And we are both perfectly aware that we live in two different worlds—quite literally. Walt's not stopping me from dating."

"I'll just have to make sure that's true." Marie let out a sigh. "But I do like him. It's a shame he's dead."

Danielle muttered, "No kidding," and then took a sip of her drink.

After a few moments of silence, Marie asked, "I have a favor to ask you."

"What's that?"

"One bright spot in this death thing, I don't have to suffer through Thanksgiving at Seaside Village." Marie shuddered. "I've no idea why my son thought that was preferable to having dinner here."

"You think they'll make dinner at your house?"

"I seriously doubt that. And I hate thinking of Adam going to some restaurant for Thanksgiving."

"You want me to tell Adam that the invitation is still open?"

Marie perked up. "Would you?"

"Certainly. I'll tell him they're all still welcome to come."

Marie stood up. "Now that that's settled, I think I'll check in on Adam, see if he's asleep yet."

ADAM OPENED his eyes and found himself sitting on his grandmother's side porch.

"I couldn't make up my mind where to go," came a familiar voice to his right.

Turning to the voice, Adam found himself looking at his grandmother, who sat rocking in the chair next to him.

"Grandma?" Adam stammered. He knew she had died, yet there she was, sitting next to him.

"We could have met on a ship, or up on a mountaintop, or in a hot air balloon. To be honest, the idea of a hot air balloon never appealed to me. Imagine if it suddenly lost air or a wind gust came up and pushed us out to sea? But of course, none of that would matter now, so maybe I should have gone for a hot air balloon."

Adam frowned. "What are you talking about?"

"For this dream, Adam. You're dreaming, haven't you figured that out yet? After all, I am dead."

Adam considered her words a moment and then shook his head and leaned back in the chair. "I guess this has to be a dream," he muttered. "Doesn't feel like a regular dream. But it has to be."

"That's what I was told, that it would feel different from normal dreams. Maybe next time we can try the hot air balloon. It's probably best I stick to something familiar for my first go at this."

Adam looked over at his grandmother and smiled sadly. "I wish you really were here, and this wasn't a dream, which would mean you'd still be alive."

"That's sweet, dear, but you have to admit, I bet you're a bit relieved to have me out from underfoot. You won't have to be bothered anymore with changing my lightbulbs, taking me to the grocery store or checking on me."

Adam leaned back in the chair. "I have to admit you were sometimes a pain in the ass—"

"Adam!"

He chuckled. "It's my dream. Anyway, it doesn't mean I'm not going to miss you."

"If I was really sitting here with you, what would you want to tell me?" Marie asked.

Adam considered the question a moment. Finally, he said, "I guess I would want to ask why you took Dad off as a signer on your checking account."

Marie frowned. "I'm surprised you already know that. Doesn't it take a few days before you can access my checking account?"

"I told Dad we'd have to wait until after the death certificate was issued. Until then, we can't really do anything. But that's not really true. He went down to the bank and tried to withdraw money and was told he wasn't a signer on the account anymore."

"What was the point? He was never here, and you handle my properties."

"That's what I told him."

"Well, I'm not really here to discuss my finances. I need you to do something for me."

"What's that, Grandma?"

"I need you to request an autopsy of my body."

Adam sat up straight in the chair and turned to Marie. "Now I have no doubt this is a dream. Grandma would never want an autopsy."

"That was before I was murdered."

"Ahhhaa! Now I know why I'm having this dream." Adam chuckled.

"What are you talking about?" Marie asked.

"Danielle tried to talk me into requesting an autopsy. Something about you claiming someone wanted to kill you." Adam paused a moment and then shook his head. He leaned back in the chair. "Why am I telling all of this to Grandma, like she's really here..."

"Because I am really here! And I was murdered, and you need to request an autopsy."

"This crazy dream is all Danielle's fault. Who would want to murder my grandma?" Adam said more to himself, looking out into Marie's side yard.

"I have no idea who murdered me. But unless there is an autopsy, no one will be looking for my killer!"

"I wonder if it was that second burrito? I should have stopped with the first one. But that second one, right before bed, that might not have been a good idea."

"Adam, this is not a regular dream."

"No kidding," he muttered.

"I'm really here, and I need you to listen to me."

"Well, I have to admit, that does sound like Grandma," Adam said with a chuckle. "I wonder if I'm going to have a lot of dreams with her bossing me around?"

Growing frustrated, Marie said, "I'll prove it to you."

Adam turned to Marie. "Prove what?"

"That I'm not a figment of your imagination. That this isn't just a dream."

"How are you going to do that?"

Marie considered her options a moment and then broke into a smile. "Because in the morning, Danielle is going to call you up and invite you to Marlow House for Thanksgiving. When she does, you'll know I was really in your dream, and that I want you to request that autopsy."

ADAM SAT up abruptly in his bed and looked around the dark room. The only light came from the alarm clock sitting on the nightstand. It was almost 3:00 a.m.

"Wow, that was a crazy dream." Adam grabbed a pillow, gave it a punch, and repositioned it under his head before settling back down on the bed and closing his eyes.

EIGHTEEN

Marlow House seemed especially quiet on Wednesday morning. There were no guests, Lily now lived across the street, Joanne had the week off, and Max was curled up asleep on the bedroom sofa. Danielle assumed Walt was in the attic; as for Marie, she couldn't be sure. Unlike Walt, Marie was not confined to the house and might be anywhere—over at Adam's, at her own house, anywhere.

Barefoot, wearing plaid pajama pants and an oversized T-shirt, Danielle made her way down the stairs. Her first stop was the front door, where she found the newspaper, wrapped in plastic, on her front stoop. The rain had stopped sometime during the night, yet the yard was still wet. Fortunately, the newspaper was not.

From the front door, Danielle walked to the kitchen. Removing the plastic cover from the newspaper, she tossed the plastic into the trash can and the newspaper on the kitchen table. She had just started the coffee pot when Walt appeared.

"Good morning, Danielle," he said brightly.

"Morning, Walt. The paper's on the table. Is Marie here?"

"I haven't seen her since last night." Walt sat down at the table and picked up the newspaper, opening it. "I think she's still over at Adam's."

"That's what I figured." Danielle stood patiently by the coffee pot, waiting for it to brew.

"Good morning!" Marie greeted them when she appeared by the kitchen table.

"Morning, Marie." Danielle filled a mug with coffee.

"How did the dream hop go?" Walt asked, turning a page. He then pushed out a chair for Marie to sit on.

"I was able to do it." Marie sat down and looked over to Danielle. "Dear, I have a favor to ask you."

"Sure, what is it?" Danielle sipped her coffee.

"Would you please call Adam and invite him for Thanksgiving dinner?"

"Sure, I said I would." Danielle took another sip of coffee.

"No. I mean now."

"Now?" Danielle frowned.

"Yes, right now. It's important."

Danielle shrugged. "Okay, I guess so." She reached for the cellphone on the counter and dialed Adam's number.

"Morning, Danielle. Rather early for a phone call?" Adam said when he answered the phone.

Danielle glanced over at the table, where Marie was now looking over Walt's shoulder, reading the newspaper and trying unsuccessfully to turn a page. "Hope I didn't wake you."

"No. What's up?"

"I wanted to let you know you're still invited for Thanksgiving. I know, now with Marie gone, you obviously won't be going to Seaside Village for dinner. I can't imagine you feel like cooking."

"You're inviting me for Thanksgiving?" he said dully.

"Sure. Not just you, your whole family is welcome. And of course, Melony is still invited. You are all welcome, and if your parents don't want to come, you and Mel can just come, your brother and his fiancée too. Whoever wants to."

"This is bizarre," Adam mumbled.

"What's bizarre?" Danielle glanced over at the table and found Marie staring at her. Marie flashed her a smile.

"Do you believe our loved ones who passed can visit us in our dreams?" Adam asked.

Danielle didn't answer immediately. Finally, she said, "Sure. Last Christmas I dreamt about my parents and Cheryl. Part of me felt like their spirits really visited me." *Actually, all of me knew they had visited me*, Danielle told herself.

"Well, I had a dream about Grandma last night. It was sort of crazy. She started talking about hot air balloons."

"Hot air balloons?" Danielle frowned over at the table at Walt and Marie, who were now occupied by the newspaper.

"And then she told me I had to request an autopsy, insisted she was murdered. This is totally your fault, Danielle."

"My fault? How do you figure that?"

"All your talk about autopsies and murder. Why else would I have that crazy dream?"

"Umm…so it was just a crazy dream?" Danielle said dully.

"It actually got a little crazier. In the dream Grandma said she would prove to me that she was really there, that it wasn't a regular dream."

"Umm…and how was she going to do that?"

"You were going to call me this morning and invite me to Thanksgiving."

Danielle did not respond immediately. They were both silent for several moments. Finally, Danielle said, "Adam, I did call and invite you to Thanksgiving."

"To be honest, a minute ago, after you called, my initial thought was, *Holy crap, Grandma really did visit me in my dream.* But that's just silly."

"Is it?" Danielle glanced over to the table. Marie was reading an article over Walt's shoulder, instructing him on when to turn the page.

"It's obvious why I had that dream. You wanted me to have an autopsy. So I had a dream about it."

"What about my phone call?"

"It doesn't really surprise me that you've extended the invitation again, considering everything. I probably unconsciously worked that into my dream."

"And what if you didn't?" Danielle asked.

"Are you suggesting my grandmother's spirit really visited me last night and told me to order an autopsy?"

"You said yourself, in the dream she told you I would be calling to invite you to Thanksgiving," Danielle reminded him.

"Like I said, a coincidence. Plus, that would have to mean our future is predestined, since she knew what you were going to do. I can't buy that. It has to be some coincidence, my subconscious working overtime."

Danielle glanced over to the kitchen table, and after seeing Marie and Walt still occupied with the newspaper, she quietly stepped into the hallway for more privacy.

"It doesn't really matter if Marie's spirit actually visited you last night. But you know what this means, don't you?"

"Uhh, no, what?" Adam asked.

"If you don't order the autopsy, you will never know for sure if Marie was murdered. Your subconscious is clearly not certain if she died from natural causes. And if you don't have the autopsy, you will never know for sure, and you could be plagued with similar dreams…dreams where your grandmother comes to you every night —night after night—asking you why you didn't listen to her. Why, when she gave you proof. Oh, Adam, do you really want to ignore what your subconscious is trying to tell you?"

Adam groaned. "Grandma could be a nag."

Danielle glanced to the open doorway leading to the kitchen. "You may not want to say that out loud."

"You really think I should request an autopsy?"

"Yes, I do."

WARREN NICHOLS and his wife arrived at the funeral home first. They were sitting in the front lobby when Jason and his fiancée arrived.

"Isn't Adam here yet?" Jason asked.

"No." Chloe glanced at her watch. "When we get out of here, I was hoping we could all go out someplace for a nice lunch."

"Yes!" Sondra agreed. "I'm starved." She took a seat next to her future mother-in-law.

"I just wish we could have had the funeral today." Warren shifted uncomfortably in his seat.

"How long does this all take? No one's ever died in my family," Sondra asked.

Chloe arched her brows and looked bemused at the younger woman. "Never?"

Sondra blushed. "I mean—well, my grandparents died when I was little, so I naturally wasn't involved in planning the arrangements. I just wondered how long it takes to plan a funeral and settle an estate."

"Ahh, looking forward to getting your hands on my youngest son's share of the estate?"

"Mother," Jason snapped, "that was uncalled for."

Chloe rolled her eyes. "Oh, come on, dear, you can't wait to get your hands on that twenty-five percent. Although, it should rightly all go to your father first. He is Marie's only son."

"Maybe if you could have gotten along better with my mother, she wouldn't have rewritten her will," Warren grumbled.

Chloe gasped. "What? You're blaming me now?"

"You two never got along," Warren reminded her.

Chloe reached out and patted Warren's hand. "Then I suppose we should all be grateful Marie died before she had a chance to carry out her threat and change her will again."

"Mother!" Jason gasped. "I can't believe you just said that."

Chloe laughed. "Oh please. Like your father said, Marie and I never got along. And the woman was ninety-one. She had a long life. I'm certainly not going to pretend to be grieving over an old woman I never really liked."

Their conversation was interrupted when Adam came walking through the front door.

"It's about time you got here," Warren said as he stood up.

"Sorry, I had to stop somewhere," Adam explained. He looked over to his brother and future sister-in-law and flashed them a smile in greeting.

Five minutes later the entire group was sitting in an office with Liz Cramer, who sat at her desk, glancing over her funeral calendar.

"What do you think about Friday morning?" Liz suggested.

"Friday morning?" Warren asked. "That would be perfect! But I thought this Friday was all booked up."

"Oh, no. I didn't mean this Friday. I meant next Friday." Liz smiled politely.

"Next Friday?" Jason and his fiancée groaned.

"That's out of the question. I thought you said Tuesday might be possible?" Warren asked.

Liz glanced over to Adam, who sat quietly in his chair. "That was before the autopsy."

Warren frowned at Liz. "Autopsy?"

"There's no autopsy," Chloe snapped. "You have us confused with someone else. My mother-in-law died of old age in an old folks' home, and there is obviously no reason for an autopsy—unless you think this is going to get you more money."

Liz nervously turned the pages of her funeral calendar. "I'm sorry, I assumed you all knew. But we aren't doing the autopsy, the coroner is. It's possible we can schedule earlier in the week, but I just assumed—"

"What do you mean the coroner?" Sondra asked.

"There has to be some misunderstanding," Warren said.

"No," Liz assured them. "I don't think so."

"Why's the coroner doing an autopsy now? I thought they said that wasn't necessary," Jason asked.

"From what I understand, a family member requested it," Liz explained.

"That's ridiculous!" Warren stood up abruptly. "No one ordered a damn autopsy. I want to talk to your supervisor!"

"Sit down, Dad," Adam said dully. Instead of looking at his father, he continued to stare ahead blankly.

"Did you know about this?" Warren snapped.

"I requested an autopsy," Adam explained.

Chloe groaned. "Oh, Adam, how could you?" Resting her forehead in the palm of her hand, she shook her head in disbelief.

"Another one of your stunts?" Warren accused.

Adam looked over to his father. "Good lord, Dad. I'm not a teenager doing crap just to annoy you."

Warren glared at his oldest son. "You could have fooled me."

"Why would you do this?" Jason asked Adam.

"I just felt we needed to know why Grandma really died."

"She died because she was an old woman!" Chloe snapped.

"What's the big deal?" Adam asked.

"For one thing, I know how your grandmother felt about autopsies," Warren answered.

"You also knew how she felt about cremation, but that didn't stop you from trying to change her funeral plans," Adam countered.

"I don't understand; why would they even do an autopsy?" Sondra asked.

"Obviously my brother thinks someone killed our grandmother," Jason said with a snort.

Liz stood up. "Perhaps I should give you all some privacy to discuss this. But if you want to schedule the funeral earlier, let me contact the coroner and find out when they plan to release the body."

Sondra reached over and gripped Jason's wrist, squeezing it. Leaning close to him, she whispered in his ear, "I can't stay until Friday. Let's go home now, please."

NINETEEN

Just as Candy Ralston was about to enter room six, Clyde Archer, the patient on the opposite side of the corridor, rang his bell—*again*. Pausing, Candy glanced from the room she was about to enter to the patient ringing for assistance. With a sigh, Candy changed course. Clipboard in hand, she headed to Mr. Archer's room. He had arrived at Seaside Village a week earlier, after knee replacement surgery. They hadn't put him in the rehab section of the hospital, because according to his family, Mr. Archer would not be returning home after rehab. He had early stages of Alzheimer's.

"Hey, Candy Striper, I need some pain meds!" Mr. Archer shouted when she entered the room.

Forcing a smile and ignoring the nickname he had given her after learning her first name, she approached his bed. "What do you need, Mr. Archer?"

"I need some pain medication! My knee hurts like hell!"

Candy glanced at her clipboard and then looked back to the patient. "I'm really sorry, Mr. Archer, but you were given pain medication just thirty minutes ago."

"Well, it isn't working!"

"Let me check with your doctor, and I'll see what I can do."

Several minutes later, Candy walked up to the front nurses'

station. There she found Sunny updating patient charts while SeAnne stood nearby, talking on the telephone.

Dropping her clipboard on the counter near Sunny, Candy said, "It's Mr. Archer again, asking for more pain meds. He's been asking for more meds the last couple of days."

Sunny smiled at Candy and said, "I'll talk to his doctor."

"Oh my god!" SeAnne cried out as she hung up the phone. Rushing toward Candy and Sunny, she said, "You are never going to believe this, but they've ordered an autopsy of Mrs. Nichols!"

"Who ordered an autopsy?" Candy asked.

"I guess the family," SeAnne said.

"But why would they do that? She obviously died in her sleep. Wasn't she in her nineties?" Candy asked.

Sunny set the file she had been holding on the counter. "It sounds to me like the family might be considering some sort of malpractice suit."

"Against us?" Candy gasped. "We didn't do anything wrong!"

Sunny shook her head. "It could be against her doctors. Maybe they suspect something went wrong in surgery that caused a problem down the road."

"Or they may think we did something wrong," SeAnne said nervously.

Sunny reached out and patted SeAnne's hand. "I don't believe any of us here did anything wrong. You're an excellent nurse, SeAnne. I see how you are with your patients. You're kind, conscientious, and they are lucky to have you. I monitor the medications, and I know without a doubt she didn't die from some overdose. They certainly won't find any lethal traces of any medication in her blood. That leaves medical malpractice from her doctors—but that really is no reflection on us. It's not like she was showing any signs of illness. Even her physical therapist said she was doing well. It was simply old age catching up to her."

"Or someone killed her," Candy whispered.

"Candy!" SeAnne snapped. "That's a horrible thing to say!"

"I was thinking about her family," Candy explained. "Remember the night before Mrs. Nichols died, she threatened to change her will. I'm not the only one who heard that argument."

"If that was the case, why would the family request an autopsy?" SeAnne asked.

"Because maybe it wasn't requested by the guilty family member?" Sunny suggested.

IT WASN'T until Danielle installed a computer in the Marlow House library—for her guests—did Walt start wondering if it would be possible for him to learn how to use it. After all, he had mastered the television, how much more difficult could a computer be? When he had been first introduced to the laptop computer, Danielle had compared it to a television. The desktop computer sitting in the library resembled the television even more than the laptop, so wouldn't it stand to reason it would be as easy to use? At least, that was what Walt surmised.

He was sitting at the computer, his hands idly resting on the keyboard, when Marie appeared by his side. "Heavens, do you know how to use one of those things?"

Startled by Marie's abrupt appearance, Walt quickly moved his hands from the keyboard and settled them on his lap. "When did you come back?"

"Just now. I was down at the funeral home, listening to my family argue." Marie stood next to the desk and looked down at the computer. "Do you know how to use that?"

"No. But I was thinking of asking Danielle to teach me."

Marie shuddered. "Oh my, why would you want to do that?"

"Danielle once told me it was a little like a library. I miss going to the library."

Marie glanced around. "You've an impressive library here. My mother used to talk about it. She was quite taken with the fact you were such an avid reader and could never understand why you got involved with that dim-witted little gold digger."

Walt stood up. "I assume you mean Angela."

"My father talked about your great love affair," Marie said with a snort.

"We both know the truth about that." Walt wandered over to the sofa and sat down. He watched as Marie took a chair across from him.

"Eva told me Angela is at the local cemetery—her spirit, that is."

"Danielle says she's under house arrest." Walt chuckled.

Resting her balled fists on her knees, Marie leaned forward. "So that means you two have never—since either of you died—seen each other?"

"More accurately, not since I died. From what I understand, Angela came here after her death and tried to stop her brother from killing me. That didn't exactly work out, and she ended up confined to the cemetery. Since then, we haven't seen each other, nor do I have any desire to."

"Isn't it frustrating to you, being confined to this house?" Marie asked.

"With death as in life, we make choices. Had I followed Eva's path, then I wouldn't have the energy to..." With a wave of his hand Walt made the chair Marie was sitting in lift into the air and then float gently back to the floor.

Marie laughed. "While I don't care about moving furniture—I had a difficult time doing that when I was alive—I do miss being able to do simple things, like turn the page of a newspaper."

"In order to do that, you have two choices." Walt waved his hand for a lit cigar. "You can move on to the other side—or stay in one location, which will allow you to utilize that saved energy, doing things like moving furniture or turning the page of a newspaper."

Marie considered the option a moment and then shook her head. "No, I can't move on. I need to find out who murdered me. As for the other option, no. Walt, you died before you had a chance to grow old. In many ways, age confined me to my house, like death confined you to yours. Before I died, I needed a walker to make it across the room. And at night, there were countless trips to the bathroom. My bones constantly ached, and I had to rely on my grandson for basic things like taking me to the grocery store."

"And now?"

Marie smiled. "My bones don't hurt anymore, and while I may discover I miss enjoying one of Old Salts' cinnamon rolls, I certainly don't miss those trips to the bathroom. I must say, it was exhilarating going from the home to the police station, to my house and then here. I love the freedom!"

"Don't you want to move on? See your parents, your husband?"

Marie smiled at Walt. "Don't you?"

Walt shrugged. "I'm not in a hurry."

"Neither am I. Plus, I need to find out who murdered me."

"I suspect you can find that out after you move on," Walt said. "Moving on doesn't mean you won't find the answers."

Marie arched her brows. "Really? According to Danielle, you initially insisted on sticking around because you wanted to find your murderer. How is that any different from me?"

"I suppose I wanted more than to just discover what had happened. I wanted the record set straight. I didn't want everyone to keep thinking I had killed myself," Walt explained.

"That's what I want...Although, no one thinks I killed myself, just that I died in my sleep."

Walt studied Marie a moment while the fingers of his right hand toyed with his cigar. "Are you sure you want that?"

"What does that mean?"

"Marie, what happens if it was someone from your family?"

Marie frowned. "What are you saying?"

"Perhaps someone from your family is responsible for your death. After all, they had the financial motive," Walt suggested.

"MORE POTATOES, MAYBE A HAM..." Danielle muttered to herself as she added items to her grocery list. She sat alone in the kitchen. Yet she wouldn't be alone for long.

A crash and thump of the doggy door, followed by Sadie diving through the small opening into the kitchen, startled her. The golden retriever was already at Danielle's side, pressing a wet nose into her wrist, begging for attention, when the kitchen door opened. In walked Ian and Lily.

"You ready to go to the store?" Lily asked.

"In a few minutes. I was just updating my list now that Marie's family is coming," Danielle said. "I was thinking maybe we should get a ham just to make sure we have enough. I already have the turkey thawing."

"When you called to tell me Marie's family was on again, we stopped by Old Salts and picked up two more pies, pumpkin and pecan," Lily said.

"I can't believe they had any left." Danielle scratched pies off her list.

"Heather's bringing rolls. Do you think we should let her know the others are coming?" Lily asked.

"I already called her. She said she has more than enough."

"Is Marie here?" Ian asked in a whisper, glancing around.

"I saw her talking with Walt in the library. They might still be in there. You want to go say hi?" Danielle grinned.

"Yeah, right," Ian said with a grunt as he took a seat at the table. "You just want me to go into the empty library and start up a conversation so you and Lily can laugh at me."

Lily reached out and patted Ian's arm. "Now you have some idea how I've been feeling the past year. Starting up conversations and finding out no one is there. I'm just glad I'm not alone in all this anymore." Lily took a place at the table. In the next moment, Sadie dashed from the room.

"Say hi to Walt and Marie," Ian called out to Sadie.

Lily glanced to the doorway. "Marie hasn't seen Sadie yet, has she?"

"Not unless she stopped over at our place and we didn't know," Ian said. "Sadie's been with me since Marie passed."

"What about Max?" Lily asked.

"I don't think so." Danielle scribbled another item on the list.

"Why do you care?" Ian asked.

"Because they're animals, and Marie is a ghost now," Lily said as if her explanation made complete sense.

Ian frowned. "What am I missing?"

Danielle set her pen down and looked across the table at Ian. "Because most spirits I know are able to communicate with dogs and cats."

"I know, but—"

Danielle interrupted Ian with, "It can be a little startling for a new spirit to realize he—or she—understands what the dog or cat is thinking."

As if on cue, Sadie started barking, the sound drifting from the library to the kitchen. By the volume and intensity, it sounded as if Sadie had cornered a rat—or a startled ghost.

TWENTY

Sadie was still barking when Ian, Lily, and Danielle ran into the library a few moments later. With her attention riveted on the top bookshelf, Sadie continued to bark, her tail wagging.

While Ian and Lily couldn't see why the dog was barking, Danielle could, and she didn't understand why Walt sat on the sofa, chuckling, and made no attempt to quiet Sadie.

"What are you doing up there?" Danielle asked Marie. She then looked at Walt. "And why are you sitting there laughing?"

"Sadie, quiet," Ian admonished. Sadie stopped barking. Sitting down, the dog began to whimper while she continued to stare up toward the ceiling.

Lily looked curiously up at the top bookshelf. "What's up there?"

"Marie," Danielle explained. They all looked up to where Marie was supposedly hovering, inches from the ceiling.

"It's that dog!" Marie exclaimed. "I swear it talked to me! Maybe not in words, but she talked to me! That's not right. Animals don't talk to people."

Danielle glared over at Walt. "Really, Walt? You couldn't just explain to poor Marie what was going on? You just sit there and laugh and let Sadie bark? Didn't anyone teach you to respect your elders?"

"Phonus balonus!" Walt said with a laugh.

Danielle frowned. "Huh?"

"Marie isn't my elder. I knew her when she was born." Still chuckling, he looked up at Marie. "It's okay, Marie. One of the perks of being dead."

"Humpf...well, it's almost demonic!" Marie grumbled. In the next moment she drifted down from the bookshelf, her feet landing on the floor.

"What just happened?" Ian asked.

"I think Marie was a little spooked when she realized she could read Sadie's thoughts," Danielle explained.

"I'm sorry Sadie startled you, Marie," Ian said.

"Are you sure Ian can't see and hear me?" Marie asked, noting the way Ian seemed to be looking directly at her.

"No, he can't," Danielle insisted.

"Marie, I just wanted to say," Ian began.

Eyeing Ian curiously, Marie moved several feet to her left and watched as Ian continued to direct his attention to the spot she had been standing at.

"I was really sorry to hear of your passing—" Ian stopped midsentence and shook his head. "I'm sorry, I'm not sure I can get used to this."

"How do you think I feel?" Marie asked.

"I think Ian means talking to someone he can't see," Danielle explained.

"It is pretty bizarre," Ian muttered. "But I want you to know, Marie, Lily told me about what happened to you. And I'll do whatever I can to help find whoever is responsible for your death."

"Thank you, Ian. Knowing the famous Jon Altar will be looking into my murder makes me feel much better. But I never understood why you don't write under your real name?"

Before Danielle could convey Marie's message to Ian, her phone rang with a text message. Removing the phone from her pocket, she looked at it. "It's Adam. He wants to know what they should bring."

"None of them can cook a lick," Marie said as she sat down on the chair across from Walt. "Although, I'm really not sure about that fiancée of Jason's. Maybe she can."

"Tell them to bring wine," Ian suggested.

"Ohh, maybe that good stuff he bought Chris," Danielle said with a giggle as she sent a text message to Adam.

"Seriously, Dani, you really didn't tell him to buy that expensive stuff," Lily asked.

"Nah. I don't think Adam is in a mood for jokes right now," Danielle said.

"Speaking of Chris, have you heard from him?" Ian asked.

"I talked to him earlier today. He wants to know when the funeral is so he can be back in time for it."

"What a sweet boy," Marie said.

Walt rolled his eyes.

Catching a glimpse of Walt's eye roll, Marie arched her brows. "I saw that, Walt Marlow."

"Saw what?" Walt asked guiltily.

Danielle remained standing in the middle of the library, ignoring the exchange between Walt and Marie, still looking at her cellphone, a curious frown crossing her face.

Noticing Danielle's peculiar expression, Lily asked, "What is it?"

"It's an email...from Walt's cousin..." Danielle's finger repeatedly moved over the display. "A long email."

"Walt's cousin?" Marie asked. "You're in communication with one of Walt's cousins? You never told me that."

Ian glanced over to Danielle. "Is that the Realtor you told us about?"

"Why is he writing you?" Walt asked.

Still looking at the iPhone display, Danielle made her way to the computer desk. "I found a distant cousin of Walt's online. But I never contacted him." Danielle sat down. "Yes, Ian, it is the Realtor. Marie, Adam came across this guy's business website. He looks just like Walt's portrait—and he share's Walt's name. It's kind of eerie how much they look alike. Adam sent him a link to Marlow House's website."

Marie frowned. "Why would Adam do that?"

Danielle set her phone on the desk and glanced over to Marie and shrugged. "He's your grandson."

"Foolish thing to do. You know nothing about this man, and now he's emailing you?" Marie said. "I need to have a word with my grandson!"

"Read the email!" Lily urged.

"I'm going to pull it up on the computer. It looks pretty long. Not sure my eyes can take reading it on my phone."

"You're getting old," Walt teased.

"Oh hush, you're one to talk, old man!" Danielle shot back, suppressing a giggle.

Several minutes later, Danielle opened the email on the library computer. Standing around her, looking over her shoulder, were Lily, Ian, Walt, and Marie. Danielle began to read aloud.

"Dear Ms. Boatman. My legal name is Walter Clint Marlow. I go by my middle name, Clint. I've always hated my first name. It sounds like a nerd—"

"What's wrong with my name?" Walt asked angrily. "He's the one that's a nerd...uhh...what's a nerd again?"

Danielle glanced over her shoulder to Walt and smiled. "I like your name, Walt."

"I do too," Lily chimed in.

Danielle began reading again. *"My parents told me Walter and Clint were names passed down in our family. While I've never been fond of my name, I will have to say I was intrigued to discover the other Walt Marlow and learn how much we look alike. That really blew me away.*

"I am a real estate agent in California. A while back, a fellow Realtor sent me a link to your bed and breakfast website. I had heard about some distant cousins settling in Oregon, but I never knew anything about them. And frankly, genealogy has never interested me. But when I saw your website, I was intrigued.

"I'm sending you a link to my real estate website. If you go to it, you'll see my picture. When you look at it, you'll see what I'm talking about. That portrait of the Walt Marlow who lived in your bed and breakfast is a dead ringer for me—"

"Dead being the operative word," Ian said under his breath.

Danielle chuckled and then continued reading. *"I would like to buy the portraits from you—of Walter and Angela Marlow—"*

"Buy my portraits? Absolutely not!" Walt interjected.

After clearing her throat, Danielle resumed reading aloud. *"I'm getting married this summer, and I think my fiancée would love the portrait of me. I know she would find the portrait, with its likeness so close to me, uncanny. I'm not particularly interested in the portrait of Angela Marlow, but I hate to break up the pair, and who knows, maybe I can get an artist to cover the wife's face with my wife's likeness. Wouldn't that be awesome?"*

"My cousin is a dimwit," Walt muttered.

"He sounds like an idiot if he wants to paint over that old portrait," Lily added.

"Of course, if you are opposed to me painting over the one portrait, and it's

a condition of the sale, I won't make any changes to it. But I just figure, if it were me, I would hate to be saddled with two life-sized portraits of two strangers. People I'm not even related to. So basically, I'm making you an offer to take the portraits off your hands for a thousand dollars. I think that's probably more than what they're worth, but I'd really like to give them to my fiancée for a surprise wedding gift.

"Let me know where I can send the money, and I will arrange to have a shipping company pick them up. Hope to hear from you soon. Clint Marlow."

"He sounds like a goof," Lily said.

"What are you going to tell him?" Marie asked.

"That I'm not interested, of course. Those portraits belong here. Plus," Danielle looked over to Walt and said, "They're not mine to sell."

Walt broke into a smile and then said, "Maybe you should reconsider."

"Reconsider? You want me to sell your portraits?" Danielle asked.

"Walt said that?" Lily asked. "He can't be serious."

"I don't know," Walt mused. "Sell it to him under the condition he has to paint over Angela's face—he can send you a snapshot when it's done. You can show Angela." Walt grinned.

Danielle rolled her eyes and shook her head. "You're bad, Walt. But we are not letting anyone paint over Angela's face. When we get tired of looking at it, we can donate it to the museum."

"Not sure Eva would appreciate sharing the museum with Angela," Walt said.

Danielle shrugged. "You're probably right. For now, the portraits stay where they are."

"Hurry up and send your no-thanks reply," Lily said. "We need to get to the grocery store. Tomorrow is Thanksgiving!"

"I REALLY SCREWED UP," Sondra whispered into her cellphone. She stood alone on Marie's side porch, glancing nervously to the door leading into the kitchen. "And now with the autopsy, crap, what am I going to do? Now I have to stay here until Friday and just hope no one finds out!"

"Sondra?" Jason called out after opening the back door. "What are you doing on the porch? It's freezing out there."

Placing a hand over the phone, Sondra called out, "I'm just talking to Georgia."

"Well, do it in here, before you get pneumonia. You don't even have a coat on!" Jason went back in the house and shut the door.

"I have to go. Jason is calling me."

TWENTY-ONE

Early Thanksgiving morning, Walt found Danielle alone in the kitchen, her hand shoved up a recently thawed turkey carcass. She had already dressed for the day, wearing orange and gold patterned leggings and a long beige cotton shirt protected by a cartoon-pilgrim-themed, cobbler-style apron.

"That doesn't look very pleasant," Walt observed as he took a place at the kitchen table and picked up the newspaper Danielle had placed there earlier.

Glancing over to the table, Danielle smiled. "Good morning to you too." She pulled the plastic bag of giblets from the turkey and set it in the sink. Next she removed the turkey neck.

"It's too bad Joanne isn't here to help."

"She's spending the time with her family. I think she's enjoyed this week off."

"What can I do?" Walt set the paper on the table and looked up at Danielle.

"I've got it under control, but thanks." After rinsing the turkey neck, she set it in a pot on the stove.

"What exactly are you going to do with that thing?" Walt asked.

"It's for the dressing. I have to cook the neck and giblets in a pot of water. After the meat is tender, I put it all in the blender, whip it up until puréed, and then add it to the dressing."

"Extra calcium with the neck bones?"

Danielle rolled her eyes. "First I remove the meat from the bone."

"Sounds like a lot of work. Are you sure you don't have something I can help you with?"

Danielle glanced over at the cutting board sitting on the counter. On the cutting board was a knife, yellow onion, and several stalks of celery. "Umm, would you mind dicing the celery and onion? The celery is already clean, and I've removed the skin from the onion."

"I don't know, Danielle, cutting onions always makes my eyes water." Walt folded the newspaper and tossed it on the chair next to him.

Danielle turned to Walt and arched her brow. "Seriously?"

Still sitting at the table, Walt chuckled and then turned his attention to the cutting board. It lifted from the counter and floated to him.

"And don't forget to tell me to wash my hands first, and be careful with the sharp knife," Walt teased.

Danielle grinned. "I suppose there are some benefits of having a cook who is a gh…spirit."

"Don't get carried away, I'm just cutting the vegetables!"

"And I appreciate the help!"

DANIELLE HAD LEFT the side gate open into the backyard, which was an easier route than going to the front door for Lily and Ian, who had their hands full. With Sadie by their side, they approached the back door leading into the kitchen of Marlow House.

Ian had opted to forgo denims and wear tan dress slacks and a brown, long-sleeved silk shirt, sans a tie. Lily made him leave his Cubs baseball cap at home. From what Lily had told him, Walt normally wore a three-piece pinstriped suit, not that anyone other than Danielle or Heather could see Walt today—except for Marie, of course.

Lily wore black slacks and an emerald green short-sleeved blouse —it brought out the green in her eyes. She had pulled her red hair up into a high ponytail, telling Ian it was best this way—less likely any of it would get into the food. There would be potatoes to mash and salads to prepare. Since Ian wasn't fond of hair in his food, he told her she looked adorable.

The kitchen blinds were open, and Ian was the first to glimpse what was going on inside. He stopped abruptly, still finding such scenes unnerving. A knife seemingly danced of its own accord over a cutting board on the kitchen table, dicing vegetables.

"I'm not sure I'll ever get used to this," Ian muttered. "And seriously, this is one of the best stories of my career, but I can't write about it."

"You could," Lily said cheerfully as she juggled the bowls in her arms to reach for the doorknob. "But then you'd lose all your credibility. No one would believe you."

"No kidding." Ian reached quickly to help Lily with the door.

"Happy Thanksgiving!" Danielle greeted them when Lily and Ian entered the kitchen a moment later.

"Morning, Dani. Who's your helper?" Lily nodded to the table and the knife chopping away at the vegetables.

"Walt." Danielle filled the pot holding the giblets and turkey neck with water.

"Morning, Walt," Lily and Ian said simultaneously.

The knife waved in the air like a salute.

Lily and Ian set the items they had been carrying on the counter, while Sadie greeted Walt.

Lily glanced around the room. "Where's Marie?"

"She went over to her house to spy on her family. I hope she doesn't hear something that she doesn't want to," Danielle told her.

"Like what?" Lily asked.

"I imagine Danielle means something like a confession to her murder," Ian suggested.

"I DON'T KNOW why we just can't go to a restaurant for dinner," Sondra told Jason as they dressed for Thanksgiving.

"I told you, Mom called around, and everything was filled up." Jason sat on the edge of the bed, pulling up his socks.

"We don't have to stay in Frederickport. Did she try someplace in Astoria? It's not that long a drive. And I would be willing to drive to Portland."

"If you still had family in Portland, that wouldn't be a bad idea."

"We could still go. I'm sure we can find somewhere to go for dinner."

"This is a done deal, Sondra. Adam already told them we would be there. We can't bail out now. I'm sorry this trip didn't work out like I'd hoped."

"Didn't it?" Sondra snickered. She looked into the dresser mirror and applied her eyeliner.

"What is that supposed to mean?"

"We both know why we came, to kiss up to your grandmother so she wouldn't do anything stupid before she died, like leave your brother all her money."

"Don't say that too loud, not now," Jason grumbled.

STILL IN HER HOUSE ROBE, Chloe sat in Marie's living room with her husband, enjoying their morning coffee. Jason and Sondra were still in the guest bedroom, getting dressed.

Neither Chloe or Warren attempted to get up from their chairs when they heard the front door open and close. They weren't surprised when Adam walked into the living room a moment later.

Pausing mid-sip, Chloe said, "Good morning, Adam. What time are we supposed to be over there?"

"Morning, Mom, Dad. Danielle said to come over around two." He took a seat on the sofa.

Lifting her mug, Chloe said, "There's coffee made. Help yourself."

"In a minute, thanks. But I wanted to tell you Liz from the funeral home called me this morning."

"Please tell me that ridiculous autopsy is cancelled," Chloe said.

"No. But she said we can have the funeral on Tuesday if you want. She spoke to the coroner, and they're fairly certain that time frame will work out after all."

"Fairly certain? What if it isn't?" Warren snapped. "You really screwed this whole thing up by bringing up this autopsy thing. I don't know what in the hell you were thinking, boy."

"I'M in my fricking forties and he's still calling me *boy*," Adam grumbled to Melony when he picked her up later that afternoon.

"I guess you could look on the bright side. It means you're still young." As Melony climbed into the passenger side of his car, she leaned over and placed a kiss on Adam's cheek and then sat down and fastened her seatbelt.

Hands on the steering wheel, Adam glanced over to Melony. "Yeah, right."

Settling back in the seat while Adam drove away from the curb in front of her house, Melony said, "Well, your mother still looks at me as if I'm some sexually permissive teenager."

"Instead of a sexually permissive adult?" Adam teased.

Playfully smacking Adam's right arm, Melony said, "Oh, shut up."

Adam snickered. "I guess my parents will never see us past high school."

Melony shrugged. "It's hard for some parents to see their children as adults."

"You know what's funny?" Adam asked.

"Funny? Humor would be nice; it's been pretty glum this week." Melony leaned back in the seat.

"Not that kind of funny."

"Yeah, I sort of got that. What?"

"Dad's under the impression my property management company is nothing more than my grandmother's properties."

Lifting her head from the seat, she turned to Adam. "You own more houses than Marie did, don't you?"

Adam chuckled. "Yes. But Dad doesn't know that. And he has no clue that the houses I own and Grandma owned are only a fraction of my inventory. He seriously has no clue what I've built here."

Melony reached over and patted Adam's arm. "He's always underestimated you. Marie saw your potential."

Adam sighed. "I'm really going to miss her. She was a pain sometimes, damn bossy, but I loved her."

"I know you did."

They drove for a few moments in silence when Melony said, her tone serious, "I'm afraid I have a problem I need to talk to you about."

"Another problem?"

"I really should have said something as soon as I found out Marie had died. But it was all so sudden, and you were dealing with the funeral and your parents. I suppose I should have sent you a certified letter, it's what I would normally do. But I figured that would just freak you out."

Adam glanced to Melony with a frown. "What are you talking about?"

"You know that argument your family had the night before Marie died?" Melony asked.

"When Grandma threatened to change the will?"

"Yes. The fact is, Marie had already changed her will."

Adam gripped the steering wheel tighter. "What?"

"She called me after the Beach Drive house closed escrow, said she wanted to make some changes to her will, asked me if I could do it, and told me not to say anything to you."

"You aren't even an estate attorney!" Adam snapped. "I can't believe you didn't tell me!"

"I couldn't, you know that. It was client confidentiality. You're a broker, you know about fiduciary duty. And I have done some estate work."

"Okay, so tell me, what is in this new will?"

"Sorry, I can't tell you right now."

Adam flashed a frown at Melony. "What do you mean you can't tell me right now?"

"Your grandmother gave me specific instructions. First, she didn't want to keep a copy of her new will in her house. She instructed me to keep it for her."

"Why would she do that?"

"She told me that the minute she died, your father would be at her house going through all her files, and she was afraid if he found the new will first, he might destroy it and try to use the previous one. I guess she had given him a copy of that one a number of years ago. I told her that even if he tried something like that, it wouldn't work because I would still have a copy of the current will, but for what-ever reason, she insisted he not know about the new will until it was formally read."

"I guess Grandma knew her son pretty well. Dad went through all Grandma's files right after he got here. She wasn't even dead yet," Adam grumbled.

"According to your grandmother's instructions, she wants the will to be read the day after her funeral. At Marlow House."

"Marlow House?"

Melony shrugged. "It's what she wanted. When everyone is

together today, I need to tell them about the reading of the will and check with Danielle. After all, it's supposed to be done at her house."

"I didn't tell you, but Dad tried to take some money out of Grandma's bank account on Tuesday. He was pretty upset he wasn't on her account anymore."

"Well, I don't imagine he's going to be thrilled when this new will is read," Melony muttered.

TWENTY-TWO

Sondra and Jason sat in the backseat of Warren and Chloe's car as they drove to Marlow House for Thanksgiving dinner. Both Sondra and Chloe had chosen to wear dresses for the occasion, while the men wore dress slacks and button-up, short-sleeved dress shirts.

"I don't understand. What exactly was Danielle Boatman to your grandmother?" Sondra asked Jason. "When Marie introduced her to me at the home, she said Danielle was practically a granddaughter. But from what Adam said, Danielle hasn't lived here that long. How did they get so chummy?"

"My mother was friends with Danielle's great-aunt," Warren called out from the driver's seat. "She's the one who left her Marlow House."

Chloe turned in her seat to look back to Jason and Sondra. "From what Adam has told me, Marie adored her. I don't think they'd met before Danielle moved here over a year ago. At least, that was my impression. She sounds like a manipulative little thing, if you ask me."

"Why do you say that?" Sondra asked.

"Seriously?" Chloe let out a harsh laugh. "Come on, a woman her age getting so cozy with someone as contrary as my mother-in-law?"

"Chloe!" Warren admonished. "My mother just died; that sounds horrible."

"Come on, Warren, you know it's true. And why do you think Danielle's aunt left her Marlow House? They were only related by marriage. She probably got all cozy with her—like she did with Marie—and then inherited her entire estate. I've read about it. Danielle had a cousin who was just as entitled, but she wasn't left a dime. It's a good thing we came here when we did, before your mother changed her will and left everything to Danielle Boatman!"

"You're actually saying it's a good thing my mother died?"

Chloe shrugged. "I won't pretend I'm relieved she didn't have time to carry through with that spiteful threat of hers. Good lord, you are her only son!"

"Mom, do you seriously think Grandma would have done that?" Jason asked. "Left everything to some woman she hasn't even known that long?"

Turning back around in the seat, Chloe said, "It happens all the time. A person gets old, their mind starts to go, and some manipulative schemer moves in and gets everything, leaving the family nothing."

"Your mother has a point. Don't forget the gold coins," Warren reminded them.

"Gold coins?" Sondra asked.

"I don't think I told you about that," Jason said. "You know that house Grandma just sold?"

Sondra smiled. "The one that went for over a million?"

Jason nodded. "Yes. They found some gold coins hidden under the floorboards. Worth a freaking fortune."

"Gold coins?" Sondra perked up.

"Don't get excited, dear," Chloe said sarcastically. "My brilliant mother-in-law gave them to Danielle."

Sondra gasped. "Why would she do that?"

"According to my brother, they technically belonged to Danielle, so Grandma couldn't keep them."

Sondra frowned. "I don't understand?"

"Something about the coins belonging to Walt Marlow's estate, which meant she got them," Warren explained. "But it sounded like a bunch of BS to me. Mother should have just kept them. They were in her house for over a hundred years. As far as I'm concerned, they belonged to us."

"Can't you do anything?" Sondra asked. "Take her to court?"

"It was already settled in court," Jason said.

"Maybe the court said Danielle was the rightful owner, but that's only because your grandmother didn't make a claim for them. She made it perfectly clear she didn't want the coins and insisted they belonged to Danielle. Foolish old woman." Chloe shifted angrily in the passenger seat.

"Wow, I had no idea," Sondra said.

"We only found out about the coins a little while ago ourselves," Chloe said. "Someone I know sent me a link to an article on it. I called Adam, and he explained what had happened."

"Which is one reason we knew we had to get out here when I heard Mother broke her hip. Adam sure as hell wasn't taking care of things."

"We should have come earlier," Chloe muttered.

Several minutes later they pulled up to Marlow House. They parked behind Adam's car.

"Wow, is that it?" Sondra asked as she looked up to the impressive Victorian house—a Second Empire-style home with a mansard roof line. Surrounded by wrought-iron fencing, with a side driveway, it stood three stories, counting the attic room.

"You know, I grew up in this town, and I've never been in that house," Warren said as he parked the car.

"It was built by the town's founder," Jason told Sondra. "It sat empty for almost a hundred years—after the last owner died. He was the grandson of the founder. Danielle runs it as a bed and breakfast."

Chloe unhooked her seatbelt. "I wasn't thrilled about coming here today, but I have to admit I'm curious to see inside that house."

MARIE SAT with Walt on the living room sofa when her son parked his car in front of the house. In the room with them was Adam and Melony, who stood by the corner bar with Ian and Lily while Ian made them all cocktails. In the kitchen was Danielle, checking on the turkey, while Heather had just gone to the front door to let in the new arrivals.

"You know what I find fascinating about this ghost thing?" Marie asked Walt.

"Spirit," Walt corrected.

"Really, Walt, ghost sounds so much...more interesting."

"Okay, what do you find fascinating?" Walt asked.

"I can smell the turkey cooking. And it smells wonderful!"

"I suspect that's because you've adapted to your state. When I first met Danielle, I couldn't smell the ocean breeze from the window. I really missed that."

"But you can smell it now?" Marie asked.

"Yes. So you didn't expect to be able to smell things as a...ghost?"

"To be honest, I never really thought about it. Never really gave much credence to the notion of ghosts. But it's not just that I can smell the turkey cooking—and it does smell heavenly—I'm not a bit hungry. While I'm enjoying the fragrance, I don't have the urge to eat."

"Probably has something to do with the fact you no longer have a body—well, at least not one attached to your spirit."

"But doesn't it take a nose to smell?" Marie asked. "And an ear to hear? I can hear what's going on. This is all very confusing."

"I have a theory," Walt told her.

"Theory? What theory?"

"Whatever we are now—our energy, or spirit—not all of our sensory abilities are attached to our physical being. For example, we have the sense of sight, sound, and smell—yet not of touch or taste. Why is that, I wonder?"

"I really wish there was some sort of rule book," Marie said.

"Like in *Beetlejuice*?" Walt asked.

"*Beetlejuice*? What's that?"

"Danielle had me watch it. Amusing little movie about a haunted house. In the movie those who die are each given a copy of the *Handbook for the Recently Deceased*. I have to say, that would have come in handy." Walt glanced up to the doorway and watched as Heather brought Adam's family into the room.

"They finally arrived," Marie huffed. "My daughter-in-law always has to be fashionably late. I find it rude."

"If we had that handbook, we'd know it's time to stand up," Walt said as he watched Adam's parents approach the sofa.

"But I like it here. It's the best vantage place in the room to see what's going on," Marie said just before her son sat on her. "Goodness gracious!" Marie leapt from the sofa.

"See what I mean," Walt said with a chuckle as he motioned to the other side of the room. Reluctantly, Marie followed him there.

Danielle joined them in the living room a few minutes later, and introductions were made. Adam's family hadn't yet met Ian, Lily, or Heather.

"You're the ones who bought my grandmother's house?" Jason asked Lily and Ian.

"Yes. Ian had been renting it for over a year," Lily explained. "We love the house."

"Oh my god, that must mean you're Jon Altar!" Sondra squealed.

Jason chuckled. "My fiancée is quite a fan of yours. In fact, I'm pretty sure you're the reason she's marrying me."

Sondra blushed. She swatted her fiancé's arm "Oh, stop that!"

Lily arched her brow. "Gee, I'd love to hear this."

"I'd been trying to get Sondra to say *I do* for months, and when I told her who was buying my grandmother's house, she finally said yes." Jason laughed.

Obviously embarrassed, Sondra shook her head. "Jason is just being silly. Yes, I've always wanted to meet you—I've always enjoyed your work—but I'm pretty sure I was going to say yes to Jason even without the possibility I might get to someday meet Jon Altar." She glanced at Jason and added, "Although now I'm beginning to question my judgment."

"See, I told you!" Jason said with a laugh. "Now that you've finally met him, you don't care about marrying me anymore. Damn, I knew I should have waited until we said our vows."

Sondra shoved Jason with her hip and mumbled, "You can be such a weirdo sometimes."

MARIE SAT at the end of the dining room table with Walt, watching her family as Danielle served the Thanksgiving meal. She felt a twinge of guilt for having asked Danielle to extend the invitation again. It looked as if she had gone to a great deal of work, and Marie doubted her daughter-in-law or Jason's girlfriend would be much help cleaning up. She knew her son and youngest grandson would be no help.

Marie thought Chloe and Warren had been rather icy since they had first arrived, although they were polite. She imagined when the evening was over, she would need to issue an apology to Danielle for the re-invite. There was considerable teasing going on between Adam and Danielle, and Sondra hung on every syllable Ian uttered. Lily seemed more amused than annoyed over the obvious infatuation, and Jason seemed oblivious. He and Heather were in a debate about essential oils. Jason insisted they were nothing more than a scam, while Heather found his claim blasphemy.

Sitting quietly by Adam's side was Melony, who looked as if something was on her mind. Just as they finished the meal, Melony cleared her throat and stood up.

"I need to tell you all something," Melony announced.

"Isn't the toast at the beginning of the meal?" Jason joked.

Melony awkwardly flashed Jason a smile and then cleared her throat again. "As we all know, Marie's funeral is on Tuesday."

No one responded. They simply looked at Melony, wondering what she was about to say.

"According to Marie's wishes, she wanted the will read the day after her funeral." Melony looked at Danielle. "At Marlow House."

"Really?" Danielle glanced over at Marie.

"I hope you don't mind, dear," Marie told her.

Warren tossed his wadded cloth napkin on the table. "That's silly. There's no reason to have some formal will reading. We all know what's in it. I have a copy, and everyone concerned has already read it."

Melony cleared her voice again. "The thing is, Warren, Marie made a new will."

"What!" Warren, Chloe, and Jason shouted at the same time.

"After Marie sold her Beach Drive house, she asked me to make a new will," Melony said.

"You aren't even her attorney!" Chloe spat.

"Technically, I was," Melony said calmly and sat down.

"What's in this will?" Jason asked.

"You'll find out at the reading," Melony said. "That's how Marie wanted it."

Warren looked at Adam. "Did you know about this?"

"Adam didn't know anything about it." Melony spoke up. "I told him on the way over here today."

"I don't understand," Sondra said. "Why did she threaten to change her will if she had already done it?"

Warren stood up abruptly and looked at Adam. "I don't believe for a minute you didn't know about this earlier." He then turned to face Melony. "I'm not sure it's entirely ethical of you to be representing your boyfriend's grandmother like this. Of course, your family wasn't big on ethics, was it? I guess the apple really doesn't fall far from the tree."

"That's uncalled for, Dad," Adam shouted.

"Dad, don't you think you need to see what's in the will before you get upset?" Jason asked.

"Don't be a fool, Jason," Warren snapped. "Your grandmother wouldn't have kept this all a secret if she didn't think I'd get upset. Unlike your brother, who she's coddled for years, she knew I wasn't a pushover."

"More like an ass," Marie grumbled. "Walt, in moments like this I wish I could do some of your tricks."

"If you could, what would you do?" Walt asked.

"I'd start by dumping that glass of wine on his lap."

In the next moment, Warren's wineglass moved from its place on the table, landing upside down on his lap.

TWENTY-THREE

D anielle was just bringing in the morning newspaper when she spied a cup of coffee floating in her direction. Suddenly Walt appeared, Marie by his side. He was holding the cup of coffee in his hand.

"I wanted to make you coffee," Marie explained. "Well, I wanted to, but as you know, I can't actually do that."

"So she asked me to." Walt handed Danielle the cup.

"Like she asked you to spill the wine on Warren last night?" Danielle handed the newspaper to Walt.

"I'm so sorry about that. I hope it didn't stain your lovely chair," Marie said.

Danielle smiled. "Don't worry about it. It was sort of worth it." She sipped the coffee and made her way to the parlor, Walt and Marie trailing behind her.

"I'm sorry, Danielle, about asking you to invite my family to come last night."

"If you hadn't done that, Adam may not have requested that autopsy."

"I'm so ashamed. They were horrible last night, just storming out before you even had a chance to serve your lovely dessert."

"Just more pecan and pumpkin pie for me. A win-win." Danielle sat down on the small parlor sofa, tucking her bare feet under her.

"I feel so bad for Adam. Once again, I put him in the middle of things," Marie said. The next moment the doorbell rang.

Walt looked out the parlor window. "It's the chief. Rather early for him to drop over."

———

A FEW MINUTES later Danielle led Police Chief MacDonald to the parlor.

"Just so you know, Chief, both Walt and Marie are in here." She pointed to the two chairs across from the sofa.

"Morning, Walt, Marie. I'm really sorry, Marie, about all this," the chief began.

"Goodness gracious," Marie exclaimed. "The chief really does buy into all this hocus-pocus!"

"It's not exactly hocus-pocus," Danielle said with a chuckle.

"If I were still alive, that's exactly what I'd be thinking right now, and I'd probably petition to have poor Edward committed," Marie explained.

"And you asked me why I never told you about all of this before?" Danielle snickered.

The chief frowned. "I don't understand?"

Danielle waved her hand dismissively at him. "Don't worry about it, Chief. It's just that Marie finds this all as bizarre as you do."

"Isn't that the truth?" The chief sat down on the sofa and looked at the chair. "But for the moment, I have to overlook all that. You were right, Marie. You were murdered."

"Of course I was murdered! Didn't I tell you that?"

"The coroner report is finished?" Danielle asked.

"Just the preliminary report, but we know she was probably smothered. Broken veins on her face and eyes are consistent with suffocation. There is also bruising on her body, as if she was held down. They also found a feather in her nasal passage, which substantiates the suffocation story, but the problem with the feather —according to the nursing home, they don't have feather pillows. I stopped by there before I came over here, to see if I could pick up the pillows from Marie's room, but they weren't feather pillows. According to Sunny, they don't use them because of allergies."

"It was my pillow from home."

"Marie said it was her pillow from home," Danielle explained.

"I wonder where that pillow is now?" the chief asked.

"I helped Adam clean up Marie's room at the nursing home. There was a pillow. The last time I saw it, it was in the trunk of Adam's car."

"I'll stop over at Adam's office, see if he can get me the pillow." The chief jotted a note down on a pad of paper.

"If there was bruising on her body, why didn't they have an autopsy without Adam requesting it?" Danielle asked.

"Good question," Walt interjected.

"Because the funeral home was told she had fallen Monday, and they assumed that was the cause of the bruises."

"I didn't fall!" Marie snapped.

"Marie said she didn't fall," Danielle told him. "Who at the nursing home told the funeral home about the fall?"

"I'm not really sure. But now that I know she didn't fall, I'll find out," the chief said. "Before I go over there, I need to ask Marie some questions."

"Amusing," Marie murmured. "Questioning the murder victim."

For the next forty minutes the chief asked Marie questions, and Danielle played spirit translator. When they were finished, Danielle walked the chief to the front door.

"Who else knows?" Danielle opened the front door for MacDonald.

"Sunny knows, but I asked her not to say anything right now. Not until I have a chance to notify the family." The chief paused a moment and glanced over Danielle's shoulder. "Is Marie here?"

Danielle looked toward the door they had just come out of and shook her head. "No. She stayed in the parlor with Walt. You want to ask her something else?"

"Not right now. According to Sunny, Marie had heated words with her son on Monday, and she threatened to change her will. Do you know anything about that?"

"Why didn't you ask Marie?"

"This is a murder investigation, and he is her son. I'm not sure she'd be that forthright with me."

"You mean try to protect her son?"

The chief nodded. "Do you know anything about the argument?"

"I know it happened. We talked about it on the phone that night after her family went home. Warren and Chloe had toured Seaside Village, the area for permanent residents, and felt that's where Marie belonged. They didn't want her to go home after she completed her rehab."

"I can't imagine Marie would be okay with that."

"No, she wasn't. I think that's why she threatened to change her will. But the funny thing was, she had already done that." Together she and the chief stepped outside. As she walked him to the sidewalk, she recounted the episode at dinner the night before.

"Basically, when Marie was killed, Warren assumed he would be getting half her estate. But now, who knows?"

"She didn't say what was in the new will?"

"No, and I didn't ask. I guess the only ones who know that are Melony and Marie."

"HOLY CRAP," Adam said for the sixth time. He sat behind his desk in his office, trying to process what Chief MacDonald had just told him. "So, she really was murdered?"

"It looks that way." MacDonald stood beside the desk, his cap in hand.

"How? Why? Why would anyone want to hurt Grandma?"

"Do you know where your grandmother's pillow is? The one you and Danielle took out of her room at Seaside Village?"

Adam considered the question a moment and then shrugged. "I suppose it's still in the back of my car. I haven't gotten around to taking Grandma's things out of the trunk yet."

"I need that pillow."

Adam stood. "Sure. I'll get it for you."

Several minutes later, Chief MacDonald stood by the side of Adam's car, waiting for him to get the pillow.

Just as Adam flipped open the trunk, he paused and looked at the chief. "What about the security cameras?"

"You mean the security cameras at Seaside Village?"

Adam nodded. "One of them had to have caught something—someone going into Grandma's room that night. I know there's a camera in the hall, not far from her room, and another one right outside the back door."

"That would be great if they actually worked." The chief took the pillow from Adam and placed it in a plastic bag.

"They don't work?" Adam slammed his trunk closed.

The chief shook his head. "I was over there this morning—one reason, to see what was on those cameras. But according to Sunny, the camera system hasn't worked for over six months."

"And they never fixed it?"

"After talking to Sunny, I have a feeling Seaside Village might be experiencing some money problems."

"Grandma did mention they were understaffed. And the entire time she was there, she was the only patient in the rehab wing."

"I need to interview everyone in your family—including you."

Adam nodded. "Certainly. You want to do it at Grandma's, or do you want us to come down to the station?"

"Why don't you have them come down to the station." He glanced at his watch. "But if they're not all there in thirty minutes, I'll send someone for them."

"Wow...you sound like you think one of us is the killer."

"Adam, Sunny told me your family had quite an argument the night before Marie was murdered. She said it got pretty vocal, and Marie threatened to change her will."

Adam let out a sigh and leaned back on his car. "It was mostly Dad and Grandma. He wanted to keep her there after she completed physical therapy, but I wouldn't have let him do that." Adam paused a moment and studied MacDonald. "Wait a minute, you don't seriously think someone in my family killed Grandma."

"They did have a motive. Marie wasn't exactly a pauper, and from what I understand, your father believed he was going to inherit half her estate."

With a grunt, Adam said, "Well, if you talked to Dad, he'd say he was entitled to her entire estate because he was her only son. And while I don't get along with him, I can't believe he'd kill his mother over money."

"Not even if he thought he might lose his half?"

Adam shook his head. "No way. I have issues with my parents, but cold-blooded killers for money? Never."

"How did your brother feel about your grandmother's threat to change her will?"

With a snort Adam said, "I think his girlfriend was more upset than him. Sure, he wasn't opposed to the idea of inheriting a quarter of Grandma's estate. But he would never kill her for it. My brother has never been into money. If he was, he wouldn't have taken a crappy associate professor job after all those years of college. He's the good one."

"So the girlfriend was upset?"

"I didn't mean it like that. I just meant he really was not upset over Grandma's threat."

"Was she?"

"Sondra?" Adam shrugged. "I suppose a little. But I can't really blame her. If she's marrying my brother, her chance for any fortune will probably have to come by way of an inheritance."

TWENTY-FOUR

A dam didn't knock. He used his key and entered the front door of his grandmother's house. As he stepped into the entry, he heard voices from down the hall. His father was in the living room talking on his cellphone; it sounded like a serious conversation involving his work. The other voices came from the kitchen.

Shoving his keys into his pocket, Adam shut the door behind him and made his way to the living room. He found his father pacing the room as he talked on his phone. Adam stood at the doorway for a moment, watching his father, who was unaware of Adam's presence.

After a few moments, Warren noticed his son. He stared at Adam a moment and then said into the phone, "He's here now. Let me see what I can do. I'll get back with you." Warren ended his call and set his cellphone on the coffee table.

"Dad, I need to talk to you and Mom. Also Jason and Sondra. Are they all here?"

"In the kitchen, but I need to talk to you first." Dressed in gray slacks and a blue golf shirt, Warren approached his son.

Adam glanced down the hallway and then back to his father. "What about?"

"Do you have any idea what's in your grandmother's new will?"

Adam shrugged. "Not a clue. According to Melony, Grandma

instructed her to wait until the day after her funeral for the will to be read."

"This is ridiculous. I'm a little surprised your grandmother made that stipulation. I don't recall her going for such theatrics. I suppose this means we have to wait until the reading of the will before we do anything with the estate—assuming, of course, your grandmother didn't do anything foolish like leave her money to some charity or that Danielle Boatman."

"Why would you think Grandma would leave her estate to Danielle? I have a feeling Danielle would be pretty annoyed at Grandma if she did something like that, and Grandma knew how Danielle felt."

"What in the world are you talking about? Boatman is obviously an opportunist. She managed to inherit Marlow House from an aunt who isn't even a blood relative, and she ended up with the gold that was found in Mother's house. Gold that should have gone into Mother's estate."

"You don't know what you're talking about, Dad. But I really need to speak to you and Mom. Please, can we go into the kitchen?"

"Fine," Warren snapped as he grabbed his cellphone from the coffee table and shoved it into his pocket. He followed Adam into the kitchen.

"Sorry, Adam, you just missed breakfast," Chloe said as she stood by the sink, filling the dishwasher, while Sondra wiped down the stove, and Jason put a new plastic liner into the trashcan.

"I need to talk to you all," Adam announced. All eyes turned to him.

Jason sat down at the table. "Are you going to lecture us again about how rude we were to leave Marlow House when we did?"

"No. I came to tell you all the preliminary autopsy is done. Grandma was murdered."

"You can't be serious!" Warren blurted.

"I'm certainly not going to joke about something like this. I came over here to let you know you need to go down to the police station. They want to interview all of us."

"Murdered? Grandma murdered? I can't believe that. How?" Jason asked.

"Suffocation," Adam said. "They believe she was smothered with her pillow. The chief just picked it up from me."

"Picked up what from you?" Warren asked.

"Grandma's pillow, the one she took with her. It was with her things that I picked up," Adam explained.

"I don't understand; why would they want the pillow?" Chloe asked.

"They believe it was the murder weapon. There was a feather found in her nasal passage," Adam explained. "Seaside Village doesn't have feather pillows, but the pillow Grandma brought with her from home does."

"That doesn't mean she was smothered," Chloe snapped. "You hear about people getting strange things up their noses all the time. It doesn't mean someone tried to kill them. She could have easily breathed in a loose feather from her pillow while she was sleeping. It doesn't prove anything."

"According to the chief, when a person is smothered with a pillow, it can leave a DNA pattern behind on the pillowcase. I guess where the eyes, nose, and mouth are," Adam explained.

"You can't be serious?" Sondra gasped.

Adam glanced at the kitchen clock. "You've got less than twenty minutes to get down to the station, or the chief is going to send someone over here to get you."

"I don't understand. I barely knew your grandmother, and I wasn't even at the care home when she died. Why do they need to talk to me?" Sondra whined.

Adam shrugged. "I don't know. But they want to talk to all of us."

Chloe picked up the hand towel off the counter and wiped off her hands. She then tossed it on the counter and glared at Adam. "This is all your fault!"

"My fault? That someone murdered Grandma?" Adam asked.

"Don't be obtuse! You requested that ridiculous autopsy for heavens knows why. Nobody killed Marie. Just because she has a feather up her nose doesn't mean anyone killed her. The idea is ludicrous."

"That's not all they have, Mother," Adam insisted.

"This is probably going to complicate things," Warren murmured. "Until they know more, we probably can't touch her estate."

"Seriously, Dad, you just found out your mother was murdered and you're worried about getting your hands on your inheritance?" Adam asked.

"Don't be ridiculous. Your mother's right, she wasn't murdered. No one would want to kill your grandmother. You really did screw things up, boy," Warren grumbled.

"Dad," Jason said, "it's obvious the police think one of us might have killed Grandma, since they want us to go down there."

Chloe walked over to the far counter and picked up her purse. She turned to Jason. "Don't be stupid. They obviously want to find out if we know who might have had a problem with your grandmother at the nursing home. While I don't believe for a minute she was murdered, if the police seriously think she was smothered during the night, they obviously believe the killer was someone from the nursing home."

"You really think so?" Sondra asked with a sigh of relief.

Chloe turned her attention to Sondra and said dryly, "Unless of course you snuck over there when you were supposed to be jogging, so you and Jason would have a little extra honeymoon money."

"DID YOU FIND YOUR PILLOW?" Sunny asked Chief MacDonald when he returned to the nursing home later Friday morning. She sat at the main nurses' station, doing bookwork.

"We found a pillow, not sure it's the same one," the chief told her.

"Do you seriously believe Mrs. Nichols was murdered? There has to be some kind of mistake," Sunny said.

"It looks like it. I was wondering where I could find Herman Garcia."

"Herman?" Sunny frowned.

"I understand he's a nurse here?"

"Yes. He's been with us for about six months. You don't think he had anything to do with Mrs. Nichols's death, do you? He doesn't even work in the rehab area. I doubt they even met. She didn't get out and socialize much, pretty much stayed in the rehab section."

The chief glanced at the notepad in his hand. "I understand he helped move her body when the funeral home picked her up."

"Oh, yes, he did. I forgot about that."

"I just have a few questions for him," he explained.

"Would you like to use my office?" Sunny offered.

"I'd appreciate that." He closed his small notepad and slipped it into his shirt pocket.

"Let me see where he is." Sunny picked up the desk phone.

"Thanks."

When Sunny got off the phone a few minutes later, she said, "He'll be about ten minutes. He's just finishing with a patient. I told him to come to my office when he's done."

"Thank you, Sunny."

"Would you like some coffee or something while you wait?" she offered.

"No. I'm fine, thanks." He glanced at his watch.

"Umm...I've been meaning to ask you, have you heard from Carol Ann?"

"Carol Ann? No." MacDonald shook his head. "That bridge has been burned."

Sunny grimaced and then smiled guiltily. "I wrote her a letter a while back. I know she was wrong, but I just feel it was that brother of hers. He always had such control over her. He practically raised her."

MacDonald shrugged. "She was your friend. You need to do what you think is right."

"It didn't really matter. She never wrote me back. I don't take it personally. I feel she's probably just embarrassed about what she did."

CHIEF MACDONALD and Herman Garcia reached Sunny's office at the same time. Sunny had given the chief a key, so he opened the door and let them both in.

"I understand you were the one who helped the funeral home when they picked up Marie Nichols's body," the chief said after he shut the door and sat down behind Sunny's desk. Herman sat in a chair facing him.

Herman nodded. "Yes."

"From what I understand, you told them about Mrs. Nichols taking a fall the day before she died."

Herman shrugged. "One of them asked me if there was anything I knew about the patient that wasn't on her chart. Something that might have caused her death."

"And you told them it might have been a fall?"

"No. I said I knew she'd taken a fall in the dining room the day before, but it wasn't anything that would have killed her. Maybe bruised her up a little bit. It's not like she hit her head or anything. She fell on her walker; it slammed into her chest."

"You saw this happen?"

"No. I wasn't even there when it happened. Candy told me. And I figured since it wasn't in her chart, it must not have been a big deal."

"Candy?"

"One of the other nurses."

"YES, I DID TELL HERMAN THAT." Candy cringed. She had been called to Sunny's office to talk with the police chief after he was finished interviewing Herman.

"So you saw Marie Nichols fall in the dining room?"

She shook her head. "I was wrong. I mean, someone did fall in the dining room, but it wasn't Marie Nichols, it was Betty Nichols, one of the full-time patients. She got bruised up pretty bad when she tripped and fell, knocking over her walker. When Herman told me Mrs. Nichols had died during the night, I thought he meant Betty Nichols. I told him what had happened to her the day before." She shrugged. "It wasn't until I saw Betty Nichols when making my rounds—and about jumped out of my skin—did I realize it hadn't been the same Nichols who had died."

"YES, we have a patient named Betty Nichols, why?" Sunny asked the chief when he stopped by the nurses' station to return her office keys and ask about the patient who had fallen in the dining room.

"Do you know if she fell the day before Marie was killed?" he asked.

With a frown, Sunny considered the question a moment. Finally, she said, "Why yes. It happened in the dining room. Betty has a bad habit of pushing her walker away from her chair, so that when she stands up, it's not where it needs to be. From what I understand, she stumbled and ended up knocking the walker over and falling on it.

She got a nasty bruise on her chest. Why did you ask? Does this have something to do with Marie Nichols?"

"Marie had some bruising on her chest. The funeral home initially ignored the bruising, believing it was from the earlier fall."

Sunny frowned. "Bruising? She was bruised?"

"Yes. Probably when her killer was holding her down."

"Oh…my…" Sunny stammered.

TWENTY-FIVE

"Hello, Chloe, it's been a long time," Brian Henderson greeted Adam's mother when he entered the interrogation room. She sat alone at the table. Before leaving for the police station, Chloe had changed into navy capris and a white blouse, her black hair pulled up into a bun atop her head.

"Hello, Brian," she said lazily as she leaned back in the chair and crossed her legs, folding her arms across her chest. "I suspect you're the oldest one at the Frederickport Police Department—in years and tenure—but I see you never made it to chief?"

Brian forced a smile and sat down across from her at the table. "Good to see you too."

With a bored sigh she asked, "Why am I being questioned in here? And was it really necessary to separate us? It's not like any of us was responsible for my mother-in-law's death. I certainly don't believe that cockamamie story about her being murdered. She was ninety-one, for heaven's sake."

"Elderly people do get murdered," he reminded her.

Chloe shrugged. "So what do you need to know?"

"When was the last time you saw your mother-in-law?"

Chloe shifted in her chair. "Monday night. We stopped in to visit her after dinner. Left about nine."

"And you didn't see her again?"

"I haven't been back to Seaside Village since I left that night, so, no."

"Where did you go after you left?"

"We went home." Chloe shifted in her chair again. "Back to Marie's house. That's where we've been staying since we got in town."

"Did you go anywhere else that night?" he asked.

She shrugged. "No. Went to bed. Heard about Marie the next morning when Adam called from the care home."

"Who can verify your alibi?"

Uncrossing her legs, Chloe scooted up in the chair and pulled herself closer to the table, leaning toward Brian. "You seriously asking me if I have an alibi? You think I murdered my mother-in-law?"

"I'm just trying to understand where everyone was at the time Marie was killed."

Chloe shrugged and leaned back in the chair, stretching her legs under the table. "All of us were at the house—Warren, Jason, and Sondra, Jason's fiancée. Ask them, they'll tell you."

"I understand there was an argument between Marie and your husband that night."

"When didn't Marie and Warren argue? Lord, if he didn't kill her before, I don't know why he would now."

"Maybe because Marie threatened to change her will?"

Chloe stared at Brian for a moment before saying, "Marie was just angry because Warren didn't believe she was capable of living by herself—and she wasn't. He only wanted what was best for his mother. He certainly would never hurt her."

"I UNDERSTAND you tried to get the funeral home to have your mother cremated. Why did you want to go against her wishes?" Brian asked Warren Nichols when it was his turn in the interrogation room.

"It just seemed silly to spend the money on a coffin." Warren paused a moment and frowned at Brian. "Wait a minute, you certainly don't think I killed my mother and wanted to destroy the evidence? It wasn't even my idea to change her burial plans."

"Whose was it?"

Warren shrugged. "Sondra, Jason's girlfriend. She just said it was better for the environment."

"And you were concerned with the environment?"

Warren shifted in his chair and uncrossed and recrossed his legs. "Not really. But I did think it would probably be cheaper."

"So that last night, when you all left Seaside Village and returned to Marie's, none of you went out again until morning?"

Warren shook his head. "No."

"Did your mother ever say she had a problem with anyone at Seaside Village?"

"Fact was, Mother had a problem with everyone there. She thought the lady that runs that place was too cheerful. I mean seriously, too cheerful? She was constantly complaining about the fact there wasn't a lock on her door. Said anyone could just walk in on her. And she was convinced half of the residents who lived there were crazy."

"Knowing that, knowing how much Marie hated that place, you wanted her to stay there?"

Warren glared at Brian. "Are you saying this is in some way my fault? My mother checked in to that place. I didn't pick it out. And she was there for rehab. I had nothing to do with it. If it really was murder—which I don't believe—if one of the patients did this to her, it was not my fault."

"I'm just trying to understand why you wanted her to move there full time, knowing how much she hated it."

"Oh, come on, Brian, you knew my mother. She wouldn't have been happy at any assisted-care facility. But she had no business living alone. The woman was ninety-one. Hell, she broke her hip by just trying to answer her phone."

"I understand you had an argument the day before she died. She threatened to change her will."

"Yeah, well, the funny thing about that, she had already changed her will," Warren scoffed.

"Do you know what's in the new will? Who inherits now?"

"None of us will know until the will is read on Wednesday. That was what my mother wanted."

"Do you know who was to inherit before this new will?" Brian asked.

"Yes. Mother had the trust set up where I would get half of her estate, and my sons would split the other half."

"So you had a vested interest in your mother not changing her will?"

"She had already changed it," Warren snapped.

"But you didn't know that."

Warren glared at Brian. "I told you, we all left the home together at nine that night. You can ask the staff there. Hell, I'm sure they already told you all about it, considering Mother wasn't especially quiet when she started yelling at me. But that doesn't mean I killed her. We all left at nine, went to my mother's house, and went to bed. End of story."

"WAS MY GRANDMOTHER REALLY MURDERED?" Jason asked Brian. The two sat alone in the interrogation room.

"Yes. It appears she was smothered. They believe with a pillow, considering the feather they found in her nasal passage. She also had bruising where someone held her down."

Jason shook his head. "I guess she was right."

"Who was right?" Brian asked.

"Grandma kept saying anyone could walk into her room and kill her while she was sleeping. I thought she was just being paranoid."

Brian sat up straighter in the chair, the pen in his hand ready to jot down notes. "Did she ever mention anyone she was having problems with? Anyone she was afraid of?"

Resting his hands on the tabletop, Jason's fingers fidgeted nervously. "Not really. She used to say half the people who lived there were out of it, and the other half spent all their time complaining about how much pain they were in. But she never mentioned having a problem with anyone specifically."

They discussed the Seaside Village staff for a few more minutes; then Brian switched the direction of the conversation. "Did you have any idea your grandmother had changed her will?"

Jason shook his head. "No."

"Do you think anyone knew?"

Jason shrugged. "To be honest, I find it difficult to believe Adam didn't know. I'm certain Grandma used to tell him everything, and he's dating Melony. Well, I think he is. One minute he tells the family they're good friends, but when they're together, they don't seem like casual friends."

"How did you feel when your grandmother threatened to change her will? I understand in her last will she was leaving you a quarter of her estate."

"Grandma was mad at Dad, not me. I honestly didn't think Grandma would write Adam or me out of her will because of something my parents did. Of course, Mom was convinced Grandma might do something crazy like leave everything to that wacked cult that Adam's old girlfriend was involved in."

"So your mother was concerned that Marie might change her will?"

Jason frowned. "Sure, I can't blame her. But it wasn't like she was going to kill Grandma to stop her."

"I BARELY KNEW HER, but to be honest..." Sondra paused a moment and glanced over to the two-way mirror. She was alone in the room with Brian. "Is anyone in there, watching us?"

"You mean like Jason or his parents?"

Sondra nodded.

"No."

Letting out a sigh of relief, she turned her attention back to Brian. "I don't want to speak ill of the dead, and I certainly don't want to say anything bad about Jason's grandmother, not when she just died. And while I know his parents didn't get along with her that well, she was still Warren's mother."

"But?" Brian asked.

"Well, she didn't seem all that nice. She was kind of crabby. Her family came all this way to see her, and she didn't seem to appreciate it. I feel bad for Jason. It was so important for him that I meet his grandmother now, before she passed away. He didn't think she would make it to our wedding."

"Why was that?"

"Her age, of course. Plus, the fact she had just broken a hip. You know, for a lot of elderly people, breaking a hip can be lethal. Jason was afraid his grandmother wouldn't be around that long, and he wanted me to meet her. But I'm afraid she wasn't that interested in getting to know me. But she seemed pretty fond of that Danielle Boatman."

"Danielle? Yes, Danielle and Marie were close."

Sondra shifted in her seat. "I don't think Jason's grandmother was that friendly to the people at the home. I guess that's why one of them killed her."

"So you think someone from the home killed Marie?"

Sondra shrugged. "If she was really murdered, then yeah. Had to be someone from that place. Maybe someone who was a little crazy to begin with, and Marie made them mad."

"When you went to Seaside Village on Monday, did you all drive together?"

"Jason and I went in his parents' car. Adam was already there. He had driven his own car."

"And you all left together?"

"Yes. Everyone but Adam."

Pen in hand, Brian glanced from the pad of paper before him back to Sondra. "What time was that?"

"It was nine when we left—me, Jason, and his parents. I don't know how much longer Adam stayed. He was still there when we left."

"And where did you go?"

"We went back to Mrs. Nichols's house, that's where we've been staying."

"And no one left the house again until morning?" Brian asked.

Sondra started to say something and then shifted in her seat. "I guess that's right."

"I HATE TO SAY THIS," Adam told Brian during his questioning. "But according to my brother, one of my parents left the house Monday night after they returned from visiting Grandma. They got into a fight, and one of them stormed out. I don't think for a minute whoever it was drove to Seaside Village and killed Grandma. My parents have always had a volatile relationship. It's not uncommon for one of them to take off after a fight, drive around, and then come back as if nothing happened."

"Do you know which parent left?"

Adam shook his head. "Jason didn't know either."

"I THOUGHT WE WERE DONE?" Warren asked when he was brought back into the interrogation room.

"I have a few things I need to clear up," Brian explained when he took a seat back at the table. "I understand you didn't just argue with your mother that night, you had a fight with your wife after you got back to Marie's house."

Warren frowned at Brian a moment before responding, "So? Who told you that? Jason? Sondra?"

"I also understand one of you left your mother's house."

"So?"

"According to you, your wife, Jason and Sondra—none of you left the house that night after you got home from Seaside Village."

"Then how did you—" Warren didn't finish his question.

"It doesn't matter. I just do, and you all lied about it. Why is that?"

"We didn't lie," Warren said, shifting nervously in his chair. "It just had nothing to do with my mother's death."

"I believe I asked if anyone had left Marie's that night. You all said no. Sounds like you lied."

"We forgot. It was not a big deal. And I doubt Jason or Sondra even knew one of us had left for a few minutes."

"Just a few minutes?"

Warren shrugged. "Yeah, you know, to drive around the neighborhood, cool off."

"Which one of you left the house?"

Warren stared at Brian a moment, finally he said, "Chloe did. But she was only gone for a short time, drove around the neighborhood. She certainly wasn't gone long enough to get to Seaside Village, kill my mother and get back to the house."

TWENTY-SIX

Chief MacDonald was reviewing the notes from Brian's interviews when Danielle stepped into the open doorway. She knocked lightly. He looked up from his desk and waved her into the office.

"Adam called me. Said you interviewed his entire family." Danielle closed the door behind her before taking a seat.

"I was just going through the notes." He set the paper he was holding down on the desk and said, "I thought of something."

"What?"

"Where's Marie? She's not with you, is she?"

Danielle shook her head. "No. She's back at the house with Walt. He's telling her old stories about her parents."

"Couldn't we simplify things if she just hung around her family...eavesdrop?"

"You think one of them did it?"

"They have a motive, and I already caught them in a lie. Maybe she could overhear something—"

"Serious? You want her to do your job? Wow, you're getting kind of lazy, Chief."

He stared at Danielle, uncertain if she was serious or teasing.

Finally, she smiled. "It's not an option anyway."

"Why not?"

"Marie doesn't believe her family was involved—not even her

162

daughter-in-law, who she's not fond of. But Chloe is Adam's mother, and Marie adores Adam. She wouldn't do anything to hurt him. I actually did suggest she go over there, see if she could pick anything up. She refused."

"She's afraid of what she might overhear?" the chief asked.

"Marie didn't actually say that. But she made some lame excuse why she couldn't go over there right now. I talked to Walt about it. He doesn't think Marie wants to know if one of them was responsible."

"But she's the one who pushed for the autopsy."

"Yes. Because she thought someone from Seaside Village was involved. She still does."

MacDonald absently tapped the end of his pen against his desktop. "To be honest, that doesn't surprise me. It's why I didn't ask Marie about the argument she had with her family on Monday night. If she did find out something, she probably wouldn't tell you. Agatha didn't when it was her grandson."

"True." Danielle leaned forward. "So tell me, what do you have so far?"

The chief picked up some papers from his desk and arranged them in a neat pile. "We have the time of death. Not from the coroner, but from Marie. Of course, Brian and Joe don't know that, so the window for the time of death is broader for them."

"Yes, three in the morning."

"I know Adam's parents, brother, and Sondra left together at nine that night. Adam left about twenty minutes later. Staff at the home confirms those times."

"Oh, did you know Sondra was from Portland?" Danielle interrupted.

"Portland? I thought she was from Colorado?"

Danielle shook her head. "No, she grew up in Portland, lived there all her life. She only moved to Colorado about six months ago, where she met Jason. Jason told us that yesterday. Anyway, you were saying?"

"After they went back to Marie's house, they got ready for bed, and Warren and Chloe went to their bedroom, and Jason and Sondra went to theirs. Adam's parents got into a heated argument, and around midnight, Chloe stormed out of the house. She claims she just drove around the neighborhood for about fifteen minutes to cool off and then came right home. Warren backs up her story."

"Not enough time to drive to Seaside Village, smother Marie, and then go back to Marie's house."

"My only issue with the story, they all lied about Chloe leaving the house. But Jason had mentioned the fight and the fact one of their parents took off in the middle of the night when Adam stopped by the house that morning, before finding out Marie was dead."

"Did they say why they lied?"

"Warren and Chloe insisted they didn't think it had anything to do with Marie, it was a personal issue and she had only been gone for a few minutes, while Jason and Sondra claimed they forgot."

"Interesting," Danielle muttered.

"When Adam arrived at Marie's on Tuesday morning, his parents' car was parked in front of the house, and they were still up in their bedroom. Jason's rental car was gone, along with Sondra. According to both Sondra and Jason, she left early that morning to go jogging and then to get something to eat."

"How early?" Danielle asked.

"She said she left just before sunrise. Jason was still sleeping, so he didn't know for certain what time she left that morning."

"Did Brian ask Sondra if Warren and Chloe's car was parked in front of the house when she left that morning?" Danielle asked.

"If Chloe was the killer, I'd assume she would have been back by then. But Brian did ask. Sondra said it was still dark, and that she didn't notice."

"We know at least two of them left Marie's house early Tuesday morning. So none of them have a terrific alibi. But maybe Marie is right." Danielle let out a sigh. "Actually, I want Marie to be right. I don't want Adam to learn someone from his family killed his grandmother."

THE DRIVE from the police station back to Marie's house was uncomfortably quiet. It was obvious Chloe had something on her mind. When they got back to the house, Chloe tossed her purse on Marie's sofa and turned around to face her husband, youngest son, and future daughter-in-law. Adam hadn't returned to the house with them, but had instead gone back to his office.

"I thought we agreed not to mention the fact I went out that night. There was no reason for anyone to know, and I certainly had nothing to do with Marie's death."

"I didn't say anything," Sondra insisted. "At least not the first time they talked to me. But then I couldn't really lie, could I? As it was, I told them I forgot. Not sure they believed me."

"So it was you, Jason?" Chloe asked angrily.

"No, Mother. It had to have been Adam."

"Adam? How did he know?"

"I...I must have mentioned that one of you left the house that night after an argument."

"Wouldn't it have been a good thing to let us know that?" Warren asked. "Before we all agreed not to say anything about your mother going out for a few minutes?"

"I'm sorry, Dad, I forgot I told Adam."

"Great, just great." Chloe plopped down on the sofa next to her purse. "If I had known that, I would have simply told the chief I'd gone out for a few minutes!"

Ringing came from Sondra's purse. She picked it up from the coffee table and removed her cellphone and looked at it.

"If you will excuse me, I have to take this. It's my mom." Sondra dashed out of the living room, leaving her fiancé with his parents while they argued.

"I TOLD you not to call me. Please!" Sondra whispered into the phone. Standing in the kitchen, she glanced warily to the doorway. "This was all a huge mistake. No. I told you. Absolutely not! You don't understand, now that the police know his grandmother was murdered, we're all suspects, and what happens if they start asking me questions? What? You would like that, wouldn't you!" Sondra abruptly hung up on the caller and turned off her phone.

TWENTY-SEVEN

On Saturday morning, Danielle walked into the library, a cup of freshly brewed coffee in one hand and the morning newspaper in the other. She found Walt sitting in front of the guest computer, the tips of his fingers poised to touch the keyboard.

"What are you doing, Walt?"

"Nothing." His hands dropped to his sides. He stood abruptly, facing Danielle.

"I brought the paper in, if you want it." She tossed the newspaper onto the desk and took a seat on the sofa. "Have you seen Marie this morning?"

Walt moved to the chair facing Danielle and sat down. "She left for Seaside Village about thirty minutes ago."

Cradling her warm coffee mug in her hands, she took a sip and then asked, "Seaside Village? Why?"

"To look for clues on her murder, of course." Walt waved a hand and summoned a cigar.

"Ahh...I guess I can understand that. Last night she wasn't happy the chief's focus seemed to be on her family, but she has to understand they have to consider everyone close to her. I just wish she wouldn't have gone over there this morning, at least not without talking to me first."

"Why's that?" Walt took a puff off his cigar and then blew a smoke ring.

166

Distracted by the smoke ring, Danielle watched as it drifted up to the ceiling and disappeared. "Could you do that when you were alive?"

"You mean blow smoke rings?" Walt took another puff off his cigar and blew another ring. "Yes."

"If smoking wasn't so bad for you, I'd think that was cool. And if that brand of cigar you smoke was as offensive as many of them, we'd have to have a talk about expanding your no-smoking policy beyond the bedrooms."

"Is it *really* that bad for you?"

"Unfortunately, yes. But I've always said campaigns against smoking approach the problem all wrong." She took a sip of coffee.

"How's that?" Walt flicked his cigar; it vanished.

"I'm pretty sure my idea would work for girls. It might work for boys too. You see, some teenage girls can be very vain."

"Ahh...I see you grew out of that phase."

Danielle frowned at Walt. "What is that supposed to mean?"

He shrugged and smiled. "Just that you seem very comfortable in your own skin. It's actually a compliment."

Danielle glanced down at her clothes. She was still wearing the flannel pajama bottoms and T-shirt she had worn to bed the night before. The plaid pajama bottoms had seen better days. *Perhaps I've grown too complacent about my looks*, she wondered.

"So what do vain girls and antismoking campaigns have in common?" Walt asked.

Attempting to smooth out the wrinkles in the fabric of her faded pajama bottoms with one hand while holding her mug of coffee in the other, she glanced up to Walt. "Because smoking prematurely ages and wrinkles your skin. I say show vain girls before and after pictures of women who've smoked."

"You forget, Danielle, a teenager never imagines that would be them."

Cocking her head slightly, she studied Walt a moment. "How about you, Walt? If you knew then what you know now, would you quit smoking?"

"You mean if my fairy godmother showed up and said I had a chance at life again, would I keep smoking?"

"Something like that."

"Not that I believe in fairy godmothers, but if I had another chance at life, I suspect I'd cherish it too much to want to do anything to shorten it."

"Why is it we never truly appreciate something until we lose it?"

"Human nature, I suppose." Walt shrugged. "Did I ever tell you how I used to smoke buggy whips?"

"Buggy whips?" Danielle grimaced.

"Buggy whips were made from hemp. I remember George and I were just kids at the time. Some of the older boys had showed us that if you cut a whip into small pieces, you could smoke it, like a cigarette."

"Yuck!"

Walt chuckled. "We felt pretty grown up, until one of my grandfather's employees caught us down at the beach smoking. He showed us how black and nasty the inside of one of those pieces were, and told us we were taking all that into our lungs. Was the end of our smoking—for a while."

"I don't imagine smoking cigars were much of an improvement —health wise."

Walt shrugged and then waved his hand for another lit cigar.

With a sigh, Danielle pulled her bare feet up on the sofa and snuggled down comfortably as she sipped the coffee. They sat in silence for a few moments, each lost in private thoughts.

"Why did you say you wish Marie hadn't gone over to Seaside Village without talking to you?" Walt asked a few minutes later.

"Because the chief called me this morning. He wanted to come over and talk to Marie, ask her some more questions. I told him I'd call him back after I talked to her, make sure she'd be here. Unlike you, she's not a captive audience."

"I see…" Walt blew a series of smoke rings—eight total. They drifted to the ceiling.

"Now you're just showing off."

Walt chuckled. "I have to admit, I had to use a little spirit energy to do that."

Danielle repositioned herself on the sofa and rested her half-empty mug of coffee on one knee. She looked at Walt. "So tell me. What were you really doing sitting in front of the computer a minute ago? It looked like you were getting ready to type."

"I want you to teach me how to use the computer," Walt announced.

"Teach you to use the computer?" Danielle frowned.

"Yes. Why are you looking at me like that? You think I'm too mired in the past I can't learn how to use one of your modern contraptions? I figured out the television fast enough."

"Umm...well, a computer isn't exactly a television." Danielle leaned forward for a moment and set her mug on the coffee table. She then sat back in the sofa again and studied Walt.

"That's not what you once told me."

"Why do you want to learn how to use the computer?" Danielle asked.

"Why not? You once told me it was a little like a library. I always enjoyed visiting the library."

"We're sitting in the library," Danielle teased.

Walt rolled his eyes. "You know what I mean."

"You hate when I do that," Danielle scoffed.

"Do what?" Walt frowned.

"Roll my eyes."

"Come on, Danielle, I'm serious. And I would like to have an email account."

"Email?" Danielle choked out, trying her best not to start laughing.

"Certainly. While I can call someone on the telephone—the person on the other side can't hear me. But if I could send them an email, I could communicate with the outside world while still being confined to this house."

"You want to communicate...with the living world...via email?"

"What's wrong with that?" Walt asked in all seriousness.

No longer able to hold back, Danielle broke into laughter. "A ghost with an email account," she said between sputters of laughter.

"You know what I think about the word *ghost*."

It took Danielle a moment to regain her composure. When she finally did, she said, "I know. But you have to admit, saying a spirit with an email account doesn't sound nearly as funny as a ghost with an email account. Maybe I could turn it into a book."

"Book?" Walt frowned.

"Sure. I always wanted to write a book...*The Ghost Who Sent an Email*." Danielle started laughing again.

Narrowing his eyes, Walt glared at Danielle. "This really isn't that funny. I don't know why you're so amused."

With tears of laughter in her eyes, Danielle glanced over at Walt and noticed he really did seem annoyed. Forcing herself to stop chuckling, she wiped the moisture from her eyes and smiled sheepishly at Walt. "I'm sorry. It just really tickled my funny bone. The entire thing seemed so…so…"

"You don't think it's a good idea?" He sounded disappointed.

Once again calm, Danielle took a deep breath. "Actually, it's rather brilliant."

"Brilliant?"

"I don't know why we never thought of it before. I mean, there have been times when you needed to contact someone from the outside world…like when we were hijacked. And an email would be the ideal solution."

"Then why all the laughter?" he asked.

Danielle shrugged. "I guess because on the surface, it seems rather bizarre. But it has potential."

"Does that mean you'll teach me how to use the computer?" Walt asked excitedly.

"I suppose. You want a lesson now?"

"Yes!" Walt stood up. "Can you set me up an email account?"

"Umm…sure." Danielle stood up and walked over to the computer with Walt. "Now that I think about it, there are a number of people you could correspond with. Lily, Ian, Heather, Evan, the chief, Chris…"

"What do I do first?"

"Why don't we just start with me turning on the computer and opening my email account. I'll send an email to Lily and you can watch. It'll give you an idea of what you need to do before I start taking you through the steps." Danielle sat down in front of the computer. Walt stood behind her, watching.

A few minutes later, after Danielle opened her email account, she called out, "He wrote again!"

"Who?" Walt leaned down and looked at the monitor.

"Your cousin. He's sent me another email." Danielle opened the email from Walt's cousin. Together, Danielle and Walt silently read the letter.

I was rather bummed that you turned down my offer so quickly. I would like you to reconsider. Walt Marlow is nothing to you, but he is in essence my namesake and a cousin. Not to mention the fact he could be my twin. I understand you run his house as an inn, so I guess you see the portraits as some sort of prop. I notice you're big on exploiting his misfortune on your website to bring in business. While I question how you managed to end up with my cousin's estate, you really have no business keeping those portraits. They should remain in the family. However, I am willing to compromise. I am still offering the thousand dollars for both portraits, but I am also willing to commission an artist to duplicate the portraits, and your guests will never know the difference. I would have written as soon as I received your email, but I wanted to find an artist qualified to duplicate the portraits. I have. Please let me know when we can finalize this transaction, I would really like to have it completed before my wedding. Clint Marlow.

"Wow," Danielle stammered. "Your cousin is kind of a jerk."

"He seems convinced you're going to just fold and do what he wants."

"I suppose I can kind of understand." Danielle closed the email and turned around in the chair to look at Walt.

"What do you mean?"

"If your spirit wasn't here—if we had never met—I probably would agree with him. Those portraits belong in the Marlow family."

'They belong to me!" Walt snapped.

"I understand. And I have no intention of selling them. I'm just saying I sort of get what he was saying."

"Aren't you going to write him back, tell him you aren't interested?" Walt asked.

"I will. But I want to think about what I want to tell him."

In the next moment Marie appeared in the library, standing next to Walt.

"Marie!" Danielle said in surprise.

"I must say it is exhilarating, moving from one place to another without a cane or walker! Or even an automobile!" Marie beamed.

"Did you find out anything to help the investigation?" Danielle asked.

"Unfortunately, no," Marie said with a sigh. She and Walt each moved to a chair, while Danielle sat back down on the sofa.

"I'm glad you're back. The chief wanted to come over and ask you some more questions."

"I really hoped I could track down that woman who saw my killer."

"You mean the spirit?" Danielle asked.

"Yes. But I didn't see a glimpse of her anywhere."

"Maybe she has moved on," Danielle suggested.

"Which won't help me!" Marie reminded them. "I need to find

out who over there killed me before the chief pins this on someone in my family. I'm starting to regret pushing for the autopsy."

"Marie, if it is someone from Seaside Village, we need to start with the people you had contact with over there—especially anyone who might have had an issue with you."

"My first thought was Crazy Earl, but as you mentioned before, he seems to be confined to a wheelchair, and it was footsteps I heard that night, not a wheelchair."

"What about some of the other patients? One that had the password to the back door," Danielle suggested.

"I never really socialized with anyone over there."

"What about the woman you used to visit at night?" Danielle asked.

Marie frowned. "What woman?"

"One of the permanent residents. She told me you used to visit her room at night."

"I never visited anyone's room at night."

TWENTY-EIGHT

"Walt with an email account?" Lily considered the possibility as she sipped a cup of hot green tea. She sat with Danielle on the front porch swing. The chief had left a few minutes earlier after interviewing Marie—with Danielle playing spirit interpreter.

"It really is ingenious. I'm not sure why we didn't think of it before." The toe of Danielle's right shoe gently pushed the ground, keeping the swing in motion.

"Couldn't he also use the landline?" Lily asked.

"The landline?"

"Sure. He can use his energy to pick up the receiver, dial out. Maybe he couldn't call me, but he could call Heather or Chris. Why didn't we think of this before? He could call you on your cellphone when you're out and he needs to get ahold of you!" Lily said excitedly.

Danielle shook her head. "Because it doesn't work that way. What I'm hearing when Walt or Marie talks, well, that sound isn't carried to me in the same way as your voice is. It's hard to explain, but I'm not using my ears to hear Walt."

"So if Walt talks into the telephone, and you're on the other end of the line, you won't hear him?"

Danielle nodded. "Pretty much."

Lily let out a sigh. "I suppose the email is a rather brilliant way to get around that. I know one person who will love this. Ian. I can see it now. He'll be on the computer more than he already is, bombarding Walt with questions."

Danielle chuckled.

"Oh my gosh," Lily gasped. "He can't be the only ghost who's thought of this!"

"What do you mean?"

"Using energy to manipulate a computer in order to communicate with the living! Who's to say all the tweets out there on Twitter are coming from living people?"

Danielle giggled. "You saying there are a bunch of spirits sitting around sending out tweets?"

"It could be true! What about public forums?"

"Public forums?" Danielle frowned.

"Or Facebook comments? Maybe some of those are from ghosts!"

"A ghost with a Facebook account?" Danielle asked.

"And why not? Walt's getting an email account! Who knows, maybe a bunch of those internet trolls and bullies are really pissed-off ghosts!"

Danielle chuckled. "Calm down, girl. I think you're getting carried away."

"I don't know." Lily shrugged. "The next time I'm online and talk to a stranger, I will not only wonder if it's really a serial killer, I'll now wonder if it's a dead person."

"Seriously, when you chat with someone online, you wonder if they're a serial killer?"

"Don't you?" Lily asked. "Especially when I post at one of those political sites."

"While it all sounds interesting, the truth of the matter is, finding a spirit online is more an anomaly."

"Why do you say that?"

"First of all, I believe the percentage of spirits lingering on this plane compared to living people is a small fraction. Most spirits move on."

Lily gestured behind her. "You say that, but there are two ghosts inside the house right now. And I know of one hanging out at Pilgrim's Point, another at the cemetery, and then there's Eva, not to mention all the other ones who've passed through here in the last year and a half."

"True. But those other spirits that passed through have since moved on, and none of them could harness their energy like Walt has—therefore they wouldn't be able to use a computer."

"Are you saying there aren't any spirits like Walt out there, who have harnessed their energy enough to use a computer?"

"Spirits capable of moving objects like Walt does are typically confined to one location. And those spirits are normally confused, like Lucas was before he came here. After Lucas was killed, his spirit got stuck in an office building. Heck, he had access to computers, and unlike Walt, he knew how to use them. But he also didn't understand he was dead. He was confused, in a fog. His ability to move objects was confined to pushing over a waste basket or slamming a door. That's typically where those types of spirits are at."

"I never really considered all that."

"So you feel better now?" Danielle asked.

"What do you mean?"

"Now you don't have to worry about being harassed online by ghosts."

"Ha-ha," Lily said dryly, and then broke into a giggle. "Yeah, I do feel a little better about it. But now you need to get Walt a cellphone."

"What would Walt do with a cellphone?"

"He could text message." Lily grinned.

"IS HE GOING TO WAIT?" Chloe asked Warren when he got off the phone. They were alone in the master bedroom at Marie's house.

"I talked him into holding off until Wednesday. I explained her funeral was Tuesday, and we couldn't do anything until we have Mother's death certificate. Which isn't entirely true."

"Did you tell him that was the day they're reading the will?" she asked.

"Hell no!" he roared. "I'm not crazy. I didn't tell him Mother had another will made. As far as he knows, I'm still inheriting half of her estate. And maybe I am."

"Or maybe you're not," Chloe snapped.

"But for now, he figures even if I don't have the death certificate by Wednesday, I can go to the bank and use my inheritance as collateral."

"He's threatening to call in the loan before you can get your inheritance? He actually expects you to take out another loan?"

"Like you said, I may not even have an inheritance. And if that's the case, then we're screwed." Dejected, Warren sat on the edge of the bed.

"Money is the least of our problems," Chloe reminded him. "I really don't want to get sent to prison for your mother's murder. Do they still have the death penalty in Oregon?"

JASON STOOD ALONE in Marie's garage, the cellphone by his ear. He hadn't bothered turning on the light, but daylight made its way in the side window, its venetian blind partially open.

"I'm not sure when I can get back. Not with the ongoing murder investigation…I suppose if I want to look on the bright side, I don't have to worry about losing my job, since I already did that… no…I haven't told Sondra yet…Hell no, my parents would be the last ones I'd tell about getting sacked. I thought I had this all under control.

"She had even more money than I thought. Did I tell you she sold her parents' old house for over a million bucks?…Yes, you heard me. Over a million, and she owned it free and clear…No. I don't think we'll get that much for the house she lived in, but she has five other houses in town…I know!…I was so looking forward to that nice little nest egg. But now with Grandma changing her will, I might end up with nothing."

WHEN ADAM WALKED into Marie's house on Saturday afternoon, he found Sondra alone in the living room on her cellphone. The moment she saw Adam, she abruptly ended her call and shoved her cellphone in the pocket of the hoodie jacket she wore with her fitted blue jeans.

Adam didn't think much of the abruptly ended phone call, but he did notice Sondra's bare feet propped along the edge of Marie's coffee table. *Grandma would hate that*, Adam thought.

"Good morning," Sondra greeted him.

He glanced around. "Where is everyone?"

"Your parents are in their room, and Jason went outside. I saw him go into the garage."

Adam walked over to a chair and plopped down. "I wanted to talk to them about Grandma's funeral on Tuesday."

"I thought your grandmother had that all planned."

"There is the wake afterwards. I was thinking we could have it here." He glanced around the room. Feet on the coffee table would not be the only thing to annoy Marie if she could see how her family had taken care of her house. Empty and abandoned water glasses and coffee mugs and crumbs littered various tables in the room. A plate with stale food remnants sat on the coffee table, while a pile of newspapers was shoved in the corner with a pair of someone's shoes. Adam was fairly certain that someone was not Marie. Discarded jackets and hand mittens adorned various pieces of furniture. The place was a mess.

"Wake?"

"Of course, this place needs to be cleaned up first."

Sondra glanced around the room, surveying its condition. "You going to hire a housekeeper?"

"I was thinking the people staying here could do that."

"What are you doing here?" Chloe asked as she and Warren walked into the living room.

"I came to talk to you about Grandma's funeral. I thought we should have the wake here."

"Do you really think we need a wake?" Chloe sat down on Marie's rocking chair. "It's not like your father and I kept in touch with anyone from Frederickport."

"Mother lived here all her life," Warren reminded her. "Of course we'll have a wake. It's expected. And considering the turn of events, it would look bad if we didn't have one."

Chloe let out a sigh. "I suppose you're right. But Adam needs to get someone over here and have the place cleaned first."

"Can't you just do that?" Adam asked. "After all, it was perfectly clean when you got here."

"I'm not playing housekeeper when your grandmother's estate can clearly afford to have the damn house cleaned for her wake."

"Fine. I'll order some sandwiches from the deli and pastries from Old Salts. And I'll pick up something to drink," Adam grumbled.

"Won't people bring food?" Chloe asked. "From what I remember, that's what normally happens."

"I still want to have something. And don't worry, I'll pay for it myself," Adam said.

"Considering that commission you earned from Beach Drive, I guess you can afford it," Warren said with a snort.

Before Adam could respond, his brother joined them. "What's going on?" Jason asked as he walked to the sofa and sat next to Sondra.

"We were talking about Grandma's funeral. Afterwards, we'll have a wake here," Adam explained. "I'll send someone over to clean the house on Tuesday morning, and I'll order the food and have it delivered."

"So organized," Chloe snarked.

"Why are you acting so bitchy, Mom?" Adam asked.

"Don't call your mother a bitch," Warren shouted.

"I didn't. I just asked her why she was being so bitchy toward me."

"Same thing," Warren grumbled.

Chloe glared at her oldest son. "How do you expect me to act toward you, dear son? After all, you practically accused me of murdering your grandmother!"

"When did I do that?" Adam asked.

"When you told them I left the house on Monday night. Why was it any of their business what I did that night, unless you actually believe I killed Marie?" Chloe asked.

"Mom, I couldn't lie. They asked me what I knew…what happened that morning. I didn't know it was some secret."

"It wasn't a secret," Chloe snapped. "It just wasn't necessary to tell the police. The fact is, all of us are now suspects in your grand-mother's murder. Even if none of us inherit a dime, at the time she died, we all thought we were in her will."

"So you now believe Grandma was really murdered?" Adam asked.

On the sofa Jason and Sondra sat quietly, attentively listening to the conversation. Chloe exchanged glances with her husband and then let out a weary sigh before saying, "Yes. I do. I will admit, when I first heard she was murdered, I didn't believe it. It all seemed too outrageous. I mean, who would really bother killing an annoying old woman who was probably going to die any day now anyway? Unless, of course, the killer had a financial motive."

"Like one of us," Warren muttered.

Chloe looked to her husband and nodded and then turned her attention back to Adam. "Exactly. It seems like everyone at that care home overheard Marie threatening to cut us out of the will. I imagine the police are right now thinking someone in this room murdered Marie, and they're trying to figure out who, and how to prove it. Since I was the only one who left that night—and lied about it, I'm probably the one they're focusing their attention on."

"What about Adam?" Sondra blurted. "He could have gone back over there!"

Chloe glared at her future daughter-in-law, her eyes narrowed. "Don't be stupid. Adam is the very last person who would hurt his grandmother. "

TWENTY-NINE

On Sunday morning, Danielle sat at her vanity, looking into its mirror and weaving her dark hair into a fishtail braid, when Marie popped into her room.

"Sorry I didn't knock, dear, unfortunately I haven't figured out how to do that yet." Marie stood by her side. "Walt said you were getting ready to go out for breakfast."

Still weaving her hair, Danielle's eyes darted toward Marie. "Morning. Yes, I'm meeting Heather at Pier Café. We usually have guests on Sunday, so it's kind of a treat to go out for Sunday breakfast." She turned her attention back to the reflection in the mirror.

"Heather? Perfect! Would you invite Adam, please? And may I go? I won't eat much." Marie laughed at her joke about not eating much.

Danielle fastened her braid and turned to Marie. "You're more than welcome to join us. In fact, I was going to ask if you'd like to come along. But why Adam?"

"There are a few things I need to tell him about my service. I need to make sure he doesn't forget anything."

"Ahh…you want me to play translator?"

"Something like that. But I understand you can't tell him it's actually coming from me."

"No, he thinks I'm ditzy enough," Danielle muttered.

"DEATH REALLY BECOMES YOU," Heather told Marie, who sat next to Danielle in the booth at Pier Café. "I swear, you look...*younger.*"

"Not as young as I could be," Marie whispered, leaning over the table toward Heather. "When I first tried this, I focused on the age I was when I got married. Unfortunately, since mirrors don't really work for me anymore, it seemed a little silly for me to look like someone no one around me could even recognize."

"Marie was pretty hot," Danielle said with a wink to Heather.

"Oh, Danielle!" Marie chuckled.

"So how many years did you shave off with this look?" Heather asked.

"I went for eighty," Marie told her. "I didn't shave off eighty years, I went for the age eighty."

"Yeah, I got that...eighty looks good on you." Heather picked up her coffee and took a sip.

"Thanks for inviting me for breakfast," Adam said when he joined them five minutes later. Danielle was relieved when he took the empty seat by Heather, as opposed to sitting on his grandmother.

"Melony couldn't join us?" Heather asked.

"I called her, but she woke up with a sore throat this morning. Said she was going to take something and go back to bed."

"I have the perfect oil for that!" Heather said. "A couple of drops in a glass of water, and it will knock it right out."

Adam smiled at Heather. "Then maybe after breakfast I can pick some up from you and drop it off at Mel's."

Heather smiled happily and took another sip of her coffee.

Marie studied her grandson. "Adam looks like he hasn't been sleeping. Ask him how he's been sleeping."

"How are you doing, Adam?" Danielle asked. "You look kind of tired."

"I just can't wrap my head around the idea someone murdered Grandma. I know the chief is looking at my family, but I don't believe for a moment any of them was responsible."

"Of course not!" Marie agreed.

Adam looked to Heather. "Chris sent me an email, said he

would be back for Grandma's funeral. I thought that was nice of him."

"He's coming back tomorrow," Heather told them.

"How's Hunny doing?" Danielle asked. Heather, who was Chris's employee, was dog sitting his pit bull, Hunny.

"She's sweet, but still terrified of Bella." Heather shook her head at the thought. Her calico cat, Bella, was less than half the dog's size.

"I need to ask Adam some questions about my service," Marie interrupted. Heather and Danielle glanced to Marie.

"So the funeral is Tuesday?" Danielle asked.

"Ten in the morning," Adam told her.

"Find out if he's planning a wake," Marie urged.

"And afterwards, are you having people come to your house?" Danielle asked.

"I thought it would be best to do it at Grandma's. But I need to send one of my cleaners over there early Tuesday morning. I'm afraid my family hasn't done a terrific job keeping up the house since they got here."

"I was going to suggest that. Smart boy," Marie said.

Adam went on to tell of his other plans, including the food he intended to order, while Marie occasionally chimed in and Danielle subtly conveyed the information to Adam, sometimes with Heather's help.

"I guess the chief called Mel, wanted to know what was in Grandma's new will," Adam said after the waitress brought their food and left the table.

"Does he think whoever is in the new will might be the killer?" Heather asked.

"That's what I'd have to assume," Adam said as he picked up his fork and set his napkin on his lap.

"That's just ridiculous," Marie snapped. "Whoever benefits from my new will did not kill me." She turned to Danielle. "And you have to tell Edward that! He needs to stop wasting his time looking in the wrong places for my killer. He needs to go back to Seaside Village. My killer is there!"

ON MONDAY AFTERNOON, Hunny entered Marlow House

first, pushing through the doggy door leading into the kitchen, her butt wiggling and tail wagging. She ran from the kitchen, making her way to the library, where she found Walt sitting at the computer.

Danielle hadn't locked the kitchen door, so Chris opened it without using his key. He had already figured out Danielle wasn't home, since her Ford Flex was not parked in the driveway. It didn't take him long to find Hunny and Walt in the library.

"Breaking and entering now?" Walt asked.

Chris flashed Walt a smile. "It was easy. Doesn't Danielle ever lock her doors anymore?"

At first glance, Chris Johnson looked more beach bum, with his sandy colored hair, vivid blue eyes, and model good looks, than who he really was, billionaire philanthropist Chris Glandon. While his real surname was Glandon, he had taken his mother's surname, Johnson, for anonymity's sake. Most people assumed he simply worked for the Glandon Foundation, not that he *was* the Glandon Foundation.

"Now that you're back, I'll be sure to remind her," Walt said sternly. He then broke into a smile and asked, "How was your trip?"

Chris pulled a chair over to the desk and sat down next to Walt. "It was alright. But I'm sort of over traveling. I liked it a lot better when I was younger."

"You're only a couple of years older than me," Walt reminded him.

"Yeah, if we only count the years you were alive, gramps." Chris chuckled and asked, "So where is Danielle?"

"She and Marie went out to help Adam prepare for the wake. He ordered the food, but he forgot about buying paper plates, cups, ice, that sort of thing."

"So how is Marie adapting to the hereafter? Is she moving on after the funeral? You going with her?" Chris grinned.

Walt ignored Chris's comment about him moving on. Instead he said, "Don't tell Danielle, but I don't think she is."

"She isn't moving on?" Chris frowned. "Seriously?"

Walt shook his head. "No. Marie was talking to me last night, and she's not prepared to move on."

"Is it because of her murder?"

"That may be part of it, but not entirely."

"Do you think this means she hasn't adapted to her death?

Normally someone her age has no problem moving on. But murder can throw a monkey wrench into things," Chris said.

Walt chuckled. "As far as adapting, I'd say she's enjoying herself —especially the mobility and lack of aches and pains. Although, I suspect if she weren't able to communicate with Danielle and Heather, I have a feeling she would be going right after the funeral, or when she felt confident she didn't need to stick around to witness the outcome of her murder investigation."

"You have a point." Chris glanced at the computer. "I saw Lily at the service station when I got back into town. She told me you were learning how to use the computer. Is that such a good idea?"

"Why wouldn't it be?"

Chris studied Walt. "I just wonder how wise it is for you to bond with things from this era—not just the people, but the technology, the things that make our time different from yours. Every day you're becoming more and more part of this time in a way I've never witnessed another spirit do. And I have to wonder, is that good for you? Is it good for Danielle?"

"You'd really like me to move on, wouldn't you?"

"To be honest, I think I would miss you if you moved on. I like you, Walt. This house—even Frederickport—wouldn't be the same without you. And I will confess, I had—have—feelings for Danielle. We both know that. But I think that window of opportunity to be more than friends has gone by. Even if you suddenly disappeared, I don't see a future for her and me. The best we'll ever be is good friends."

"Are you saying you don't have a personal motive for wanting me to move on?" Walt asked.

"It's Danielle's happiness I wonder about. I don't know if you realize it, but the two of you have fallen into this comfortable relationship that reminds me of an old married couple. Like two people who are still in love after fifty years, who are happier in each other's company than with anyone else. But a couple who has moved past the physical side of their relationship, and they're okay with it, because they're just happy to be together."

"Does that sound so bad?"

"Maybe not if Danielle wasn't still a young woman. A young woman who may still have dreams of a life those physical pleasures can bring her—like children."

THIRTY

On Tuesday morning, the church was full for Marie Nichols's funeral. Marie had lived her entire ninety-one years in Frederickport. It was where her parents had married, where she had met her husband, and where they had raised their son. It was even where her son had raised his family for almost two decades.

However, many of Marie's close friends had already passed on; therefore, it might be suggested that one reason for such a large attendance was the curiosity factor. News had spread through town —Marie Nichols had been murdered in her sleep at Seaside Village. It wasn't a great advertisement for an already struggling care home, yet it did help boost funeral attendance.

Knowing how fond Marie had been of Danielle, Adam had invited her to sit up front with him, Melony and his family, but she declined when she saw how her presence seemed to annoy his parents. She didn't know why, but they didn't seem to like her. Of course, they didn't seem thrilled with Melony either, especially Adam's mother. Danielle suspected the parents still harbored animosity toward Melony for running away with Adam when they were just teenagers. She wasn't sure what problem they had with her.

Danielle sat in the pew between Chris and Lily. Heather sat on the other side of Chris, while Ian sat next to Lily. It was difficult for Danielle, Heather and Chris to concentrate on what the minister was saying, because Marie kept buzzing around the church, reminding Danielle of a hyperactive preschooler.

Chris leaned toward Danielle and whispered, "Marie can sure get around now that she's dead."

"I wish she would land somewhere. She's making me dizzy, moving from one place to the next."

"She's probably eavesdropping, trying to hear what people are saying about her," Chris suggested.

"I never think that's a good idea," Danielle murmured. "Sometimes it's best not to hear what others think of us."

Danielle spied the chief and his two boys. They sat two rows back from Marie's family. Like Danielle, Chris and Heather, Evan was watching Marie, not the minister. Danielle elbowed Chris and nodded toward the young boy.

MARIE MADE her way through the church, curious to see who had come to say goodbye. She spied several people from the museum, including Ben Smith and his wife. While she had never had much use for the museum group, she had to admit she was touched they had come. She continued on until she found an empty seat. Sitting down, Marie looked to the front of the church and her casket; she assumed her body was inside. The casket was closed, just as she had requested. Marie didn't think anyone wanted to look at her dead body. She certainly didn't want to.

She noticed Sunny Hartman sitting several rows ahead of her. Marie wasn't the only one to notice. The woman sitting to her right —a woman from Marie's church—whispered to her companion, "Isn't that Sunny Hartman from Seaside Village?"

The companion craned her neck to get a better look. Marie leaned closer to hear what the women had to say.

"I think so," the companion said.

"Damage control?" the woman scoffed. "Trying to make Marie's family think they care?"

"As if that will prevent the family from suing the pants off Seaside Village!"

"As they should!"

THEY HAD all driven with Lily and Ian to the funeral—Heather, Chris, and Danielle. It made sense, since they were neighbors. Ian and Chris had left their dogs at Marlow House with Walt. Bella stayed at her house. Heather figured poor Hunny needed a break from her cat, and at Marlow House she would have to deal with Max; the dog didn't need two felines terrorizing her.

From the church they went to the cemetery for the gravesite service. Only a fraction of those who had been at the church showed up. Yet when they drove over to Marie's house, they could see by the cars parked up and down the street and around the corner that many of those who had gone to the church service and skipped the cemetery had come to the wake.

Adam greeted them when they walked in Marie's front doorway. He shook both Ian's and Chris's hands—thanking Chris for making it back to the funeral—and then gave the women each a quick hug. He had no idea his grandmother stood by his side.

"I was a little surprised no one was asked if they wanted to get up and say something about Marie," Lily said.

"Grandma specifically requested we not do that. She left instructions when she made her funeral arrangements," Adam explained.

Danielle and Heather looked to Marie for a further explanation.

Marie shrugged. "I didn't see the point. Most people who would've actually had something to say are already dead. And how awkward for Adam if only a couple of people got up there? No, he'd feel compelled to get up and say something, and he's never been fond of public speaking."

"I have to admit I was a little relieved," Adam whispered. "If Grandma had wanted that, I would have felt obligated to get up there myself. Speeches aren't my thing."

"See, I told you," Marie said with a nod. She smiled at her eldest grandson.

IT HAD BEEN A LONG DAY, and the last guest had just left. Adam gathered stray cups and paper plates from throughout the house, taking them to the trash can in the kitchen. His mother had gone upstairs to lie down, and his father was in the bathroom.

In the kitchen he found Jason and Sondra sitting at the kitchen table, quietly sharing a slice of chocolate cake.

Adam shoved the paper plates and cups into the trash can. "Has this messed you up with work?" he asked his brother.

"How do you mean?" Jason took another bite of cake.

"I remember when you first arrived, you said you'd have to fly out on Saturday after Thanksgiving at the latest because of work."

Jason shrugged. "It's no problem. Work's fine."

Sondra tossed her fork on the plate and glared at her fiancé. "Just stop it, Jason. I can't take it anymore!"

Startled by Sondra's outburst, Adam stared at the couple. He hadn't seen his brother look like that since the time he had almost been caught swiping ten bucks out of their mother's wallet.

"What are you talking about?" Jason asked guiltily.

"I know about work. I know you lost your job," she told him.

"You lost your job?" Adam blurted.

Jason looked at Sondra. "How long have you known?"

"I'm not stupid," Sondra snapped. "I've known all along."

"Why didn't you say anything?" Jason asked.

"I was waiting for you to tell me," she said.

Adam took a seat at the table. He looked at his brother. "When did you lose your job? Why didn't you say anything?"

"It's not something I wanted to broadcast." Jason dropped his fork on the plate with Sondra's and slumped back in the chair. "The department had some major budget cuts, and I was low man on the totem pole. I was told the week before Grandma broke her hip. My last day at work was the day before we got here."

"Why did you say you had to get back for work?" Adam asked.

"I needed to get back and start looking for another job." Jason turned to Sondra. "I'm sorry I didn't tell you. But I just hoped I'd have something lined up, and I didn't want you to think this would interfere with our wedding plans."

"So when are you going back?" Adam asked.

"Chief MacDonald wants us to stick around, but he really can't make us stay, and I know Dad's got to get back to work," Jason said. "I'm just waiting to see what Grandma's will says before I make any more plans."

Sondra reached across the table and took Jason's hand in hers. "I don't believe your grandmother wrote you out of her will. It's going to be okay."

"WHY EXACTLY DID you ask Melony to read the will here?" Walt asked Marie on Wednesday morning. The two were in the attic, looking out the window, waiting for Marie's family to arrive.

"I considered requesting she read it at Adam's office. My intention was to give Adam a home-field advantage, since his father is not going to be happy with the new will. I didn't want him alone with Adam when he found out what was in it. Adam doesn't deserve his nonsense. But then if they were at Adam's office, he might still fly off the handle, and I didn't think that would be good for Adam's business. Here, he would have Danielle's moral support."

"Marie, what did you do?" Walt asked.

MELONY DECLINED Adam's offer to drive with him to Marlow House. Of all days, she did not want to present herself as Adam's girlfriend, and frankly, she didn't know if that label accurately described their current relationship.

She arrived first, just parking in front of Marlow House when Adam's parents pulled up behind her, Jason and Sondra in the car with them. Just as she got out of her vehicle, Adam drove down the street, parking behind his parents' car.

Fifteen minutes later, they were all gathered in the dining room, Melony sitting at the head of the dining room table. While taking their seats, Danielle had offered them all a beverage, which they had all declined, save for Melony, who had asked for a glass of water. Unbeknownst to everyone but Danielle, Marie and Walt sat at the table with them.

Setting down the file she had brought, Melony folded her hands on it and looked down the table, a somber expression on her face. "Several days after the Beach Drive house closed escrow, Marie called me up and asked me if I could stop at her house." She looked to Adam. "She expressly asked me not to say anything to Adam about the visit."

Warren let out a little grunt as if he didn't quite believe that.

Licking her lips, Melony took a breath and continued. "Marie wrote a letter that she wanted me to read before I go over the contents of her revised will." Unfolding her hands, Melony opened the file and removed a piece of paper.

Melony cleared her throat and began to read. *"As they say in the movies, if you are all gathered here that must mean I'm dead. I'm not really afraid of dying. I've had a good, long life, and frankly, I'm a little tired. But before I go, I need to make sure my estate is in order for those of you I leave behind.*

Warren, as you know, after you moved away, I changed my will. When I sent you a copy, you were pretty upset. At the time I wondered why you assumed you were entitled to my entire estate just by virtue of being my son, and now that I think about it, perhaps I was wrong. Your father was rather old-fashioned and believed a person's estate should go entirely to the eldest son. Which would mean any other siblings would be left with nothing. Fortunately for you, you have no older siblings."

Warren expelled what sounded like a sigh of relief and settled back in his chair, a smile on his face. Both Adam and Jason remained stoic, while Sondra furrowed her brow and fidgeted with the table's edge. Chloe hadn't altered her expression since sitting down, aside from a slight twitching at the edges of her lips as if she resisted smiling.

Melony continued. *"Jason, in the last fifteen years I don't think I've seen you more than five times. I can't remember the last time you sent me a birthday card or even called just to say hello. Yet I must say you have been prompt in sending me thank-you cards for the money I sent you for your birthdays and Christmas. For that, I thank you."*

Color drained from Jason's face. He shifted nervously in his chair.

"Adam," Melony continued reading, *"you were a rascal as a young boy, always giving your parents fits. But even when you were at your worst, you were always the best to me, taking care of me after your grandfather died, seeing that I had what I needed. I want you to know how proud I am of you. The only thing I ask of you—"* Melony paused and cleared her throat before reading the next part *"—is that you settle down, get married, and give me some great-grandchildren."*

Adam chuckled and shook his head. "Grandma, you never stop, do you?"

"Not until you give me what I want!" Marie told deaf ears. Danielle flashed Marie a smile.

"Danielle…" Melony began reading again. All heads at the table turned to Danielle. *"You have no idea how grateful I am you came into my life when you did. I was feeling a little alone. Not that I didn't appreciate Adam, but you were like the daughter I never had. You and Lily made me feel useful*

again. I think you needed me. Please look after Adam for me. I think he will need it."

Tears glistening in her eyes, Danielle looked to Marie and smiled.

"Oh, don't get all maudlin on me!" Marie snapped. "If I knew I would have been sticking around, I wouldn't have gotten all mushy."

A smile twitched the corners of Danielle's mouth.

"When Melony finishes reading my letter, I have instructed her to hand out the copies of my revised will to each of you. However, before she does that, I will cut to the chase and give you a summary of what is in the will.

"To Warren, when your father died, our estate was worth approximately fifty thousand dollars. Had I died when your father had, the entire estate would have gone to you. Therefore, I am leaving you fifty thousand dollars." Melony paused and took a drink of water.

"Fifty thousand? Are you serious? Is that it?" Warren shouted.

"That can't be all!" Chloe protested.

"Yes, that's all," Marie said with a nod.

"Please go on," Jason said nervously.

Melony gave Jason a nod and then continued. *"To my youngest grandson, Jason, who I loved in spite of his inattentiveness. I suppose I shouldn't be surprised a young man is not interested in spending time with an old woman. I am leaving you twenty thousand dollars. It should be enough to help you buy a house someday."*

"Twenty thousand? She didn't leave Jason just twenty thousand, did she? That's all?" Sondra said with disbelief, shaking her head.

Marie glared at Sondra. "If I were about to get married, I would be thrilled to know my fiancé had a twenty-thousand-dollar nest egg. What's wrong with young people these days? They want everything handed to them!"

"To Danielle—"

Warren stood up and shouted, "I knew it!" Melony stopped reading and all eyes turned to Adam's father. "I had this little gold digger's number all along! If you think you're going to get a dime of my mother's estate without a fight, you are wrong, sister!" He glared at Danielle.

"Sit down, Warren, you're making a fool of yourself," Marie snapped.

"Please, Warren, let me continue," Melony said calmly.

Glaring now at Melony, Warren reluctantly sat down.

Clearing her throat again, Melony continued. *"To Danielle, I would like you to have my tea set, the one I used during our visits. I hope you think of me when you use it. To Adam—"*

"Wait," Warren interrupted. "Is that all she left Danielle?"

"Yes," Melony said.

"Gee, Dad, are you going to take Danielle to court over a tea set?" Adam snickered.

"To Adam," Melony continued, *"you were more than my grandson; you were my business partner. I have never for a moment underestimated your role in not just overseeing my estate, but keeping me from making foolish mistakes. Five years ago, I was approached by a buyer who wanted to purchase my parents' house for a fraction of what it was worth, and like a foolish woman, I was prepared to sell. If it hadn't been for you, I probably would have. But that is only one example of how you kept me out of trouble. You didn't just make sure I had food in my pantry and that the lightbulbs were replaced without me climbing on a ladder, you made sure I wasn't taken advantage of. To you, I leave the remainder of my estate.*

"A final message to Warren, while you might believe you are entitled to more of the estate, you should thank your eldest son for so wisely handling my finances. Had he not been so diligent, I suspect there would have been nothing of real significance to leave anyone."

Melony folded the letter and slipped it back into the folder and then removed copies of the will from the file to disperse.

"That's it?" Chloe asked.

"So Adam gets almost everything?" Sondra whined.

"It's none of your business," Marie snapped. "Useless women, the two of you!"

THIRTY-ONE

C arla, the waitress at Pier Café, was just about to serve Joe and
Brian their lunch when Beverly Klein walked into the diner
alone. Seeing the widow of the man she had been having an affair
with, Carla almost dropped the plates she was carrying, yet
managed to salvage the meals before losing more than three French
fries. Without expressing her apology, she slammed the plates on the
table in front of the officers and scurried away.

Startled by Carla's abrupt behavior, both Joe and Brian frowned
down at their plates before looking up to see what the waitress
seemed to be running away from. They spied Beverly coming in
their direction, a smile on her face.

"Good afternoon, gentlemen," Beverly greeted them when she
reached their table. She flashed Brian a warm smile.

"Afternoon, Beverly." Brian beamed. "You look lovely today.
Meeting someone for lunch?"

Joe chuckled under his breath and picked up one of his French
fries before giving Beverly a polite hello.

"I never eat here anymore." Beverly glanced briefly in the direction in which Carla had disappeared, and then smiled back down at
Brian. "I come down to the pier sometimes. It's where I go when I
want to talk to Steve." As they all knew, her husband, Steve, had
died at the pier when he had fallen into the ocean after going into
anaphylactic shock from accidentally eating shellfish and finding his

epinephrine injection mysteriously missing from his tackle box. What they didn't know, Beverly was the one who had slipped shellfish into her husband's tamale and had removed his epinephrine injection. Of course, she had not been trying to kill him, just to punish him for having an affair with Carla. His death came as an added bonus.

"You're welcome to join us," Brian offered, scooting over in his seat.

Smiling at Brian, Beverly sat down. "Just for a moment. I was wondering, is there anything new on Marie Nichols's murder?"

Brian and Joe exchanged glances. Brian said, "Nothing I can discuss."

"I still can't believe Marie was murdered." Beverly shook her head. "Do you think it was someone in her family? I understand she was worth a considerable amount of money. I heard she got a good price for the Beach Drive house."

"Like I said, I can't really discuss it," Brian said.

"Did you know Marie very well?" Joe asked.

Beverly shrugged. "I suppose I knew her as well as anyone in town. We went to the same church, although she didn't go that often. I went to her funeral. I didn't go to the cemetery or wake. After all, the only one in her family I really know is Adam. I've never met her son and the other grandson. They'd left before I moved to town. Funny thing, I ran into the girlfriend of the youngest grandson the same night Marie was killed." Beverly picked up Brian's water and helped herself to a sip.

"Sondra?" Joe asked.

Beverly set the glass back down. "I guess that's her name. I asked someone at church who she was, because I recognized her. We were never formally introduced."

"Where did you run into her?" Brian asked.

"That all-night mini-mart on my side of town," Beverly explained. "I woke up with the devil of a headache, and there wasn't an aspirin to be found in my house, so I ran down there. When Steve was still here, he would have gone for me." Beverly let out a sigh and smiled at Brian. "I ran into her going out of the store—I mean I literally ran into her. We collided in the doorway."

"What time was this Monday night?" Joe asked.

Beverly considered the question a moment before answering. "I suppose it wasn't exactly the middle of the night like I said. More like early in the morning, before sunrise."

"Do you have any idea what time in the morning?" Brian asked.

Beverly glanced from Brian to Joe. "Why? Is it important?"

"It might be," Joe told her.

"It had to have been before three thirty, because that's what time I got back home. I remember, because I looked at the clock, took three aspirin, and then went back to bed. Why?"

CHIEF MACDONALD FOUND Danielle sitting alone in the porch swing when he arrived at Marlow House Wednesday afternoon.

"Kind of cold to be sitting outside, don't you think?" he asked when he reached her.

Danielle glanced up to the blue sky, not a cloud in sight, and then smiled at the chief. "What do you mean? It's a beautiful afternoon."

Shivering in his jacket, MacDonald muttered, "If you say so," before sitting down on the swing with her.

"Did you stop by to see how the reading of the will went?"

"Partly. How did it go?"

"Warren was willing to fight me for the tea set, but I think he's going to let me keep it." She chuckled.

"What?"

Danielle shrugged. "Never mind. I guess you woulda had to have been there. Basically, no one was happy. Well, maybe Adam was, but I think he was more in shock than happy at this point. I don't think he really expected Marie to leave him the bulk of her estate. But it really doesn't surprise me, considering everything."

"How did Jason and Sondra react?"

Danielle leaned back in the swing, her arms folded across her chest. "It was kind of hard to hear over all Warren's bellowing and threats to contest the will. But it doesn't sound like there's much that he can do. I don't think he has the resources to fight it in court, and I think Melony as an attorney is thorough."

"Was Sondra upset?"

"A little bit. But they went outside with Chloe and waited for Warren, who was still railing at poor Adam. Why, is the focus on Sondra now?"

"Joe and Brian had an interesting lunch conversation with Beverly Klein today." He then went on to recount what Beverly had said.

"You think it's true? I don't think Beverly would lie about it, but do you really think the woman she ran into was Sondra?"

The chief nodded. "Brian went to the mini-mart and got a copy of the surveillance recording for that time frame. It was Sondra, and one of the cameras picked up her rental car in the background. According to the time stamp, it was 3:20 a.m. Just like Beverly said, Sondra plowed into her when she was leaving, knocked her sack out of her arms. Sondra didn't even stop and say excuse me or help Beverly pick up her bag, she just ran straight to the restroom."

"Maybe she just had to go to the bathroom really bad?"

MacDonald raised his brow at Danielle. "There was definitely something on that girl's mind when she ran into the mini-mart. And where it's located, if Sondra left Seaside Village a little after three in the morning, it would have taken her about twenty minutes to get there. I already timed it."

"Oh my," Danielle muttered. She turned to MacDonald. "I think you should know something."

"What?"

"After the reading of the will, Melony and Adam stuck around for a while and we talked. According to Adam, his brother was let go from his teaching position right before they came here. Something about budget cuts. I think he was counting on that inheritance. And I suspect Sondra was banking on it."

"You think he came here to collect the inheritance? Maybe get his grandmother to hurry up and die?" the chief suggested.

"Maybe. But if Sondra did kill Marie, and Jason was in on it, that's going to suck for both Adam and Marie," Danielle grumbled.

"For Marie and Adam's sake, I'm hoping Jason wasn't involved. I know how devastating it can be learning someone close to you would sacrifice people you care about for money."

Knowing MacDonald was referring to his incarcerated ex-girlfriend, Carol Ann, Danielle reached over and patted his knee. They sat in silence for a few minutes.

Finally, Danielle said, "You know, I just thought of something. Maybe Sondra is alone in this."

"Why do you say that?"

"I remember on Thanksgiving, Jason made a joke about how

Sondra only agreed to marry him after she learned Ian—aka Jon Altar—had purchased Marie's Beach Drive house. But maybe Sondra wasn't impressed with who bought the house, but how much he paid for it."

"You think she knew how much it went for?" the chief asked.

"Marie once mentioned she wasn't going to tell her family what she got for the house. Obviously, she didn't mean Adam, since he handled the transaction. But it's not hard these days to go online and find out what real estate is going for. It's possible when Jason mentioned his grandmother had sold beachfront property, it piqued Sondra's interest."

"Which might mean Sondra decided to marry Jason after she realized how much he might eventually be inheriting," the chief suggested. "Considering Marie's age, that could have been any day. Of course, once there was talk of changing the will, Sondra may have panicked and decided it best to hurry Marie along."

"Possible. Where do we go from here?"

"Did they mention when they were going back to Colorado?" MacDonald asked.

"Adam said his brother and Sondra would be leaving as soon as they can book a flight. Jason is anxious to get his résumés out there. As for Sondra, I don't think she has to get back for her job. After all, she just does temp work, and from what I understand, she's between jobs. But I have a feeling she's anxious to leave; and if she is responsible for Marie's death, I understand why."

"Unless I arrest her, I can't make her stay, which will make investigating this murder more difficult," he grumbled. "The best I can do is bring her in for questioning, but I hate the fact she could just disappear once she gets back to Colorado."

"You don't have enough to arrest her on?"

"Not unless I can get her to confess during questioning."

They sat there a few moments, considering options. After a few minutes, Danielle sat up abruptly, her right foot pressing on the ground, stopping the swing. She turned to the chief. "I have an idea!"

MacDonald studied Danielle, his eyes narrowing. "I'm not sure I will like this. I've seen that expression before."

Danielle smiled, reminding the chief of the Cheshire cat. "I think I know of a way I can get her to confess."

THIRTY-TWO

Shoving her soiled clothes in a trash bag on the bed, Sondra paused a moment and looked at Jason. They were alone in the guest bedroom in Marie's house. "We can't get a flight out until Friday?"

"Sorry. But it's the first one in the morning."

"Whatever," she muttered.

"Adam invited us all out to Pearl Cove for dinner."

"What, to celebrate his big inheritance?" she snapped.

"Sondra, he is my brother. He had no idea Grandma was leaving him everything."

Letting go of the plastic bag, she looked at her fiancé and arched her brows. "Seriously? He is dating the lawyer who wrote the new will. You really believe he didn't know anything about it?"

"All I know is Adam wants to talk to us. Mom and Dad have agreed to go. If it makes you feel any better, Melony isn't going. Adam said he just wanted it to be family."

Sondra sat down on the edge of the bed. "Then I shouldn't go. I'm not family."

"He didn't mean you weren't invited. You're practically family. He just said that's why Melony wasn't going."

Sondra considered his words a moment and then shook her head. "No, I don't want to go. To be honest, I've a bit of a headache. There are enough leftovers in the fridge from the wake to feed an army, so I won't starve. You go. Have this family discussion without me."

———

"THIS MIGHT WORK OUT PERFECTLY," Danielle told Walt and Marie. "I just talked to Adam, and they're all going to Pearl Cove for dinner, and Sondra is staying home."

"If she's the one who killed me, I don't believe for a minute poor Jason had any idea what she was up to. The little gold digger," Marie grumbled.

"Is she going to be able to get over here?" Walt asked.

"I don't think Jason is going to take his rental car when he can ride with his parents. After all, he drove with them when they came over here to read the will." Danielle glanced at the time.

"When are you going to call her?" Walt asked.

"Adam said their reservation was at six thirty, so I'll call her then, just to be sure she's alone."

When six thirty rolled around, Danielle dialed Marie's landline.

After several rings, Sondra answered the phone. "Hello?"

"Hello, Sondra, this is Danielle Boatman."

"If you're looking for Adam, he's not here."

"No, I wanted to talk to you."

"Umm...what about?" Sondra asked.

"I need you to come over to Marlow House right now. I'm alone, and I want you to come alone. I don't want you to tell anyone you're coming over here."

"Why would I do that? What is this about?"

"I know your secret, Sondra."

Silence.

"Did you hear me?" Danielle asked.

"I don't know what you're talking about."

"I know where you really went on Tuesday morning—early Tuesday morning, very early."

"I don't know what you're talking about," Sondra repeated.

"Yes, you do. And if you don't want me telling everyone what you were really doing around three on Tuesday morning, then you better get yourself over here, now!" Danielle demanded.

There were several moments of silence, and Danielle began to wonder if they were wrong, and Sondra had nothing to do with

Marie's death. After all, they all knew Sondra had supposedly gone out early that morning to run on the beach. Perhaps it was all innocent and she had simply left earlier than they had thought, and her reason for running into the mini-mart was just to use the bathroom. Danielle knew from personal experience that sometimes when nature called, there wasn't time to hang around and exchange social pleasantries with a stranger you had just bumped into.

But then Sondra blurted, "Why are you doing this to me?" She was obviously sobbing on the other end of the line. If Danielle didn't think the woman had killed her friend, she might be feeling guilty for making the woman cry.

"Just be here within ten minutes," Danielle ordered before hanging up the phone.

"Well?" Marie asked.

"Danielle, you scare me." Walt chuckled.

Flashing a guilty smile at Walt, she turned to Marie. "I guess we wait and see if she shows up. And also hope she doesn't call Adam and tell him what I just said to her, because then he'll think I've gone nuts." Danielle plopped down on the parlor sofa.

"What happens if she did kill me, and she brings a gun? Oh no, maybe she found mine!" Marie gasped.

Danielle frowned. "You have a gun?"

"Actually, it belonged to my husband. But yes."

"Fortunately, I have Walt," Danielle chirped confidently.

I like the sound of that, Walt thought to himself.

EXACTLY ELEVEN MINUTES later the front door bell rang. Danielle peeked out the side window of the parlor.

"It's her," Danielle whispered.

"Maybe this isn't a good idea. She could be a killer," Marie suggested.

"Marie, even if she didn't find your gun, I expected her to come armed. Maybe not a gun, but a knife. Or perhaps something heavy to bonk me over the head with. After all, that is sort of the point."

"It is?" Marie frowned.

"Certainly. If she's guilty and she thinks I'm her only witness, then she'll want to get rid of me. But Walt's here. He'll make sure she doesn't hurt me."

"Ahh, I think I understand," Marie muttered. "Crafty."

DANIELLE OPENED THE FRONT DOOR. As expected, Sondra stood on the front stoop. Without a word, Danielle opened the door wider so Sondra could enter. Looking dejected, Sondra walked down the hall and into the living room. Instead of taking a seat, she stood in the middle of the room.

"Why am I here?" Sondra demanded, her voice trembling.

Flashing Sondra a smile, Danielle assumed a low and confident tone as she walked around the trembling woman, seemingly not paying attention to her surroundings. It would have been a foolish posture to take with a killer you were intending to blackmail, unless of course there was a spirit nearby prepared to block any lethal threat.

"You told the police you left the house right around sunrise to go jogging, but you left earlier than that, didn't you?" Danielle asked.

"So..."

"What you don't know, I was out that morning too."

"I don't understand?" Sondra stammered. "Why were you out that morning?"

"It doesn't really matter why I was out. It just matters that I saw you. I took pictures."

"You saw me?"

"I was really surprised to see you leaving that place. I wondered why you weren't at Marie's...with Jason."

Sondra shook her head. "I don't believe you."

"Afterwards you stopped at a mini-mart. I followed you there. You were so preoccupied you didn't even notice me. You also didn't notice that woman you ran into when you walked into the mini-mart. Knocked her bag right out of her arms and you didn't even stop to apologize."

Danielle's back was to Sondra, and Walt was prepared to intervene as soon as the woman lunged, but to his surprise, instead of rushing to Danielle, she threw herself on the sofa and began to sob.

Startled by the unexpected reaction, Danielle turned to Sondra and frowned.

"I love Jason. Please don't tell him! It only happened once and I immediately regretted it," Sondra sobbed.

"Huh? It only happened once?" Danielle took a step toward the sofa.

Sondra's tearstained face pleadingly looked up to Danielle. "Please don't tell Jason. I love him. I promise it will never happen again!"

Confused, Danielle stared at Sondra. "You won't kill Marie again? I think you only need to do it once."

With a sniffle, Sondra looked at Danielle while wiping tears from her face with the back of her sleeve. "Kill Marie? What are you talking about?"

"I was talking about you leaving Seaside Village at three in the morning after smothering Marie."

"Huh?" Sondra sat up on the sofa and shook her head. "I didn't leave Seaside Village at three in the morning. I left the Seahorse Motel."

DANIELLE AND SONDRA sat together on the living room sofa, each with a glass of Merlot. Marie and Walt sat on the chairs facing them, quietly listening.

"We dated for six years," Sondra explained. She took a sip of her wine and then continued. "When he broke up with me, I was devastated. That's why I moved to Colorado. I needed to get away from Portland and all the memories. And then I met Jason."

"So why did you agree to see him?" Danielle asked.

Leaning back in the sofa, Sondra let out a sigh and propped her bare feet up on the coffee table. She had removed her shoes after Danielle had handed her the glass of wine. "He saw on Facebook that I was coming to Frederickport. We hadn't really talked since we broke up and I moved away. I suppose I should have unfriended him when we broke up, but I thought that would seem juvenile. After all, we were together six years, couldn't we remain civil and friends?"

"So what happened?"

"He called me when I got here, told me he needed to see me. I guess he had read on Facebook that Jason and I had gotten engaged. He insisted we needed to talk before I got married. So we agreed to meet at two in the morning at the motel. I figured it would be impossible to see him during the day."

"How in the world did you get away that early without Jason wondering what you were doing?

Sondra chuckled. "I like to jog early in the morning and Jason doesn't."

"Yeah, but two in the morning early?"

"You don't know Jason. When he falls asleep at night, you can't get him up. I could seriously have a party in the house and he would sleep through it."

"He was like that as a boy," Marie interjected.

"I left him a letter telling him I had gone out, in case he woke up. That way he would just assume I'd gotten restless and decided to take a drive before taking my morning run."

Danielle reached for the wine bottle on the table and refilled their glasses.

"Why did you think I killed Marie?" Sondra asked.

"Someone I know saw you at the mini-mart. And the police think Marie was killed right before that."

"You thought I was just going to confess?"

Danielle shrugged. "Something like that."

"Weren't you worried I might do something crazy, like get ahold of a gun and shoot you? After all, you did think I smothered Jason's poor grandma."

"I was willing to take my chances for Marie."

"It was a reckless idea." Sondra took a gulp of wine. "I suppose the police will need to talk to my old boyfriend since he's my alibi. I was hoping Jason wouldn't have to find out."

"I won't tell him."

Sondra looked at Danielle. "You won't?"

"Nah, that's between you and Jason. None of my business. But I'm afraid you will need to tell the chief and let him check out your story."

The two women sat in silence for a few minutes, sipping their wine while the spirits across the room watched.

Finally, Sondra said, "I don't really know Adam well. I know he's your friend and everything, but do you think he could have killed his grandmother?"

"Absolutely not!" Marie snapped.

Danielle shook her head. "No. Never."

"Are you really being objective? I know I have an alibi, and I don't see how Jason could have gotten over to the home without getting into his parents' bedroom while they were sleeping and taking their car keys. And I'm pretty sure Adam's folks were in the house during that time. But Adam inherited a lot of money with his grandmother's death."

"You're right, you don't know Adam well," Danielle said with a calm voice. "Adam and I have had our issues. But I've come to consider him my annoying little brother—who happens to be older than me."

Sondra chuckled.

"And one thing I know, he loved his grandmother."

THIRTY-THREE

C hief MacDonald sat alone at a booth in Lucy's Diner, sipping coffee while waiting for Danielle to join him for breakfast. The previous night she had called him after Sondra had left Marlow House, insisting Sondra wasn't the killer. Danielle was meeting him this morning to give him a detailed report of what had transpired the night before.

"Chief," a voice interrupted his thoughts. MacDonald looked up to find Stu Holt standing next to the booth.

"Morning, Stu," the chief greeted him.

"I just heard about Marie Nichols," Stu said as he took the empty seat across from the chief, without asking if it was okay if he sat down. "Murdered? Was she really murdered?"

MacDonald set his coffee cup back on the table. "I'm afraid so."

Stu shook his head at the thought. "I just can't believe it. Who would want to hurt Marie? She and I have been neighbors for years. Are there any leads?"

MacDonald studied Stu a moment and then asked, "I'm curious, how is it you just found out about it?"

Stu leaned back in the bench seat and looked across the table at the chief. "I've been in California. Went there to spend Thanksgiving with my sister's family. I just got back this morning. My next-door neighbor told me. Couldn't believe it. Not that her death would come as a particular surprise, considering her age. Although, with her family leaving before Thanksgiving, I figured she must be doing a lot better. But now with this…"

"What do you mean her family leaving before Thanksgiving? They're still here."

"Yeah, I saw them over there this morning. I just figured they came back."

"Came back?" MacDonald frowned.

Stu shrugged. "Maybe I'm wrong. I left for California early Tuesday morning, when it was still dark, and I noticed there weren't any cars parked in front of her house or in the driveway, and the house was all dark. I'd noticed they'd had two cars over there on Monday, and Marie only has a one-car garage. I just naturally assumed they had gone home. At the time, I thought that was a good sign for Marie, meant she must be doing better."

"Do you remember what time it was?" the chief asked.

"Sure, it was around three in the morning."

The chief frowned. "Are you certain of the time?"

Stu nodded. "Yeah. I wanted to get to California Tuesday morning, and I was too tired to travel on Monday, so I just figured I'd get up real early and leave. I know I left the house a few minutes past three."

BY THE TIME Danielle arrived at Lucy's Diner, Chief MacDonald was again alone. "Morning, Chief," she greeted him while taking the seat Stu had occupied minutes earlier.

"Morning, Danielle."

Before they could continue the conversation, the server arrived with coffee for Danielle and took their orders.

"I really don't think Sondra had anything to do with Marie's murder," Danielle said after the server left the table. Picking up one of the creamers, she ripped off its lid and poured cream into her coffee.

"Maybe not. But I think I have to take another look at Warren and Chloe." The chief went on to tell Danielle about his conversation with Marie's neighbor.

Danielle leaned back in her seat, her right hand absently stirring her coffee with a spoon. "We know where Jason's rental car was—at

Seahorse Motel. Of course, I imagine you'll want to talk to Sondra's ex-boyfriend to verify her story."

"Brian already did that this morning. After you gave me the ex's information, I had Brian check up on it. He drove out to Portland early this morning and talked to the guy at his work. He substantiates Sondra's story."

"Maybe Chloe parked the car in Marie's garage?" Danielle suggested.

The chief shook his head. "When Adam was interviewed, he told us that when he arrived at Marie's early Tuesday, looking for his cellphone, Sondra was gone—in the rental car—and his parents were still upstairs in their bedroom, and their car was parked in front of Marie's house."

Danielle cringed. "This doesn't look good for Warren and Chloe. And frankly, if they were responsible for Marie's death, it's going to devastate her."

"I have to assume if one of them murdered Marie, the other one had to have known, since one of them left the house to kill her," the chief said.

"Unless it was Chloe, and Warren is like his son and can sleep through anything."

MacDonald shrugged. "I suppose it is possible."

"If one of them did it, I hope it was Chloe, not Warren, for Marie's sake."

"I'm going to have to talk to them again."

Danielle sipped her coffee and considered what he had just told her. After a moment, she set her cup back on the table and looked at him. "I have an idea. There is one witness we haven't been able to talk to. Let me see if I can find her again."

The chief arched his brow. "I assume you're talking about the ghost who saw Marie's killer leave the building after smothering her?"

Danielle nodded. "She's an eyewitness. I know you can't really use what she says against the killer, and even if she can't identify the killer, she can at least tell us if it was a man or woman."

MacDonald considered Danielle's suggestion and nodded. "It would help me to know if I need to focus on Warren or Chloe."

"After we eat, I'll head right over there."

"Only problem, I don't think you can just show up at Seaside Village and start going through the rooms looking for your ghost."

Danielle considered her options for a moment. Finally, she said, "Before I go over there, I'll stop at Old Salts and pick up some cinnamon rolls. When I was over there before, I met a sweet little lady who lives there full time, and she loves cinnamon rolls. Her husband used to bring them to her. I'll use that as an excuse if anyone asks. And I know what room the ghost hung out in. It's at the back of the building, and there's a good chance I can slip in and out of there without anyone seeing me if I wanted to. That section is usually vacant."

"Only problem, how do you get inside without being seen?" Instead of waiting for an answer, he reconsidered the question and then added with a shrug, "Of course, I guess that's what the cinnamon rolls are for, you don't really have to avoid being seen."

"I'll be going through the back door. I know what the password is. So maybe I won't need the cinnamon rolls to get in."

"You can try that. But I suspect they've changed the password, especially considering the recent murder. I can't believe they wouldn't have."

Danielle shrugged. "True. But I'll try the back door first. I'd rather enter that way, because if I come through the front door, they might wonder why I'm going to the back of the building, since the patient I supposedly want to see has a room in the front section of the complex."

LESS THAN AN HOUR LATER, Danielle was pleased to discover the password had not been changed. Entering the back door of Seaside Village, she found herself standing alone in the back lounge, a sack of cinnamon rolls in her right hand and the strap of her purse slung over her left shoulder. Glancing down the long hallway leading to the front nurses' station, she saw several people milling around, but it was too far a distance to tell who they were.

Hastily she made her way to the corridor to her left, and to the patient room where she had last seen the ghost. Like before, the room appeared to be unoccupied. Shutting the door behind her, she focused her attention on the bed, now neatly made with crisp sheets and a clean blanket, waiting for a new patient.

"Hello!" Danielle called out in a loud whisper. "Please talk to me. I want to talk to you about my friend, who ran out of here the other night."

In the next moment the elderly woman appeared, sitting on the side of the bed, still wearing her nightgown, its fabric a print with blue roses.

"It's you," the ghost said.

"Please don't leave again," Danielle begged. "I want you to tell me about the person who ran out of here before my friend left the other night. I need to know if it was a man or woman."

The ghost flashed Danielle a smile. "Is that all you want? Why, that's easy. It was a woman. She was in a hurry, and then your friend ran after her. Did she find her?"

"Do you know who the woman was?" Danielle asked.

"Your friend really shouldn't have run after her, you know. It's not safe," the ghost whispered.

"Why do you say that?" Danielle asked.

"Because I've seen things. Sometimes seeing things can get you in trouble." The ghost vanished.

Danielle called after the spirit several times, and when she didn't reappear, Danielle pulled her cellphone out of her pocket and called the chief.

"Any luck?" the chief asked when he answered the phone.

"Sort of. I spoke to the spirit again, but like the last time, she vanished before I could ask any more questions. But I did find out the gender of the person who ran out the back of the building before Marie did. It was a woman."

"So it was Chloe?" the chief muttered.

"It's beginning to look that way. I just hope Warren didn't have anything to do with Marie's death. It's going to be bad enough Adam will have to deal with the fact his mother killed the grandmother he loved. I don't want it to be both of his parents."

"I understand your feelings. But I can't worry about that. My job is to find Marie's killer. Even if it is one or both of Adam's parents," the chief told her.

After Danielle got off the phone a moment later, she opened the door and peeked into the hallway. It appeared to be empty. Just as she stepped out into the hall and took two steps, a nurse walked around the corner in her direction, coming from the front nurses' station. It was SeAnne Easton, the nurse who had broken the news of Marie's death to Adam and her.

"Danielle Boatman?" SeAnne said in surprise, a frown furrowing her brow. "I thought that was you I saw coming in the back door."

Quickly holding up the sack of cinnamon rolls, Danielle flashed SeAnne an awkward grin. "Hi. I was looking for Mabel. I brought her some cinnamon rolls. She loves them, you know. Her husband used to bring them to her."

Still frowning, SeAnne glanced at the open doorway where Danielle had just come through. "Why are you down here? This section is just for rehab."

"Oh, I know," Danielle said brightly. "But I thought I saw someone I knew. Small town, you know."

SeAnne studied Danielle. "Not sure what you could have seen. We only have two patients staying in this wing, and I just saw them leaving breakfast for therapy."

"Do you know if Mabel is still at breakfast?" Danielle asked, desperate to steer the topic from why she was poking through rooms on the rehab wing.

"She's back in her room. I took her there myself."

"And what room number is that?" Danielle forced a grin.

SeAnne considered the question a moment. Danielle wasn't sure if it was because SeAnne didn't remember the room number, or if it was that she didn't want Danielle traipsing through the facility unsupervised. Finally, she gave Danielle the room number.

THIRTY-FOUR

C hief MacDonald stood at the front door of Marie's house and rang the doorbell. A few minutes later, Chloe Nichols answered.

"Chief, what can I do for you?" She stood in the house, not inviting him inside.

"I need to ask you a few more questions."

"Warren just ran to the market, and Jason and Sondra went out for breakfast."

"It's you who I wanted to talk to," he explained.

She stared blankly at him for a moment, seemingly considering his request. Finally, she let out a sigh, opened the door wider, and made room for him to enter. Motioning to the living room, she turned in that direction after shutting the front door.

"Is there anything new on Marie?" Chloe asked as she entered the living room.

"That's why I'm here."

Chloe took a seat on the sofa and motioned to the chair facing her. The chief sat down.

"Does that mean you have a lead on her killer?"

"I understand you left the house Monday night—or more accurately early Tuesday morning."

Chloe leaned back in the sofa and crossed her legs. She had already dressed for the day, wearing dark slacks and a hip-length royal blue silk blouse. Folding her hands together, she studied the chief and smiled. "I believe we went over that. I left around midnight, drove around the block a few times and came right home. Not enough time to go to the nursing home and murder my mother-in-law. Although, considering her will, I would like to wring her neck."

"I've a witness that says you weren't home at three in the morning—around the time when we believe Marie was murdered."

With a frown, Chloe shook her head. "That's ridiculous. I was home in bed at three. You can ask my husband." As if on cue, the front door opened and Warren entered.

"Warren! Come in here!" Chloe called from her place on the sofa, making no attempt to get up.

"Chief?" Warren said when he poked his head in the living room a moment later.

"Warren, please tell him I was asleep in bed at three in the morning on the day your mother was killed."

Warren walked into the living room. With a frown he glanced from his wife to the chief. "What's this about?"

"It's my understanding your car was parked in front of this house, early Tuesday, before either of you got out of bed that morning," the chief said.

Still frowning, Warren muttered, "So?"

"I have a witness who claims your car wasn't parked in front of the house at three on Tuesday morning. And according to your wife, she returned home before one that morning."

Chloe broke into a harsh laugh. "Seriously, this is what this is all about? The fact my car wasn't parked in front of the house at three in the morning?"

Expressionless, the chief stared at Chloe. "Can you explain where it was?"

"Certainly, it was across the street." Chloe rolled her eyes and shook her head.

The chief frowned.

Chloe continued. "When I came back, someone was parked in front of the house. Considering the condition of the car, I assume it belonged to the boy that teenage girl next door is dating. So I parked across the street."

"The next morning I got up and moved it," Warren explained. "Tuesday is trash day on this street, and where Chloe had parked, it was blocking the neighbor's cans. After I moved the car back to our side of the street, I went right back to bed. You can check with the neighbors. I'm sure they'll back up my story."

SEANNE ENDED up taking Danielle to Mabel. The elderly resident sat in one of the two chairs in her small room, watching television.

"You have a visitor," SeAnne told Mabel as she entered the room, Danielle trailing behind her. "Looks like she brought you some cinnamon rolls."

"Cinnamon rolls!" Mabel said excitedly, her gaze darting to the paper sack in Danielle's hand. She quickly turned off her television.

Flashing Danielle a departing smile, SeAnne left the two women alone.

"Do you remember me?" Danielle asked.

Mabel's expression went somber. "You were here visiting your friend—the one who died last week."

Danielle nodded.

The elderly woman's mouth twitched into a smile. "You're also the one who gave me a cinnamon roll."

Danielle walked to Mabel and handed her the paper sack. "I thought you might want some more."

Jerking the sack open, Mabel looked inside. "They're not all for me, are they?"

"Sure." Danielle sat down in the empty chair.

Pulling a roll from the sack, Mabel handed it to Danielle. "You have to have one too."

With a smile, Danielle accepted the roll. Grinning, Mabel took a second one from the sack and then carefully folded the top of the bag together before setting it on the side table. "This is very nice of you."

"I just remembered how much you enjoyed them." Danielle smiled at the elderly woman.

"You're nice like your friend." Mabel took a bite from the roll and then let out a satisfactory sigh as she chewed.

Danielle then remembered Mabel had claimed to have been friends with Marie—even telling her Marie had snuck into her room at night to talk to her. Yet, according to Marie, she had never visited the woman.

"Can you describe my friend, the one who you say visited you?" Danielle asked.

Taking another bite of the roll, Mabel considered the question a moment while she chewed. After she swallowed her bite, she said, "You don't think it was your friend who visited me? She told me she was staying in the rehab section, and your friend was the only one staying there. Plus..." Mabel let out a sigh and added, "She hasn't been back to see me. So I have to assume she's the poor woman who died last week."

"Can you tell me what she normally wore when she visited you?"

Mabel shrugged. "Actually, she always wore the same thing—her nightgown. Of course, she only visited me late at night, so that's what I'd expect her to be wearing." Mabel took another bite of her roll.

"By any chance, was the fabric of the nightgown a rose pattern?" Danielle asked.

"Blue roses," Mabel said as she popped the last of the cinnamon roll in her mouth and then licked her fingers.

Blue roses, Danielle thought. *Like the ghost I just saw. I wonder what Mabel is going to think the next time she visits?*

"Would it be bad of me to have another?" Mabel whispered, eyeing the paper sack sitting on the side table.

Danielle grinned. "Certainly not. They're yours."

With a giggle, Mabel snatched up the sack and removed another cinnamon roll.

"Can I ask you a crazy question?" Danielle asked.

"Keep bringing me cinnamon rolls and you can ask me anything!" Mabel bit down on a roll.

"Do you believe...umm...in the possibility of ghosts?"

Chewing her bite, Mabel eyed Danielle and arched her brow. After swallowing, she asked, "This is because of your friend who died, isn't it? You wonder if you might see her ghost?"

Danielle shrugged. "I suppose. A little."

"Well..." Mabel returned the sack to the side table while holding onto her roll. "After my mother died, she came to see me. Of course, my sister said that was nonsense. And after my husband died, he came to me to say goodbye. I'm not sure they were really here, but it's rather comforting to imagine they were." Mabel smiled kindly.

"Has there been anyone else?" Danielle asked.

With a shrug, Mabel said, "Maybe."

Danielle sat quietly while Mabel finished her second cinnamon roll. She understood now that the woman who had visited Mabel hadn't been Marie. It had been the ghost who had seen Marie's killer leave the building. What Danielle wondered now, just how sensitive was Mabel to spirits? She suspected it was somewhere between Lily and Heather—Lily who had seen the ghost of Pilgrim's Point, and Heather, whose sensitivity had increased over the last year.

"I must say, your friend had a vivid imagination," Mabel said after finishing her second roll.

"How is that?" Danielle asked.

"She was very concerned one of the nurses had been stealing medication from the patients and replacing the pills with placebos. Of course, I can't imagine anyone here doing that. I told my nurse what your friend had said—what she had claimed to have seen— and she promised me she would look into it."

"Did she?"

Mabel nodded. "Yes. She came back and told me I had nothing to worry about. It was all a misunderstanding. I told your friend that, but she insisted she was right. Told me she was going to report the nurse to the authorities."

"Umm…did you ever tell anyone what she said, about reporting the nurse to the authorities?"

Mabel shrugged. "Well, yes. I thought they should know."

"Mabel, which nurse was this?"

Mabel frowned. "Which nurse was what?"

"The one who my friend claimed had been tampering with the medication?"

"She refused to tell me who it was. That's why I thought she was probably imagining it all. Sometimes people in this place imagine things, even the nice ones."

"Which nurse did you talk to about it?" Danielle asked.

"I told you. My nurse," Mabel explained.

"Which one is your nurse? Her name?"

Mabel blushed. "I'm sorry. I always get the names mixed up in here. I'm not very good with names."

"Mabel, ready for your physical therapy?" a male voice called out from the doorway.

A FEW MINUTES LATER, Danielle found herself walking down the hallway, away from Mabel's room, as the elderly woman went off to physical therapy. Heading toward the back door, she passed a man in a wheelchair complaining to SeAnne about his pain medication. It was the same man who had been complaining during her last visit.

"I need another pain pill," he insisted.

"I'm sorry, but you had one thirty minutes ago," SeAnne told him.

Walking by the arguing pair, Danielle heard her phone buzz, signifying an incoming text message. While still walking, she pulled her phone from her purse and read the message. It was from the chief.

Warren's car was across the street. I don't think it was Chloe. Back to square one, read the text message.

"Damnit, I am tired of this!" the man shouted. "My leg hurts like hell, and you promised you would talk to my doctor about changing the pain medication!"

Danielle stopped abruptly and glanced back at SeAnne and the man. What had Mabel said? *Someone was stealing medication and replacing it with placebos? Medication like pain pills?*

Without another thought, Danielle rushed down the hallway and ducked into what appeared to be the first empty room. Shutting the door behind her, she quickly dialed the chief.

"I don't think it's Chloe or Warren. The neighbor across the street remembers looking outside Tuesday morning and seeing Warren moving his car back across the street before the trash truck arrived," the chief said when he answered the phone. "And according to Marie's next-door neighbor, his daughter's boyfriend had parked in front of Marie's house when he brought the daughter home after midnight. So their stories corroborate what Chloe is telling me."

"Chief, I think I know who might have had a motive to kill Marie," Danielle whispered.

"Who?"

"One of the nurses here, but I'm not sure which one. I'll come to the station and explain there; I can't talk here. But I need you to do something for me while I'm on the way there."

"What?"

"Do you still have Marie's nightdress, the one she was wearing when she died?"

"Yes. It's in evidence. Why?"

"I need you to check the pockets."

"Why?" he asked. "But I'm sure the lab has already done that."

"Marie told me she put a pain pill in the pocket of her nightdress. I need you to see if it's still there, or if the lab found it. They need to check and see what kind of pill it is."

"What's going on, Danielle?"

"I'll explain when I get to the station."

THIRTY-FIVE

Chief MacDonald stood at his desk, reviewing the list of items held in the evidence box regarding Marie's case. Danielle had been right. There had been a pill in the pocket of Marie's night-dress. According to the lab, it was a vitamin. He wasn't sure what the vitamin had to do with Marie's murder. Tossing the list on his desk, he picked up his phone and dialed Danielle. After several rings, her voice message picked up the call.

"Damnit, Danielle, answer your phone," the chief grumbled. He hung up and sat back at his desk. According to Danielle, she was on the way over to his office. He would just have to wait until she arrived to find out what significance the vitamin held.

Fifteen minutes later, when Danielle did not arrive at the police station, MacDonald tried calling her again. As before, her voice message answered his call. Another fifteen minutes went by, and he tried calling her again. But like before, her voice message picked up. Annoyed, he dialed Lily.

"Hey, Chief, what's up?" Lily answered her cellphone.

"I'm trying to get ahold of Danielle. She was supposed to be on her way over here, but that was over half an hour ago, and she hasn't shown up, and I keep getting her machine."

"It's possible her phone is dead," Lily suggested. "She's been complaining about her battery not holding a charge. Is there a problem?"

"I hope not," MacDonald grumbled. "By any chance, do you see her car at her house?"

"Hold on. Let me check." The line went quiet for a moment and then Lily returned. "Sorry, Chief. I don't see her car. It doesn't look like anyone's over at her house." Lily chuckled and then added, "Well, except for Walt and maybe Marie."

"If she shows up over there, would you have her call me?" he asked.

"IF DANIELLE BOATMAN SHOWS UP, tell her to wait for me in my office and call me immediately," the chief told Holly Parker as he left the police station after talking to Lily on the phone.

When MacDonald arrived at Seaside Village fifteen minutes later, he didn't park his car. Instead, he drove around the complex, looking for Danielle's red Ford Flex. He didn't see it in any of the parking lots or along the street. He could only assume she had already left.

Instead of going back to the police station, he headed to Marlow House. When he pulled up in front of the property, he didn't see any sign of Danielle's red car. After parking and turning off his ignition, he tried calling Danielle again.

"You've reached Danielle Boatman. If I'm not answering this call, I've either misplaced my phone or forgot to charge it. Please leave a message, and I will get back to you as soon as possible. Have a great day!"

With a sigh, he dialed Lily.

"I see you over there," Lily answered with a laugh.

MacDonald glanced across the street. He spied Lily looking out her front window, waving at him.

"You still have a key to Danielle's house?" he asked.

"What's going on?" The playful tone disappeared from Lily's voice.

"I need to talk to Marie—if possible."

"I think we can figure out something," Lily told him. "I'll be right over there."

MARIE SAT on the attic sofa, her arms folded across her chest, as her gaze locked with Max's. He perched on a box several feet from the sofa, his tail twitching behind him.

"It's just rude, Max," Marie insisted.

"Are you still arguing with him?" Walt asked when he appeared in the room.

"I'm just trying to make him understand why it's a bad idea to use someone's flower garden as a litter box. But he insists the soil there is easier to dig in, and he enjoys the fragrance."

Walt shrugged as he made his way to the window to look out. "Two valid points."

Marie scowled at Walt's comment and then turned to him. "What are you looking at?"

"A police car is parked in front of the house," Walt said, still looking outside.

Leaving the sofa, Marie joined Walt at the window. "Looks like Edward. Is Danielle back yet?"

"No. I was expecting her home by now."

"Wasn't she meeting him for breakfast?" Marie asked.

"Yes, to discuss what she found out about Sondra. But they should have finished breakfast a couple of hours ago."

"I feel a little guilty believing that poor girl had something to do with my death."

As they looked down to the street, they watched as the chief got out of his vehicle. Several moments later, Lily and Ian came dashing toward the chief, Sadie trailing behind them.

"Looks like they're coming to the front door," Marie said a moment later.

Walt frowned. "I wonder what's going on."

———

THEY GATHERED IN THE PARLOR, Lily, Ian, MacDonald, Walt, and Marie, with Sadie sitting on Walt's feet and Max perched on the windowsill, watching. While the three living humans in attendance couldn't see the two spirits, they knew they were there. Walt had already confirmed that fact by scribbling a response on the piece of paper Lily had placed on the desk after entering the room.

Before asking any questions, the chief recounted the events of the day, beginning with breakfast with Danielle at Lucy's Diner, to the last phone conversation he'd had with her.

"And she wasn't at Seaside Village?" Lily asked.

"I drove by before coming here, but her car wasn't there. If she doesn't show up before I leave here, I intend to go back over there and talk to them. Someone must have seen her leave. Maybe she decided to go somewhere else before coming to the police station, and if her phone is dead, she'd have no way of calling."

"I told her to get a new phone," Lily grumbled.

MacDonald looked to the wall where Sadie sat, believing that was where Marie and Walt stood. "Marie, do you have any idea why Danielle would ask about a vitamin in the pocket of your dressing gown?"

Marie shrugged. "You said Danielle asked about a pill I'd put in my dressing gown that night. But it wasn't a vitamin. It was a pain pill. That place forced pain pills on me even if I didn't want one! They loved to keep us drugged up."

Walt glanced over to Marie and sighed. "You do realize he can't hear any of what you just said."

Marie pointed to the paper on the desk. "You can write it out for me."

Walt rolled his eyes. The next moment the pen seemingly moved of its own volition across the sheet of paper.

When the pen dropped to the desk, rolling gently back and forth before coming to a complete stop, the chief stepped closer and read the words.

It was a pain pill. Not a vitamin.

The chief frowned. He looked up at the wall. "Are you sure? According to the lab, it was a vitamin."

"That's what they told me it was," Marie said. "I can't imagine why they would give us vitamins right before we go to sleep at night."

Again the pen moved across the paper.

That's what they said it was. A pain pill.

IF NOT FOR the night-light plugged into the far wall, it would have been pitch dark in the windowless storage room. Wearing the pale pink jogging suit she had worn to physical therapy, Mabel stood over the laundry cart with Doris and looked down at Danielle. Nestled in the pile of dirty linens, Danielle seemed to be sleeping peacefully, in spite of the fact she looked a little like a pretzel, the way her knees pushed against her chest while her arms wrapped around the back of her thighs, held together with a zip tie.

"She's going to be awful sore when she wakes up," Mabel said with a cringe.

"If she wakes up," Doris corrected. "I don't see much of a future for this poor girl. It's all your fault!'

"How is it my fault?" Mabel asked.

"You didn't have to blab, did you?" Doris leaned into the laundry cart, studying Danielle's forehead. "That nasty bump is getting bigger," Doris said with a sigh. "Surprised it didn't kill her the way your friend clobbered her with that lamp."

"She isn't my friend!"

"It would have been nice had you figured that out sooner!" Doris grumbled.

"Quiet!" Mabel gasped. "Someone's coming! Quick, hide!"

THIRTY-SIX

The van from the funeral home was pulling out of the driveway of Seaside Village when MacDonald arrived. He parked the police car in the front parking lot and entered through the main entrance. He wondered briefly why the funeral home had been there. Had there been another death? Considering the ages of the Seaside Village residents, he imagined it was a fairly common occurrence.

Walking up to the front nurses' station, he spied Sunny behind the counter on the telephone. She was the only one manning the station. He stood quietly, waiting for her to end the call. When it ended, she smiled up at him.

"Hello, Chief. What can I do for you?"

"I'm looking for Danielle Boatman. She was here this morning and called me, said she was on her way to the police station. But she never showed up. I was wondering if anyone knew where she went. Maybe she changed her mind about coming to the police station and said something to someone?"

"Danielle?" Sunny frowned. Shaking her head, she said, "I'm sorry, I haven't seen her. Do you know who she was here to see?"

"Umm…" the chief racked his brain for the name of the patient Danielle had mentioned. He decided he either couldn't remember, or Danielle hadn't mentioned the resident's name. "I believe she was going to bring her cinnamon rolls."

"Cinnamon rolls?" Sunny smiled sadly. "I guess that explains the cinnamon roll in Mabel's room. Danielle must have brought it to her."

The chief glanced down the hall. "Where is Mabel's room? I'd like to talk to her."

"I'm afraid Mabel passed away today. In fact, the funeral home just left with her body."

"She's dead?" The chief frowned.

"It's not really a surprise—Mabel was well into her nineties, and she had been suffering early stages of Alzheimer's. So I suppose it's a bit of a blessing."

"How did she die?" he asked.

Sunny shrugged. "I suspect a heart attack. Mabel had a bad heart."

"When did all this happen?"

Sunny paused a moment and glanced down the hallway at what had been the door to Mabel's room. She then looked back to the chief. "I know after breakfast she went back to her room to watch a little television before her physical therapy. She usually does that. If Danielle was here to see her—which I imagine she was, considering I found a sack with a cinnamon roll in her room—it would have had to have been before Mabel went to physical therapy. I know that after physical therapy, she went back to her room to take a nap. I stopped in to give Mabel her medication, and that's when I found her. Looks like she went peacefully in her sleep."

"Like Marie?"

Sunny reacted as if she had been slapped. She stared at the chief a moment before muttering, "I can assure you, Mabel died of natural causes."

"I need to speak to the physical therapist."

"YES, Mabel had a visitor. A young brunette, attractive, early thirties," the physical therapist told the chief twenty minutes later. "Same woman who was here the other day when I picked Mabel up for her therapy. Mabel told me she brought her cinnamon rolls from Old Salts." The therapist let out a sad laugh and added, "Mabel acted a little guilty about eating two cinnamon rolls this morning, but said they were really good. I told her not to feel guilty; if she enjoys something, she should do it."

"Did you see where she went? The visitor?"

The therapist shrugged. "Not really. After I got Mabel, they said goodbye, and I noticed the woman heading down the hall, toward the back entrance. But I didn't see her leave the building. The therapy room is in the opposite direction."

The chief thanked the physical therapist and then went down the hall, asking other residents and staff if they had seen Danielle. He couldn't find anyone who remembered seeing her—not until a man in a wheelchair pulled out into the hallway from his room, almost running into the chief.

"Yeah, I remember seeing her," the man told him. "I didn't really see where she went, I was too busy giving SeAnne an earful about that damn pain medication the doctor prescribed."

The chief arched his brow. "Pain medication?"

"They are damn useless around here, if you ask me. I wouldn't be surprised if that stuff they give us is nothing but sugar pills!"

"Why do you say that?" the chief asked.

"Because my damn leg hasn't stopped hurting since surgery!" he shouted. "My doctor insists it doesn't have an infection, says it's just natural pain from physical therapy."

The chief glanced down at the man's legs. "Knee replacement?"

"Yeah. I suppose I should be using my walker, but it doesn't hurt as bad when I use this thing."

"YES, I SAW DANIELLE BOATMAN EARLIER," SeAnne told the chief when he found her in the rear nurses' station. "She brought Mabel cinnamon rolls. I thought that was sweet. Did you hear about Mabel?"

The chief nodded. "Sunny told me she passed away after she saw Danielle."

"Not directly after seeing Danielle," she corrected. "I saw Mabel saying goodbye to Danielle after the physical therapist came to get her."

"So you saw Danielle leave?"

SeAnne shrugged. "I didn't see her leave the building. Just

Mabel's room. I saw her heading to the back door, but I didn't see her leave the building."

"And you didn't see her again?"

SeAnne shook her head. "Sorry."

Just as the chief stepped away from the rear nurses' station, he was approached by a janitor.

"Excuse me, Chief," the man called out.

MacDonald stopped and faced the janitor. "Yes?"

"I'm Jeb Guthrie. I'm one of the janitors here. Someone told me you were asking about Danielle Boatman?"

"You saw her?" the chief asked.

"Is she the one who owns Marlow House? Drives around in that red Flex?" he asked.

"Yes. Did you see her today?"

Jeb smiled. "I thought that was her. I followed the story in the paper when she was arrested for the Gusarov murder. I used to work for the Gusarov family. Well, not the family exactly, but at one of their care homes in Portland. I remember reading how they tried framing her by using another red car."

"So you did see her this morning?"

Jeb nodded. "Sure. I pulled up about the same time as she did, in the parking lot, when I got to work today. Cute little brunette, early thirties, wears her hair in a fancy braid. She was carrying a white paper sack."

"Did you see her again?"

"Only when she left. But I didn't actually see her again, just the back of that red car of hers. I'd forgotten something in my car and came out to get it. When I did, I noticed her pulling out of the parking lot."

"Do you know what time you saw her leaving?"

Jeb gave him a time. The chief glanced at his cellphone, looking for the call Danielle had made to him that morning. She had called him about twenty minutes before Jeb saw her car leaving Seaside Village.

THE CHIEF STOOD in the front parking lot of Seaside Village, next to his police car. He dialed Lily on his cellphone.

"Tell me you've found her," Lily answered the phone.

"I take it you haven't heard from her?" the chief asked, glancing over to the front of the care facility.

"I'm getting worried. This isn't like Danielle to just disappear."

"I talked to someone who saw her leaving here about twenty minutes after I talked to her on the phone. She was supposed to go to the police station, but Holly hasn't called me, and I have to assume she didn't show up there."

"She still isn't answering calls," Lily said. "I keep getting her damn voicemail. I called around to see if anyone has seen her. No one has."

THIRTY-SEVEN

B rian Henderson felt old. It wasn't just that the new dispatcher, Holly Parker, was young enough to be his daughter, it was that pink streak in her otherwise raven-colored hair. He just didn't get it. Carla, the waitress at Pier Café, regularly changed her hair color; he had seen it every pastel shade imaginable. But he thought Carla looked like someone who should have a pink streak in her hair —*not Holly*.

In spite of the pink hair, he thought the new dispatcher a cute little thing, with her pixy haircut accentuating enormous brown eyes, heart-shaped face, and petite turned-up nose. She might make an adorable Santa's elf come Christmas, if it wasn't for the green serpent tattoo winding around her upper right arm. He didn't get the serpent tatt either.

Brian had just walked in the station when Holly waved him over.

"Could you do me a big favor?" she asked.

Brian wasn't sure how anyone could turn down a request from someone with her eyes—in spite of the age difference, pink hair, and serpent tattoo.

"Sure, what do you need?"

"Would you mind holding down the phone for a minute while I run to the restroom?"

Brian flashed her a smile. "No problem."

Holly got up from her desk and grabbed her purse from the

back of her chair. She started to walk away but paused a moment, turning back to Brian. "Oh, if Danielle Boatman comes in, tell her to wait in the chief's office."

"Danielle?"

Holly shrugged. "Yeah, the chief's been waiting for her all morning." Flashing Brian a parting smile, she turned her back to him and continued on her way.

Just as Brian sat down at Holly's desk, the phone began to ring. He answered it.

"Brian, is that you?"

"Hey, Chief," Brian greeted him. "I'm covering the phone for Holly while she uses the bathroom."

"Any chance Danielle is there?"

"No. Holly told me if she came in, to have her wait in your office. What's up?"

"I'm not sure. Danielle was supposed to be on her way to the station over an hour ago. No one's seen her."

"Where was she coming from?" Brian asked.

"Seaside Village."

"I assume you've tried calling her?"

"Yes. She's not answering her phone. I keep getting her voicemail."

Brian sat up straight in the chair. "That doesn't sound good."

"According to Lily, her battery hasn't been holding a charge, so her phone going straight to voice message is not as ominous as it sounds."

"With all Boatman's money, she can't pick up a new cellphone?" Brian snickered.

"You be sure and ask her that when you see her."

"I will," Brian said with a laugh.

After Holly returned to her desk five minutes later, Brian took off to the break room to grab a cup of coffee. He found Joe Morelli there, making a fresh pot.

"Good, I was hoping someone had made coffee," Brian said as he grabbed his cup and stood by the pot, waiting for it to brew.

"I thought you were going to stop drinking coffee during the day?" Joe asked.

"Shut up and don't remind me of the stupid things I say," Brian grumbled.

The phone began to ring.

Still chuckling over Brian's comment, Joe answered the phone. It was Holly.

"We need to go down to the north beach," Joe told Brian when he hung up the phone a minute later.

"What's going on?" Brian filled his cup with coffee.

"Looks like a vehicle went off Pirate's Bluff. Some fishermen found it. It's in about twenty feet of water. They can just see the top. The fire department's there now."

"Did they see it go off?" Brian took his cup and headed out the door with Joe.

"No. But they said it wasn't there this morning. Must have happened sometime in the last couple of hours."

"Damn, did they get the people out of the car?" Brian asked, now hurrying with Joe toward the exit door.

"Doesn't sound like it. They have the divers out."

"Any idea who it might be? A local? Tourist?" Brian asked as he opened the door for Joe, letting him exit before following him outside.

"No. All I know it's some sort of red wagon."

Brian froze. "Did you say red?"

Joe stopped and looked back at Brian. "Yeah, are you coming?"

"Joe, Seaside Village is about two blocks from Pirate's Bluff."

Joe frowned. "So?"

"The chief's been looking for Danielle all morning. She was supposedly on her way over to the station from Seaside Village. She never arrived, and he can't get her on the phone."

"Oh crap!" Joe shouted before racing toward the squad car, Brian close behind him.

"I'm calling the chief. You drive," Brian ordered as he jumped in the passenger seat of the vehicle.

ACCORDING TO LOCAL LEGEND, during the dead of night, pirates once used lanterns to lure unsuspecting ships to the rocks below Pirate's Bluff. After hitting the jagged shoreline, the broken ships washing up to the nearby shore made easy plunder for the pirates. If the stories were true, Chief MacDonald had no idea.

He stood with Joe and Brian on the nearby beach, the other first responders standing close by. They waited for the diver, who made his way toward them, removing some of his gear while he emerged from the ocean. In one hand he carried a woman's purse.

"There's no one in the car," the diver told them. "But the driver's door was open, so whoever was in the car probably got out after it went over the cliff." He handed the chief the dripping wet purse. "I found this."

MacDonald recognized the handbag. He had seen Danielle carrying it at breakfast that morning. Yet it didn't surprise him; he already knew the submerged vehicle belonged to her. He unzipped the wet purse. Inside he found her cellphone. He pulled it out briefly and looked at it before putting it back inside the handbag.

"It's Danielle's," the chief said dryly.

"How can you be sure?" Joe snapped. "You didn't check the ID."

"It's her car, Joe," Brian reminded him.

Joe grabbed the purse from the chief and opened it. MacDonald didn't stop him. He watched as Joe fished the wallet from the handbag and opened it. It was Danielle's.

Combing his fingers through his hair, Brian looked out toward the submerged vehicle. "Where did she go?"

"You know the driver?" the diver asked.

"We know who owns the vehicle. Same person who owns the purse you brought up. She's a friend of ours," the chief explained.

"I'm sorry," the diver muttered.

Joe looked out to the submerged vehicle. "Where is she?"

"Assuming she was in the car when she went over the cliff, her body will probably wash up down the beach. That's what typically happens. Sorry to be so brutally honest, but that's normally what I've seen in situations like this. If she had made it out of the car alive, I'd expect her to be on the nearby beach," the diver said.

Stuffing the wallet back in the purse, Joe said, "Maybe she wasn't in the car when it went off the cliff."

All four pair of eyes looked up to Pirate's Bluff.

"Then where in the hell is she?" the chief asked.

BY SUNSET ON THURSDAY EVENING, most everyone in Frederickport had heard the owner of Marlow House had driven her car off Pirate's Bluff. Her body had still not yet been found. When

Adam heard the grizzly news, he called the chief and asked him if it was true.

"Her car went off the bluff, but we're still trying to find out what happened to her," was the chief's cryptic reply.

Danielle's housekeeper, Joanne, had arrived back in Frederick-port that morning, after visiting her family for Thanksgiving. She had planned to come over Thursday afternoon to get Marlow House ready for the guests who were arriving late Friday. Lily had called Joanne and asked her not to come over, but instead come early Friday to ready the house for the visitors. Lily then promised she would help with the weekend's guest if Danielle was not yet back.

Joanne thought that was a peculiar thing for Lily to say, since everyone knew Danielle had driven off the cliff into the ocean, and they were still looking for her body. The chances the young woman had survived were slim to none. Yet Joanne didn't question Lily. She assumed she needed time to grasp the reality of her best friend's death.

But the fact was, Lily didn't believe Danielle was dead—and neither did Ian, Chris, Heather, MacDonald, Evan, Marie and Walt. It was all very simple, really. If she were dead, they had no doubt her spirit would have already made its way to Marlow House. And so far, none of them had seen her.

The mediums, along with the believers in the close-knit group, gathered at Marlow House. Walt had closed all the blinds to maintain the appearance of an empty house, since most everyone in the community believed its lone occupant was somewhere in the ocean. They could have met at Ian's, but then Walt would not have been able to attend.

The chief had dropped his eldest son off at his sister's. He felt it was important to take Evan with him. If they were wrong and Danielle had been killed, there was always a chance Evan might see her and not immediately understand, and he wanted his son fully prepared for anything. MacDonald's sister didn't quite understand where he was going Thursday evening with just one son, yet he hadn't stuck around her house long enough for her to adequately pump him for information.

"I hate to be the one to bring this up," Ian began. He sat on the living room sofa with Lily and Chris, with Heather and MacDonald sitting on the chairs facing them. Marie and Walt stood nearby at the fireplace, with Sadie sleeping at Walt's feet, Evan sitting next to the dog, and Max dozing in the corner. All the blinds were drawn, and the only light came from a half-dozen flickering candles perched in brass holders along the fireplace mantel. All eyes turned to Ian.

"You wonder why we're so certain Dani is still alive?" Lily told him.

"How did you know I was thinking that?" Ian asked.

Lily shrugged. "An obvious question, I think. Especially from someone like you."

"Someone like me?"

"Not just that you always question everything, but you're kind of new to all this. I know it's a question I would be asking if I were you," Lily said.

"I'd just be really surprised if Danielle didn't come here first," Chris told Ian. "If she had died."

"Because it's her home?" Ian asked.

"No." Chris looked over to Walt, his expression somber. "Because Walt's here."

"Interesting," Marie muttered, eyeing Walt and Chris curiously.

Walt's gaze met Chris's. "She's alive. If she were dead, I'd know it."

Heather spoke up. "But we're forgetting one thing. We all know how new spirits can get confused, not understand what's happened to them. Just because Danielle can see spirits—that she has more of a grasp on all this than the average person—doesn't mean that when she dies, especially if that death is from something unexpected and tragic—"

"Like driving off a cliff into the ocean," the chief reluctantly muttered.

Heather looked to him and nodded. "Yes. If something like that happened, then who's to say she might not react like any other person? Her spirit could be wandering and confused right now, especially if she detaches from her body at an unfamiliar location?"

Like the bottom of the ocean, Lily thought, but refused to voice.

"I still don't believe she's dead," Chris insisted. "Even if she was confused, she'd still come back here. In fact, this is the first place she'd come to in either case."

"Then where is she?" Ian asked.

"When she called me this morning, she insisted she knew who

233

might have been responsible for Marie's murder," the chief reminded them.

"That doesn't make me feel any better," Lily grumbled. "It could mean the killer has Dani now!"

"If she is alive or dead, what does it matter? Shouldn't someone be looking for her in either case?" Marie asked. "What good are we all doing huddled here in the dark?"

Chris looked to Marie and nodded. "I agree with you."

"What did she say?" Lily asked.

Chris repeated Marie's words for those unable to hear them.

"Marie," the chief said, "could you go back to Seaside Village and look around? See if anyone is talking about Danielle. Maybe someone knows something they weren't willing to tell me. And if she wasn't in her car when it went over the cliff, maybe someone there knows where she is."

"You want me to spy!" Marie grinned.

MacDonald stood and looked at his son, who sat on the floor by Sadie. "I can take Evan down by the pier and walk along the beach."

"I'll search the area around where the car went off the bluff. I know the chief's men have already searched the area, but let me look again. And well...if she did...you know...I'll see her," Chris said.

"I'll go with you." Heather stood up.

"Where do you want Ian and me to go?" Lily asked.

"You should stay here in case Danielle comes home," MacDonald suggested.

"If she does come back to the house, I hope I can see her and don't have to read Walt's note to know she's here," Lily grumbled.

THIRTY-EIGHT

Whatever had been in the syringe had worn off, and Danielle was now painfully awake. Still crammed into a laundry bin, her wrists and hands numb, she figured if her attacker didn't get around to killing her, the blood clots she was bound to suffer due to the unnatural contortion of her body would surely finish her off.

She hadn't been conscious when the needle had been shoved into her arm. The only reason she knew about it was from Mabel and Doris's insistent chattering. The two spirits just wouldn't shut up.

If it were possible for them to remove the duct tape plastered over her mouth, she could send them to find help. Unfortunately, they were using all their energy talking to each other and getting worked up whenever her abductor walked into the dark storage room.

One of the last things she remembered was standing in an empty patient room, talking to the chief on her cellphone. Yet now she realized it hadn't been empty at all. Someone was in the adjacent bathroom, and it was the last person she wanted to overhear her conversation with the chief.

She had just gotten off the phone when she had heard footsteps behind her, and then felt excruciating pain before her world went black. The next thing she remembered was waking up on a pile of soiled linens, a scent of urine permeating the confined space around her. Her tenacity kept her from vomiting. If a blood clot didn't kill her, throwing up while having her mouth taped shut and then choking to death would certainly finish her off.

"Someone's coming," Mabel shrieked. "Hide!"

"Haven't I told you, we don't need to hide?" Doris said impatiently.

Danielle heard the sound of a key turning a lock and then the squeak of hinge as the door to the storage room opened, letting in a stream of light, momentarily breaking up the darkness. The person unlocking the door quickly stepped into the small space, closing the door behind her and relocking it. Once again the room was plunged into semidarkness. Yet it didn't last for long. In the next moment the person flipped on the overhead light and then stepped to the laundry bin, looking down at Danielle.

Assaulted by the unexpected bright light, Danielle blinked her eyes as she looked up into the face of her abductor.

"I got rid of your car," Sunny said calmly. "Hopefully they will assume you went with it."

With balled fists resting on her slim hips, she stood in silence, looking down at her helpless captive. After a few moments, she shook her head. "What am I going to do with you? I should just finish you now before someone finds you and you tell them about me. I suppose it would be easy enough to smother you, or maybe use the needle like I did with our little chatty Cathy. But I have to say, it doesn't feel right. You're so young. Why are you making me do this? If you were old, it wouldn't be so hard. A favor, really." Now glaring at Danielle, she stomped her foot. "Damn you for making me do this! Why couldn't you just mind your own business? I don't want to have to kill you, but what choice do I have?"

Glancing around the room in search of a murder weapon, Sunny spotted something that might work: plastic trash bags. Stepping to the shelving along the wall, she pulled a black bag from its open box.

"I didn't bring a syringe with me, and there aren't any pillows in here," Sunny explained as she walked back to Danielle, stretching the trash bag between her two hands. "But this should do the trick." Leaning over the laundry bin, Sunny positioned the bag over Danielle's face.

By reflex, Danielle began to squirm, pushing her back against the linens and inside walls of the laundry bin, attempting to put distance between herself and her would-be killer.

"She's going to smother her!" Mabel shouted. "We have to do something!"

"There's nothing we can do!" Doris countered.

Just as Sunny pressed the bag against Danielle's face, something in her pocket began to ring.

"Damn," Sunny muttered, stepping away from the laundry bin to answer her cellphone. "Yes? Now? Fine. I'll be there in a minute."

With a sigh, Sunny tossed the plastic bag on a shelf and looked back down at Danielle.

"You're just going to have to wait." Sunny checked the time on her watch. "I'm going to have to leave for home in ten minutes, or the staff's going to wonder why I'm sticking around so late. But I'll come back tonight, later, like I did with Marie. I'll take care of you then. It'll be easier to move your body in the evening, with less people around."

Several minutes later, Doris peeked out of the storage room and watched Sunny walk away. "That was close! She's safe for now. No thanks to you`."

"Don't be blaming me," Mabel snapped. "You said you were going to call the police. You obviously didn't do that."

"At the time, I didn't know I was dead!" Doris fumed. "In case you didn't notice, the phone reception isn't so terrific on this side! And if you had to tell someone, why in the world would you tell Sunny?"

"She always seemed so nice," Mabel muttered.

"You didn't believe me? Did you?"

Hanging her head in shame, Mabel mumbled, "No, not really. But please, let's not argue about this! I feel awful about Danielle. She was so nice. She brought me cinnamon rolls."

"I don't think either of you are going to be eating any cinnamon rolls in the future, now that you're on this side," Doris grumbled.

"Isn't there something we can do?"

"The only thing I can think of, we need to find someone like you," Doris suggested.

"Like me?" Mabel frowned.

Doris shrugged. "Like you used to be. But someone a little brighter."

"What is that supposed to mean?" Mabel scowled.

"Think about it, Mabel. You and I are obviously dead. And if we don't hurry up and do something, Danielle is going to join us."

"I know that." Mabel groaned. "And you're the one who keeps saying there's nothing we can do to help her."

"That's not entirely true." Doris glanced back into the laundry bin. She could see Danielle watching her. "It's pretty obvious some people can see ghosts."

"Ghosts?" Mabel shrieked.

"Yes, ghost, Mabel. What we are now."

"I always think of a ghost as someone who looks like a sheet. Or like Casper."

"Pay attention, Mabel. This is why we're in this pickle. You need to focus."

"Fine, go on," Mabel grumbled.

"Like I said, it's obvious you could see ghosts—when you were alive. And I'm pretty sure Danielle can see us. In fact, I know she can. I talked to her earlier."

"That's what I don't understand."

"What don't you understand?"

"Maybe I didn't believe you when you told me what one of the nurses was up to, but why didn't you just tell Danielle if she could see and hear you like I could? After all, I wasn't your only option."

"Because I didn't know I was dead!"

Taking a step back, Mabel cringed. "You don't have to shout!"

"Sorry..." Doris took a deep breath to calm down. Of course, the deep breath, like her blue-rose-patterned pajamas, was all an illusion—more a habit held over from when she had been alive. "You see, I didn't really understand that I was dead, or what had happened to me. Things were a little hazy."

"When did things stop being hazy?" Mabel asked.

"When I saw Sunny shove that syringe into your arm and watched your spirit step out of your body. In that moment, I realized she had killed you. Suddenly, everything made sense. I understood why people ignored me. Why most people acted like they couldn't hear or see me. Because they really couldn't. Just like you, I was dead."

"So how is this going to help Danielle?"

"We know some living people can see us. Now we have to find someone who can, and have them call the authorities to rescue Danielle."

"The last time you tried that, it got someone killed. Me!"

"That was your fault!"

MARIE HAD HOPED she might run into Eva Thorndike on her way over to Seaside Village. It had been several days since she'd seen the flamboyant spirit, and she could really use the company—and the help in tracking down clues to find Danielle. Unfortunately, she had no idea where she might find her.

Like the last time Marie had been to the care home, it wasn't necessary to key in the password. All she needed to do was walk through the back door—or even the wall, that would also work.

Once inside the building, she went directly to the room where she had originally seen the spirit. Unfortunately, there was no sign of her. Marie suspected whoever the spirit was, she had probably already moved on. Walt had explained that tended to be the natural course in this dying business.

She then went to the main nurses' station at the front of the building, hoping to eavesdrop on the staff's conversation. Perhaps one of them knew something. The first person Marie spied was Sunny, who was obviously preparing to go home for the night.

Marie stood quietly and listened to the conversation. After saying goodbye to her co-workers, Sunny made a hasty departure through the front door while bundled up in a wool jacket over her nurse's uniform and clutching her leather purse. Marie knew Sunny was more than a nurse. *What is her official title?* she asked herself. It was something like unit supervisor or director of nursing, or was it assistant director? Marie couldn't recall. All she knew was that the woman was annoyingly cheerful and some sort of supervisor.

"It's you!" a voice behind Marie shouted. Assuming whoever was shouting was talking to someone else, Marie turned around to face the person, never imagining the person was talking to her. To Marie's surprise, she found herself looking into the eyes of the spirit she had just been looking for.

"I was hoping I might find you," Marie told her.

"You can see us?" Mabel asked.

Marie looked from the spirit wearing the blue-rose-patterned nightgown to the woman in the pink jogging suit. She looked familiar. Marie then recalled seeing her a few times in the dining room at

Seaside Village. If Marie had any question about the woman in the pink jogging suit being a living woman or now a member of the spirit world, her question was answered when another patient of the facility walked through her en route to the nurses' station.

"Yes, I can see you. But what happened? The last time I saw you, you were alive," Marie asked.

"That isn't important," Mabel said in a rush. "You need to call the police and get them down here!"

Doris rolled her eyes and looked over to Mabel, shaking her head. "You really aren't very good at this, are you?"

Mabel frowned at Doris. "Exactly what is that supposed to mean?"

The next moment Mabel's question was answered when the patient who had walked through her returned from the nurses' station and walked through Marie.

"Oh…" Mabel muttered. She stared a moment at Marie. "You're dead too."

"Obviously," Marie snapped.

"She's the friend of Danielle's who died here last week," Doris told Mabel.

"You know Danielle?" Marie asked. "Any chance you've seen her?"

"She's in a pickle," Doris told her. "And if we can't find someone from the living world to help her, she'll be joining us!"

"Where is she? Can you take me to her?" Marie asked.

RELIEF WASHED over Danielle as she looked up into the comforting face of Marie Nichols. While her eyes had adjusted to the darkness, she would not have been able to see Marie if not for the dim night-light still plugged into the far wall. Her old friend's face looked rather ghostly looking down at her with the room's lack of proper lighting, and under other circumstances Danielle would have found that observation amusing. At the moment, she found nothing amusing.

"Oh dear, you look so uncomfortable!" Marie reached down in an attempt to remove the duct tape from Danielle's mouth, forgetting for a moment that would be impossible. When her hand moved through Danielle, she quickly pulled it back.

"We need to find her help before she comes back!" Mabel reminded them.

"Don't you worry, Danielle, I'll get Edward. He'll help you. I know where he is."

By Danielle's questioning frown, Marie guessed what she must be thinking. Smiling down at Danielle, she said, "Don't worry, dear, he's with Evan. They're at the pier, looking for you." In the next moment, Marie vanished.

THIRTY-NINE

B undled in his jacket, Evan walked along the beach with his
father, the quarter moon lighting their way. Taller than other
second graders his age, he might be mistaken for an older boy. Yet,
upon closer inspection, it was obvious he was much younger. His
delicate features, with thickly lashed brown eyes, gave him an innocent quality more typical in a younger child.

However, Evan MacDonald was no innocent, at least not when
it came to life and death. Unlike most children his age—or even
older ones—he had touched death. Well, figuratively, at least, if one
considered making friends with ghosts like Walt Marlow touching
death.

"I don't want to find Danielle," Evan announced when they
returned to the pier.

Edward MacDonald glanced down at his son. "Why do you
say that?"

"Because that'll mean she's dead. And I don't want her dead,"
he explained.

"I can't say I blame you, bud, but frankly I'm not sure what else
to do. No one has seen her, and we've had people out searching the
area where she was last seen. It's like she's vanished into thin air."

Just as Evan stepped onto the pier, he stopped abruptly. Seemingly staring at nothing, he said, "Oh, you scared me! Where did
you come from?"

Standing by his son's side, MacDonald looked down and said hesitantly, "Danielle?"

Evan shook his head and looked up to his father, a smile on his face. "It's Mrs. Nichols. She found Danielle. She's alive, but in big trouble. They have her tied up in a storage room. We have to hurry quick, because she's going to come back and kill her tonight!"

Dropping to his knees so he could look Evan in his eyes, he placed his hands on the boy's shoulders and said, "Who wants to kill Danielle?"

Evan shrugged. "She's not really sure. She forgot to ask who it was."

EDWARD MACDONALD never used his cellphone when driving with his sons in the car. It was far too dangerous. However, tonight he would make an exception. Calling for backup was not an option. How could he possibly explain to Joe or Brian that a ghost was leading him to Danielle. While Brian might be rethinking the possibility of Marlow House being haunted, he didn't think the officer was ready to deal with the existence of Marie's spirit.

Taking his son into a dangerous situation was not an option, in spite of the fact he was willing to use his cellphone while driving with him. That was the extent of the danger he was willing to put Evan in. His only option, call Chris. He knew Chris and Heather were already somewhere in the vicinity of Seaside Village.

"Did you find anything?" Chris asked when answering his phone.

"I need you and Heather to meet me at the back parking lot of Seaside Village."

"We're about a block away," Chris told him. "What's up?"

"I've Marie with me in the car. She's found Danielle, and she's in danger. But I need you to come with me so Marie can tell us where to find her, and I need Heather to take Evan back to Marlow House."

"Dad!" Evan cried out from the backseat. "I want to help save Danielle!"

"You've already helped, bud," MacDonald called back to his son.

When MacDonald reached the rear parking lot at Seaside

Village, it was empty save for Chris's car parked in the shadows away from the rear entrance. MacDonald pulled up beside Chris, leaving the engine running, and got out of the vehicle. A moment later Heather was out of Chris's car and in the chief's, on her way to Marlow House, where they would be waiting for news of Danielle.

"YOU DON'T KNOW who abducted Danielle?" Chris asked as he keyed in the password to the rear entry of Seaside Village. Marie had given him the password a moment earlier.

"I'm sorry, Chris, I was just in a hurry to get Edward," she said apologetically.

When MacDonald and Chris entered Seaside Village, they were relieved to find the rear lounge empty. Down the long corridor leading to the main nurses' station and front entry, there were a few people milling around, but from this distance it was difficult to tell if any of them were looking in their direction.

With Marie leading the way, Chris following her and the chief trailing behind, they stealthily made their way down a corridor to the right, perpendicular to the main hallway leading to the front of the building.

Just as they rounded the corner, they came face-to-face with Sunny, who was preparing to unlock the door of the storage room. Startled by the sudden appearance of MacDonald and Chris, she looked blankly at the two men.

"What are you doing here?" Sunny asked.

"She's in that room!" Marie pointed to the door Sunny was about to open.

"We need to get in that room," Chris told her.

Sunny frowned at Chris. "Who are you?"

"He's with me," Edward explained.

"I still don't see why he—or you—are here at this time demanding to go into one of our storage rooms." Sunny tucked the keys she had been holding into her jacket pocket.

"Sunny, I'll explain later. But please, just unlock that door for me," the chief asked.

"Do you have a search warrant?"

Sunny's request startled MacDonald. "Search warrant?"

"Yes, search warrant. I would think someone in your position would be familiar with a search warrant. I can't have you making unauthorized searches whenever you feel like it. My responsibility is to Seaside Village. I would like you to leave now and come back with a search warrant; that's if you can find a judge to give you one."

Marie, who had disappeared when Sunny started questioning the chief, reappeared. She looked at Chris, panicked.

"Chris, please, do something. Danielle's unconscious. She doesn't look good! You have to hurry before it's too late!" Marie pleaded.

In the next moment, Chris lunged at Sunny, yanking the keys from her pocket before the chief could intervene. Instead of staying and demanding the chief take Chris and leave, Sunny ran off, her parting words—*as she ran*—threatening a lawsuit and promising that MacDonald would lose his job.

"Not sure that was the best way to handle Sunny," MacDonald grumbled as Chris frantically searched for the storage room key.

"We don't have time. Don't worry about your job; if I have to, I'll pay the dumb woman off to keep her mouth shut." Chris unlocked the door and swung it open, flipping on the overhead light.

What the police chief couldn't see in the room were the three spirits huddled protectively over the laundry bin. Chris saw them, yet his attention was more focused on the unconscious woman buried in the pile of dirty linens, her complexion unnaturally pale.

DANIELLE OPENED HER EYES. She was in a hospital room, her arm hooked up to an IV. Licking her parched lips, she turned her head to the right and spied Lily and Chris sitting quietly by her bedside.

"You're awake," Lily whispered, standing up. Walking closer to the bed, she leaned over and kissed Danielle's forehead. "You scared the crap outa us. Don't do that again."

Chris, now standing, stood next to Lily. He reached out and gently touched Danielle's brow. "Hey, kid, how are you feeling?"

"Thirsty as hell," she muttered.

Lily snatched the water cup off the nightstand and positioned its straw for Danielle to take a sip. "Chris here is your hero. He practically decked Sunny to get the keys to unlock the storage room."

Finishing her sip, Danielle licked her lips again. "Sunny? She's the one who—"

"Yeah, we already know," Chris interrupted. "Mabel told me when we found you."

"Where is she?" Danielle asked.

"She almost got away," Lily explained, setting the cup back on the table.

"At first we thought Sunny was running to find someone to escort us out of the building. But she was making her escape. She made it as far as Pilgrim's Point before she was pulled over. She's down at the police station now," Chris explained.

SUNNY'S cheerful disposition was replaced with a more stoic and stubborn persona. She sat rigidly at the table in the interrogation room, her hands folded and resting on the tabletop before her.

"I want that man arrested." Refusing to meet the chief's gaze, Sunny stared blankly ahead.

"I assume you mean Chris?" The chief sat down at the table, across from Sunny.

"He attacked me."

"Danielle was locked up in your storage room, unconscious."

"Well, I didn't know that!"

"Didn't you?"

She looked briefly to the chief, her eyes narrowed. "Certainly not."

"I just spoke to Danielle. She's in the hospital, but they feel she's going to be okay in spite of the drug you gave her and the fact she could have lost a limb the way you had her tied up."

"I had nothing to do with that. And if someone gave her a drug, I would suggest you find out what it was. Drugs can cause hallucinations, and if she thinks I had anything to do with abducting her, she must be hallucinating. After all, why would I want to hurt her? I barely know the woman."

"You had quite a bad accident a few years back, didn't you?"

Sunny stared at the chief. "So?"

"You were on a lot of pain medications back then."

"What does any of this have to do with what happened to Danielle Boatman?"

"I think you got addicted to all those pain medications, and when you couldn't get them anymore—the legal route—you started taking them from your patients."

"That's ludicrous!"

"I think you believed Marie was onto your little bait and switch."

"I don't know what you're talking about." She shifted in her chair. Unfolding her hands, she stubbornly wrapped her arms around her waist, refusing to look at the chief.

"That pain pill you gave Marie the night you killed her, it wasn't really a pain pill. It was a vitamin. We found it in the pocket of the dressing gown she was wearing when you smothered her."

"I didn't smother anyone."

"And then you killed Mabel because she told Danielle about the medications being switched."

"You can't prove any of this!"

A knock came at the door. A moment later it opened. Brian Henderson walked in and handed the chief a plastic evidence bag. Inside was a used syringe.

The chief tossed the bag on the table as Brian left the room, closing the door behind him.

"We found this tonight. You didn't do a very good job covering your tracks. It has your fingerprints on it."

"So? It's a syringe. I'm a nurse."

"I'm fairly certain the test will show it has Mabel's DNA on the needle, proving you injected it in her shortly before she died."

Sunny let out a harsh laugh. "Yeah right. Good try."

It was reasonable for Sunny to assume the chief was calling her bluff. After all, what were the chances he would find the syringe that she had used to kill Mabel? While it was true, she should have been more thorough and worn gloves—or at least wiped down the syringe after killing Mabel, the fact was it all happened so fast, and she wasn't thinking straight at the time. But it really didn't matter, because she couldn't imagine there was any way he had found the syringe she had used to kill Mabel.

Unfortunately for Sunny—she was wrong. What Sunny hadn't counted on was Doris's spirit, who had witnessed where Sunny had stashed the murder weapon and then passed that information on to Chris.

The chief stood up and began reciting the Miranda rights.

"Wait!" Sunny interrupted. "You aren't really arresting me, are you?"

"That's sort of the point of reading you your Miranda rights."

"You have no proof I murdered anyone! Just because you found my fingerprints on a syringe, that's not enough to hold me. And you certainly can't hold me just because you have some far-fetched idea that Mabel's DNA will be on that needle! There's no way you could've tested that needle for DNA already."

"But I do have Danielle's testimony saying you're the one who was holding her tied up in the storage room," he reminded her.

"But she was having a hallucination!" Sunny insisted. "Check the side effects of the drug she was given!"

"You can tell that to your lawyer when you're preparing your defense." He then continued reading Sunny her Miranda rights.

FORTY

B ill Jones wrestled with the freshly cut noble pine, lugging it
toward the front door of Marlow House while its branches
persistently poked his face and scratched his forearms. In that
moment he realized shoving the sleeves of his red flannel shirt to his
elbows had been a stupid thing to do before delivering a Christmas
tree.

Danielle had the door open when he reached the front stoop.
"Oh, it's beautiful! I can't tell you how much I appreciate this!"

Bill paused at the doorway and glanced up to the top of the tree,
trying to determine if it was going to be too tall for the Marlow
House living room. Danielle had told him what height she wanted,
but he was wondering now if she knew what she had been talking
about. He didn't think she did.

"I'm going to have to cut it some more," he grumbled.

"No, it's perfect. Bring it in!"

Bill rolled his eyes but silently dragged the tree into the house
and into the living room. Much to his surprise, when he reached the
designated spot for the tree, he discovered that once in the
Christmas tree stand, it fit perfectly and didn't touch the ceiling,
leaving room to place a top ornament.

"Well, I'll be damned," Bill muttered, looking up at the noble's
top branches.

Unbeknownst to Bill, he was not alone in the room with

Danielle. Walt sat at the nearby sofa, watching. Stacked in the corner were boxes filled with Christmas ornaments, which Walt had brought down from the attic.

"I really do thank you," Danielle said, about to pull money from her wallet.

Bill waved her hand away. "Save your money. The tree's on Adam."

"Adam?" Danielle smiled.

"Yeah, when I told him I was bringing you a tree today, he said he wanted to pay for it. After all you did for his grandma and almost getting yourself killed."

"That's sweet of Adam." Danielle dug back in her wallet and pulled out some money, handing it to Bill. "But let me give you something for bringing it over."

Again, Bill brushed her hand away. "Nah, consider it my good Christmas deed. I figure with all that you've been through, it's the least I can do."

Danielle smiled at Bill and then tucked her money back in her wallet. "Gee, thanks, Bill. That's really sweet."

"I always found Bill annoying," Marie said when she appeared in the room. "But it's nice to see that someone as irritating as Bill can do something nice." She took a seat on the sofa with Walt.

"No problem." Bill shrugged.

"This really did help me. I'd planned to put up my tree over Thanksgiving, but then after Marie was killed, all that sort of got pushed aside. And now that I don't have a car…"

"When are you getting a new one?"

"The insurance company is replacing my Flex, and the one I wanted is on back order. Hopefully before Christmas."

"Well, Merry Christmas," Bill muttered before saying his final goodbye and going on his way.

ADAM ARRIVED at Marlow House an hour after Bill's departure. He found Danielle seemingly alone in the living room, just finishing putting up the lights on her Christmas tree. What he didn't see was his grandmother or Walt. It had actually been Walt who had strung the lights—with Marie freely expressing her opinion on where they should be hung.

"I wanted to see what kind of tree Bill brought you," Adam said as he inspected the evergreen.

"That was really sweet of you, paying for it."

With his hands shoved into his jacket's pocket, he gave a nonchalant shrug. "I figured it was something my grandma would want me to do for you."

"I must say, those dream hops are paying off!" Marie beamed.

Walt glanced over to Marie. "You told him in a dream to buy Danielle a Christmas tree?"

Marie shrugged. "I just suggested it would be a nice thing for him to do, considering all that Danielle's been through."

Walt chuckled.

Resisting the urge to giggle at Marie's remark, Danielle asked Adam, "Would you like some eggnog?"

"You have any brandy to go with it?"

Danielle laughed. "I'm sure I do."

EACH WITH A CUP of brandy-laced eggnog in hand, Danielle and Adam sat on the sofa facing the Christmas tree, its lights turned on. The strands of lights wrapping around the tree's branches weren't small twinkly lights, or white lights, but old-fashioned Christmas lights with larger bulbs in various colors of red, yellow, green, and blue.

"Have you talked to your parents?" Danielle asked.

"Yes. Dad was disappointed they weren't going to bring charges against Sunny for Grandma's death."

"Like the chief said, they didn't have enough evidence. But they're confident with Mabel's case, since the DNA panned out, and then mine. I don't see how she won't be going away for a very long time."

"I can't believe she murdered my grandmother to cover up her addiction."

"It wasn't just her addiction, Adam. She was stealing from her patients. Even if she had managed to avoid jail time, she would have lost her job. Probably would never be able to get another nursing position."

"I guess she doesn't have to worry about that now." Adam sipped his eggnog.

"So what are you going to do for Christmas?"

"Jason asked me to come to Colorado, spend Christmas with him. By the way, he and Sondra broke off their engagement."

Danielle arched her brow. "They did?"

"Yep. He didn't say what happened, and I didn't ask. But he mentioned she was moving back to Portland."

"Really?" *Hmm, maybe it wasn't really over with the ex after all,* Danielle thought.

"He didn't seem too broken up about it. Oh, and he found another job."

"Good. What about your parents? Think they'll go to Colorado for Christmas too?"

Adam gave a snort. "I don't think so. Not sure Dad is going to be able to save his business, even with the money I gave him."

"That was generous of you."

"Wasn't generous. It was Grandma's money, and I only gave him a hundred thousand."

Danielle almost choked on her eggnog.

Adam frowned. "What?"

Still coughing, Danielle couldn't help but laugh. "You saying *only a hundred thousand*...I never imagined I would ever hear you say those words!"

Adam grinned. "Yeah, I see what you mean. Damn, are you rubbing off on me?"

"I just think it's nice you helped your parents, even after all the heated rhetoric."

Adam's smile faded. "Truth is, my dad still sees me in the same light—a stupid teenager."

"Adam, you're a successful real estate broker, and you have a profitable vacation rental company, hardly some bum."

"You're sweet, Danielle."

"Well, don't get used to it. After Christmas I'm going to start being mean to you again."

Adam chuckled. "You've never been mean to me."

"Then I'll have to make a New Year's resolution to try harder."

"Thanks." Adam chuckled again.

They sat in silence for a few moments. Finally Adam said, "I'm really going to miss Grandma."

"She's still here, looking after you. Trust me on that."

Adam smiled at Danielle and finished the last of his eggnog.

"No, Adam, I'm serious. *She is here looking after you.*"

The corners of Danielle's lips twitched as she suppressed her grin, amused at the condescending smile Adam flashed in her direction. *He has no idea I'm serious*, she thought.

"ARE we going to finish decorating the tree now?" Marie asked after Adam left.

"We're going to do that tonight. Lily and Ian are coming over for dinner, along with Heather and Chris. They're going to stay and help with the tree after we eat."

Marie frowned. "Don't tell me Chris and Heather are a couple now."

Danielle smiled. "No, Marie. Heather just works for Chris, and they're friends...and neighbors."

Marie eyed Walt while addressing her comments to Danielle. "I just think Chris and you make a good pair. You've a lot in common, he's very good looking, and he did save your life."

"Marie has a point," Walt begrudgingly admitted.

Danielle arched a brow at Walt. "Really? You playing matchmaker now?"

"I have to give him credit for not backing down and getting those keys from that deranged nurse. He didn't take no for an answer when your life was at stake. How can I not respect that?"

Danielle took a seat on the sofa. "While I appreciate both your opinions on my love life, I think I'll have the final say in where my relationship with Chris goes—and frankly, I don't see it going beyond close friendship. But you..." Danielle turned her attention to Marie.

Startled, Marie asked, "Me what?"

"Everyone knows you were really murdered, and while it can't be proven in court, everyone pretty much knows who killed you and why."

"I'm not following you..." Marie frowned.

"I love you, Marie. I'm going to miss you. But it's okay for you to move on. You'll be with your husband again, and I know how much you've missed him..."

"Oh...that..." Marie slumped back in her chair and let out a sigh.

"Oh that what?" Danielle asked.

Marie let out another sigh and then sat up straight. Primly folding her hands on her lap, she looked at Danielle and smiled. "Do you remember the *until death do us part* in the wedding vows?"

Danielle frowned. "Yes, what about it?"

"I want that." Marie's smiled broadened.

"I don't get it?" Danielle glanced from Marie to Walt, who only shrugged as if he had no clue what Marie was getting at. She looked back to Marie.

"The thing is, dear," Marie explained, "my husband was kind of a schmuck."

"Schmuck?"

"Who do you think Warren took after? It certainly wasn't me!"

"I thought you were in love with your husband?"

Marie leaned back in her chair and crossed her legs. "I suppose I was in the beginning, until I really got to know him. But, dear, we just did not get divorced in those days. It wasn't done. A woman made a binding commitment with her wedding vows and she honored them. I honored mine. *Until death do us part.* But he's dead. I'm dead. It's done."

"Are you saying you don't intend to move on?" Danielle asked.

"I will eventually. I'd love to see my parents again, and there are some friends I'd like to catch up with. But for now, I've still got things to do here."

"Such as?" Danielle asked, suspecting Adam was the reason Marie wouldn't be moving on yet.

"If left to his own devices, Adam is never going to get married. And I really don't want him to let Melony slip by. I think she might be the one." Eyes twinkling, Marie studied Danielle a moment and then added with a smile, "And after I get Adam settled, perhaps I need to see what I can do about you."

DECEMBER HAD SNUCK up on Danielle. Marie's hip surgery and then death had thrown November totally out of whack. Danielle felt as if she had missed Thanksgiving in spite of the fact her dinner table hadn't been empty for the holiday.

During the first week of December, when she had expected to have Marlow House already decorated for Christmas, she was instead being held hostage, bound tightly like a Christmas turkey. She then spent several days in the hospital, and it was almost two weeks after Thanksgiving before her Christmas tree was delivered.

Unlike the previous Christmas, she opted not to take reservations and instead spend a quiet holiday with Walt and a few close friends. The close friends didn't include Lily and Ian, who had gone to California to spend the holiday with Lily's family. Chris and Heather joined Walt and Danielle, yet Marie decided to travel to Colorado with Adam and Melony, to spend Christmas with Jason. The pair had no idea they had a ghost tagging along.

STARING WISTFULLY at the decorated Christmas tree, Danielle murmured, "Tomorrow is New Year's Eve." The only one to hear her was Walt, who sat next to her on the sofa. They were alone in the house.

"How do you feel about Marie sticking around?" Danielle asked, still staring at the tree.

"I must admit I enjoy her company, and it's not like she's always underfoot."

"I don't think she'll ever be able to harness any energy and help me get these decorations put away," Danielle mused. "Not how she's constantly running around. She mentioned something about going out with Eva for New Year's Eve."

"Good thing those two can't harness any energy. Can you imagine the havoc they would cause?" Walt grinned at the thought.

"No kidding!"

"So how about another computer lesson?" Walt asked.

Danielle stood up. "Okay, but I want to check my email first."

Several minutes later they were in the library and on the guest computer. Walt waited patiently for Danielle to finish reading her email so he could begin her lesson.

She looked up to Walt. "You aren't going to believe this."

"What?" Walt perched on the edge of the desk, looking down at Danielle.

"I just received another email from your cousin."

"Did he up his offer on the portraits?"

"No, but he accepted my offer."

"Your offer?"

"He wants to make a reservation for himself, his fiancée and the artist he has commissioned."

"Artist?" Walt frowned.

"The artist is going to make a reproduction of your portraits. I guess your cousin is no longer pressing me to sell him the originals; he'll keep the reproductions. The soonest the artist is available is March. He wants the portraits finished before his wedding this summer, since they're for his bride."

Walt frowned. "Didn't you say he's bringing his fiancée?"

"Yes. Why?"

"If the portraits are intended as a wedding gift, I just assumed he would want them to be a surprise."

"I guess not." Danielle shrugged. "What do you think about him coming here?"

"I'm not sure. But what difference does it really make?"

More than you can imagine, the Universe answered. However, neither Walt nor Danielle were paying attention to what the Universe was trying to tell them.

THE GHOST AND THE DOPPELGANGER

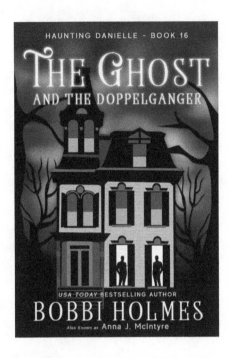

RETURN TO MARLOW HOUSE IN

THE GHOST AND THE DOPPELGANGER

HAUNTING DANIELLE, BOOK 16

They say everyone has a double. Walt's distant cousin, Clint Marlow, could be his twin. When the unscrupulous cousin arrives at Marlow House with his fiancée, he conceals his real reason for being there.

But, unknown to Walt—and his cousin—the Universe has its own plans, and none of them will ever again be the same.

NON-FICTION BY

BOBBI ANN JOHNSON HOLMES

Havasu Palms, A Hostile Takeover
Where the Road Ends, Recipes & Remembrances
Motherhood, a book of poetry
The Story of the Christmas Village

BOOKS BY ANNA J. MCINTYRE

COULSON'S WIFE

COULSON'S CRUCIBLE

COULSON'S LESSONS

COULSON'S SECRET

COULSON'S RECKONING

UNLOCKED 🔒 HEARTS

SUNDERED HEARTS

AFTER SUNDOWN

WHILE SNOWBOUND

SUGAR RUSH

CPSIA information can be obtained
at www.ICGtesting.com
Printed in the USA
LVHW092352180520
656009LV00004B/1161

9 781949 977141